From
The Games
Men Play
Series

Water Music

GEORGETTE GOUVEIA

RIVER GROVE
BOOKS

This book is a work of fiction. Any resemblance of the characters to actual persons, living or dead, is entirely coincidental.

Published by River Grove Books
Austin, TX
www.rivergrovebooks.com

Distributed by River Grove Books

For ordering information or special discounts for bulk purchases, please contact River Grove Books at PO Box 91869, Austin, TX 78709, 512.891.6100.

Design and composition by Greenleaf Book Group LLC
Cover Design by Greenleaf Book Group LLC
Cover images: (top) ©iStockphoto.com/Plush Studios and
(bottom) ©iStockphoto.com/33ft

Cataloging-in-Publication data

Gouveia, Georgette.
    Water music / Georgette Gouveia.—1st ed.
        p. ; cm.—(The Games men play series ; [bk. 1])
    Issued also as an ebook.

    1. Gay athletes—Fiction. 2. Swimmers—Fiction. 3. Tennis players—Fiction. 4. Love stories, American. I. Title.
    PS3607.O98 W38 2014
    813/.6   2013946267

ISBN: 978-1-938416-46-0
eBook ISBN: 978-1-938416-47-7

Printed in the United States of America

14 15 16 17 18   10 9 8 7 6 5 4 3 2 1

First Edition

Praise for *Water Music*

"Georgette Gouveia brings the eye of an artist and the ear of a musician to *Water Music*, her debut novel, which plunges you into the world of competitive sports to meet the men who play the games. This fascinating and spirited novel sweeps readers from Olympic swimming pools to the courts at Wimbledon. And when the swim trunks are off and the tennis rackets tucked away, she finds these athletes in the bedroom, where they fall in love and finally learn who they really are."

—BARBARA NACHMAN, AUTHOR, *Editor of the Year*

"*Water Music* is a compelling story about the language of male relationships. Georgette Gouveia's debut novel is deep, tender, perceptive, and provocative on every level. I look forward to reading more by this author."

—KAREN RIPPSTEIN, POET, CREATIVE WRITING INSTRUCTOR

"*Water Music* is modern, sleek, has great characters, witty dialogue, and a setup that will keep readers turning the page. Ms. Gouveia blends history, politics, and literary references and allusions like a classical scholar, yet she never distracts or loses the reader's rapt attention."

—SARAH BRACEY WHITE, AUTHOR, *Primary Lessons*

For Tiny

Dylan

GO AHEAD, SAYS THE VOICE IN HIS HEAD. JUMP IN. YIELD TO your greatest fears and overcome.

Submit to your darkest desires.

Surrender to the water's embrace.

He's standing on the deck, adjusting the tight white bathing cap— yet again. It feels like a second helmet around the coarse auburn curls that are just too thick no matter how often and close the stylist shears them. He shifts his goggles for the umpteenth time. The lights in the blue and white Shanghai Oriental Sports Centre flash with a pinball brilliance. The place reeks of chlorine and heat. The cheers are deafening. But all he hears is the beat of his own heart and that voice in his head.

"Be with me now, Mama," he whispers as he crosses himself. "Give me your courage, your love, and your strength."

He flaps his arms across his broad chest, and his muscles quiver like so much loose flesh. He stares at the water.

Go ahead, Dylan.

Yield.

Submit.

Surrender.

· · · ·

"GO AHEAD, HONEY. JUST LIKE MAMA TAUGHT YOU. DON'T worry. I'll watch you. I won't let anything happen."

His mother—a blond goddess in a white halter swimsuit of her own design—is encouraging his skittish nine-year-old self to jump into the deep end of the pool at their home in Malibu.

"Oh, for Chrissakes," his father is saying, disgusted. "Jump or get the hell off the diving board. Look at your little brothers."

Jordan, four years younger, and Austin, barely a year, are chirping and splashing in the attached kiddie pool.

"But you, you have to have all the attention," his father sneers. "You're such a mama's boy."

"Shut up, Tony," his mother says. "It's all right, Dylie. You just take your time."

Dylan, though, is afraid. What if he fails? What if he sinks? What if he drowns?

"He's never going to do it," his father, seated in a lounge chair on the opposite side of the pool from his mother, yells. "He doesn't have the guts."

With that, Dylan stares at his father as if his gray eyes could bore twin holes into his skull, leaps high in the air, and does a perfect swan dive off the board. He sinks like a stone and, panicking, thinks, That's it. This is the end.

But then he stills his mind and fights for control and air. He centers himself, floating on his back, and begins churning down the length of the pool. When he climbs out—exhilarated and shaking—he realizes that he's been so focused on his effort and triumph that he's unaware of the commotion around him. His parents are screaming at each other, his brothers are shrieking, and Rosa, the housekeeper, is yelling in Spanish.

"You could've killed him," his mother is saying.

"He made it, Diana, didn't he? What are you busting my balls for?"

"That's right, speak to me that way in front of my children."

"Your children? Well, I wouldn't be a bit surprised if they weren't my children."

"Oh, you'd like that, wouldn't you? That would justify the way you treat me, wouldn't it? Rosa, take Jordie and Austie into the house. Go on, babies. Rosa will give you some juice. Dylie, let Mama see you're all right."

"Yeah, that's right. Coddle him all you want. But let me tell you," he'll never be the swimmer you were. You'll never make an Olympic champ out of this kid."

. . . .

AND YET, HERE HE IS IN THE FINALS OF THE 400 IM—THE decathlon of swimming—at the world championships.

Be with me now, Mama, he thinks as he bends down to scoop up some water, splashing his arms and chest so it won't sting as much when he hits the pool. He takes another scoop, rinses his mouth, and spits it out quickly. Standing at the edge, right foot in front, toes pointed, he leans in. When the starting buzzer goes off, he knifes through the air, staying underwater as long as he can.

He loves being underwater, where it's as quiet as the grave. Loves exploding to the surface in the butterfly, sculpting huge arcs in the air. He loves the backstroke. Loves the way he can look up at the canyon clouds or a starry night, although here it's just an arched white ceiling with lots of lights. He loves the way he pushes off the wall on a turn. Loves bobbing up and down in the breaststroke. He loves giving it his all in the freestyle. Loves pushing himself to the point where his lungs burn and his body feels like a thousand knives are stabbing it. Loves the way the last 50 meters are like coming home.

But mostly, he just loves swimming, loves the purity of it, because no matter how aware you are of the swimmers undulating beside you or the crowd willing you to the finish, there really is only you and the water and the beat of your breath and your heart as you count the strokes.

He hits the wall one last time, rips off the goggles and the confining cap, and looks up at the clock and the standings. His heart is beating so fast that he doesn't think he'll ever catch his breath.

He sees his name, Dylan Roqué, just below that of Daniel Reiner-Kahn. One and two, with one 1/100th of a second separating them. He's feeling—what? Elated, annoyed—he hates losing to anyone. Yet he's satisfied. It was a near-perfect race. Nothing's perfect. That someone was better is understandable. That Dani was that someone is, well, unsurprising and gratifying. Dani is, after all, what God would've been had he been a swimmer.

Dylan bends over a lane rope where "God" is leaning against the wall, his arms spread like the wings of a condor, eyes closed, soaking it all in—or maybe just waiting for his prey. Daniel opens his eyes and grins at Dylan.

"Congrats. That was amazing," Dylan says.

"Congrats yourself," Daniel says, still breathless. "That was pretty special."

Daniel's green eyes meet Dylan's gray gaze. Together, they are the color of the sea. They embrace—their bodies seal-skin slick, at once hot and shivering, their nipples erect—and Dylan is aware of not wanting to let go and needing to.

Ivan Ivanesivic, who has finished third, necessarily breaks the spell.

"Dudes, that was awesome. I am so jazzed to be part of this trio."

Having learned English as a second language, mostly from American websites and music, the Croatian feels the need to use as many slang terms as possible in each sentence.

"Someday I tell my grandchildren about this, no?"

"Someday you tell your grandkids, yes," Daniel says, laughing, rubbing Ivan's stubbly head before he swims across the lanes, bobbing like a dolphin.

"Yeah, dude," Dylan says, patting him, "good job."

When they get out of the water, the poolside reporter, Kendra Kimball, grabs Daniel and Dylan and begins arranging them in the camera shot. Dylan feels as if he's in a dream. It's still so loud and he can hardly hear Kendra, who's saying something about "the greatest race." Daniel's laughing and Dylan starts giggling, too. The rest passes in a blur: wrapping a towel around his waist, stripping off his jammers, always a sexy moment to him; showering, more water; dressing; the medal ceremony, complete with roses and teddy bears; the anthem.

That always gets him, and he sings full out. He loves to sing, does it well, but has to fight not to let his emotions overtake it, whereas Daniel just stands atop the podium, eyes fixed on the flag, hand over heart, smiling but betraying nothing. Dylan wishes he were that cool. Then Daniel pulls him and Ivan up to the top step, and Dylan feels the electric thrill of Daniel's arm wrapped lightly around his coiled waist. More giggling.

After, they find their families in the stands. Daniel gives his flowers and teddy to his mother, Dr. Daniella Reiner—blond, freckled, glamorous. Dylan gives his to his aunt, Deidre "Dee Dee" Norquist, so like his mother and yet, so unlike her, which is what saves this moment from being truly heartbreaking. His brothers, Jordan and Austin, are there, too.

"Hugs and kisses," Daniella says to Dylan as she embraces her son. "I am so proud of you both."

"Yes, it was wonderful," Aunt Dee Dee says, whispering in his ear, "your mother would've been so pleased."

Dylan's eyes pool. "She is, Aunt Dee Dee. She is."

"So what did you think?" Dylan says to his brothers.

"It was absolutely, positively all right," Jordan teases.

"Austin, can you tear yourself away from your iPhone long enough to give me a hug?" Dylan says, feigning exasperation.

"Are you kidding?" Jordan says. "He saw the whole race on it. I mean, why should he watch the real thing when he can experience it secondhand."

"Check it out," Austin says. He's created an edited version complete with graphics and music.

"Spielberg would be so jealous," Daniel offers.

"You joke now, Dani," Austin counters, "but someday when I'm a famous filmmaker, you and Rebecca Grossman will be eating your hearts out."

Daniel and Dylan exchange quizzical looks.

"Who's Rebecca Grossman?" Dylan asks.

"Oh, she's the girl who unfriended Austin on Facebook," Jordan offers, "right after she dumped him, saying her family thought we were too weird for the two of them to date."

"Really?" Dylan says. His heart aches for his brother. "Well, that's quite an achievement. We're finally too weird even by California standards."

"Who cares what those Nob Hill snobs back home think anyway?" Dee Dee says, throwing an arm around Austin.

"That's right," Austin says, "although I may have to date down to the sophomore class at St. Francis. Still, women are like the trolley. Miss one, another will be along."

"Hey, is that what you say?" Dee Dee says, chucking Austin lightly on the back of his head. "There are ladies present."

"Yeah, it's been a big week," Jordan adds. "Austin got dumped, and Dad forgot to send the child support—again."

Dylan looks at Dee Dee, alarmed. "If you need money, Aunt Dee Dee—"

"It's not for you to worry about, sweetie. The lawyers are working it out. And this is not the time or the place," she adds, motioning to Daniella and Daniel, who are chatting between themselves.

"How about we all go out to dinner," Daniella offers.

At the restaurant in Jin Mao Tower, Austin keeps pushing the buttons on his iPhone, Jordan keeps pushing Austin's buttons, and Daniella talks to Dee Dee about creating some paintings for her Manhattan office.

So Dylan guesses no one notices him blushing as Daniel strokes his thigh under the table.

Dylan grabs Daniel's hand and holds it.

Alí

THE BALL WHOOSHED THROUGH SPACE, A TEAR IN THE AIR.
Thwomp, thwack. Forth, back.

Alí ran to the sound—he had always run to it, been comforted by its
hollow, rhythmic predictability—slipping through the green borders
and hedges that made the outer courts at Wimbledon look like secret
gardens. Quietly, he sat down courtside and watched two figures in
pristine white playing. The fairer man served, scything the space, and
just as quickly the darker one returned, as if he knew where the ball
would be even before it left his opponent's racket.

Alí marveled at the way they moved the ball, and each other, around
the court. Up and down. In and out. Side to side. Changing the pace
and direction at a moment's notice, slugging it out from the base line,
grunting. Two gladiators in heat.

Even though it was only practice, Alí sensed that there was something more important at stake than even a Wimbledon championship.
It was as if they were continuing some competition, some conversation
left off and picked up across continents and time.

And one thing more: It was if they were aware of an audience of
one—himself—for after a while, the darker player, all molten sensual-
ity, stopped, ran a hand threw his mop of thick, black hair and, grinning, pointed his racket at Alí and asked: "Do you want to hit?"

His companion looked at Alí as if he were examining the bottom of
his shoe.

"*Allons*, Alex," he said. "We're playing here."

"It's all right," Alí said to Alex, ignoring the other man. "I'd like to
watch."

"So you can learn all our secrets, no?" Alex teased.

"Something like that," Alí said.

"You're the qualifier who's made it to the round of 16. Brilliant," Alex said. "What do they call you?"

"Alí, short for Tariq Alí Iskandar."

"Alexandros Vyranos and that's Étienne Alençon."

"I know who you guys are," Alí said, laughing. Everyone knew the No. 2- and No. 1-ranked players in the world.

"Are we going to talk or play?" Étienne said, hands on hips.

"Why don't we let Alí hit with one of us?" Alex offered.

"Because we're already playing," Étienne said.

Alex and Alí locked on each other. It was hard to tell who was playing whom.

"Sure you don't want to play the grouchiest guy on tour?" Alex asked.

. . . .

"WANT TO PLAY?"

Alí sees his nine-year-old self, racing passed barricades and bombed-out buildings along the Tigris River into the Green Zone, only this time he slips not merely onto a cloistered court but into another world.

Some fifty miles south of here along the Euphrates and half as many centuries ago, Alexander—his family's namesake, for that is what "Iskandar" means—dwelled in a palace that overlooked the famed terraces of Babylon and a rectangular garden that was divided into quadrants by rills and fountains, crowned with white pavilions and filled with peacocks and pomegranates. There ladies of the court in blue and purple silks would stroll, their faces hidden by veils and parasols, their laugher echoing with the music of the burbling rills.

Saddam Hussein's former palace and gardens in Baghdad are not as handsome. But then, Alí thinks, Saddam is no Alexander, no matter how many coins with the Macedonian conqueror's exquisitely sculpted profile he has robbed from the museum in Kuwait.

Alí wonders if the Americans have those coins now. They probably eat off Saddam's cobalt blue–banded Renaissance Gold Wedgwood and sit on his golden throne, too. Alí giggles at the notion of Saddam's hairy butt on the run from his gold-plated toilet seats. It's a far cry from Alexander in his caftan and crown on the Peacock Throne, he thinks mischievously.

As for Saddam's palace, it overlooks no Hanging Gardens but a kidney-shaped pool and a tennis court, the kind Alí and his family have seen on TV.

There, two American soldiers bat a ball over an imaginary net. Alí watches them, his large eyes the color of nutmeg.

"You want to play?"

One of the soldiers hardly notices him, but the questioner looks at him with a face of enchanting sweetness.

"Here," he says, holding out the racket, "want to try?"

"Leave the kid alone," the other soldier says. "Someone might get the wrong idea."

"Don't be ridiculous. We invaded his country. The least we can do is spread a little cheer. Here, you try," the kindly soldier says, holding out the racket again. "Do you speak any English? It's all right. You don't have to be afraid."

"I'm not afraid," Alí says.

And in truth, he isn't. He's been fascinated by the Americans from the moment they rode into Baghdad, even though the bombing scared him and his four siblings. His parents, who hid them in a closet in the basement, made him, the oldest son, recite over and over again what the children were to do should their parents be killed.

Still, the Americans seem so big and healthy, well-scrubbed and friendly, full of smiles and chocolates, like this soldier. Alí ran out into the street with the other boys to greet them. His mother had been afraid for him. But his father let him go. He believes now that the Americans are here, things will change for the better.

Alí notices a cross gleaming next to the kind soldier's dog tags.

"I'm a Christian, too," Alí says, pronouncing the word with a slight French flavor.

He produces the small cross he wears on a string around his neck and keeps carefully tucked inside his thin shirt. It's not something he would reveal to just anyone, having once had a cross carved between his shoulder blades by some older boys, who grabbed him on his way from school, held him down in an alleyway, and slit his shirt open up the back, chanting, "Christian, Christian."

His father's shop, too, where he peddles carpets similar to the ones Alí's uncle sells in Paris, has been spray-painted with crosses. After that, his parents keep him, his two older sisters, and two younger brothers close, and his mother and sisters always wear their burkas outside. Still, after the Americans arrived, they had reason to hope—at least in the beginning.

So Alí feels no fear—well, maybe just a little—as he steps forward and takes the soldier's racket. He traces the arabesques around its frame and plucks the strings as if it were a violin. His mother is a music teacher.

"You ever play before?" the kind soldier, Private Michael Smeaton, asks.

Wide-eyed, Alí shakes his head.

"I play football. You know, soccer. But I watch tennis on TV. Wimbledon, when the power's on."

"He's seen it on TV," the other soldier, Patrick, says, laughing. "Come on, Mike, we're wasting our rec time."

"Here," Michael says. "You toss the ball in the air, and you meet it with the racket and hit it over the net that we don't have. Now you try."

Alí walks to the base line, bounces the ball a few times and in one fluid motion tosses it up in the air, rears back and hits it hard enough that it sails past Patrick, who is annoyed.

"Bet you can't do that again, kid," he says.

But Alí does, again and again, returning just as easily as he serves.

"He's just a little monkey," Patrick says, frustrated, "imitating whatever you do."

Michael laughs. "A little monkey who will one day whup your ass," he says.

Over the next few years in Iraq, leaders come and go on both sides—though none who lead from the front, the age of Alexander being long gone—and success ebbs and flows, like the power supply.

"I've always said if they could just keep the damn power on, things would improve," Michael says to Patrick, sweating. "The key to political power here is electrical power."

"What do we know?" Patrick says. "We're just grunts. The only certainty here is uncertainty. That and the kid."

"The kid" would be waiting for Michael, half-hidden by the hedges surrounding the court. Some days he waits and Michael doesn't appear; off on some patrol, Alí assumes. But soon he appears regularly and with him other, more official-looking men who watch as Alí easily beats Patrick and others, to Pat's chagrin and Michael's delight.

Once Alí brings his father, Makmud, to meet them.

"Thank you. Thank you for what you are doing for my boy," his father says, taking Michael's hand and kissing it.

Alí thinks it's the saddest, most embarrassing thing he has ever seen. But Michael saves the day: "I should be thanking you. He's a special little guy."

If Alí didn't love Michael like the big brother he never had, he does now. But maybe because his heart is so full, he's shy with him. One day, he works up the courage to ask, "Mike, why are you here?"

"Can't play well enough to turn pro," he says with a laugh.

He knows, though, what Alí means.

"My brother Timmy was a firefighter in New York. He died in the Twin Towers on 9/11. It's strange the things you carry with you. What I remember most now—what I carry with me—is 'The Minstrel Boy.' I remember they played it at Tim's funeral and every other firefighter's funeral after 9/11. I went to all those funerals, and I sang 'The Minstrel Boy' every damn time.

"I sang it to myself the day I enlisted. I hear it in my head when I'm out on patrol. I'll teach it to you if you like."

Alí nodded.

"Who knows?" Michael says. "Maybe someday you'll win the US Open in New York, and you'll sing 'The Minstrel Boy' to yourself and think of me and Tim and somehow, somehow all this will have been worth it."

Michael taught him "The Minstrel Boy" and a lot of other folk songs he knew, like "Wind and Rain" and "The Parting Glass."

"I take it back," Patrick says. "He's not a monkey. He's a parrot."

"But a talented parrot," Michael says. "More talented than you."

And that is the beginning, really. Soon the talk—in the Green Zone, the coffee bars, and the papers—is of a boy who has this gift and the Americans who want to help him develop it.

There is one American in particular. He comes highly recommended from everyone, including the archbishop, whose every word is precious to Alí's family and the rest of his small but hardy Iraqi Catholic flock. This American is one of the contractors, a short, thick-set, middle-aged man with reddish-blond hair, pink-white skin, and a stubby nose. He does not have a face of enchanting sweetness.

Looking back on it, Alí could not understand why they didn't all see it. Were they just so desperate that the hunger—to get out, to feel safe, to have a better life—made them blind? Maybe people see only what they want, Alí thought.

Maybe the mind simply justifies what the heart desires.

When the contractor offers to take Alí to the States to educate him, give him lessons and coaching, treat him as part of his own family, and arrange for visas for Alí's family as well, Alí's father says, "It is a gift from God."

Only the visas never come, though Alí's new "guardian" does help his family set up a new life in Paris with Alí's uncle.

And Alí does get an education, although it includes lessons no child should ever have to learn.

On the day Alí leaves for the States, he goes to say goodbye to Michael. Patrick is waiting for him instead. His eyes are as red as his hair.

"Listen, kid, you're a big boy now, so I'm going to tell you straight. Mike's been injured bad, a roadside bomb. It blew off his legs. They flew him to Germany for surgery. He told me once if anything ever happened to him, I should give you this."

. . . .

ALÍ NEVER USED MICHAEL'S RACKET. BUT BEFORE EVERY MATCH, HE'D always touch it, rubbing his fingers around the rim as if it were a talisman.

And in a way it was, a reminder of all that had been lost and that still remained. And that no matter what, against all odds, he would never quit, because the cost to himself and others had been so great.

When he smashed his way to the quarterfinals of Wimbledon, reporters latched on to the story of the kid with the gift and the Americans who helped him.

"Of course, your thoughts must be with your generous guardian, who died not so long ago," a reporter intoned. "And yet, it must still be painful for you to speak of."

Alí flashed on his guardian, looming over his bed. Then he smiled at the reporter.

"You have no idea."

Daniel

IT SEEMS TO DANIEL THAT HE AND DYLAN HAVE ALWAYS BEEN— well, what are they? Friends, lovers, husband and wife?

Whatever they are, their love, Daniel thinks, is like Henry James's "boundless deep." Except, of course, its infinity is an illusion. Everything has an end, because everything had a beginning. And if Daniel can't imagine their end, it's partly because he can't bear to think of a beginning born of sorrow and loss.

"This will be good for you," he remembers his mother, Daniella, saying to his seventeen-year-old self before his first senior national championships, in Denver. "You'll test yourself, be with people your own age, make new friends."

He didn't have the heart to tell her that making new friends implies having old ones. There had never been anyone except his mother and his twin, Arianna—Ani—that is, until Dylan.

Daniella is so relentlessly sunny, though, that it seemed pointless to bring it up. Daniel loves his mother, perhaps more than anyone he has ever known, but it has always amazed him how a champion of women's health in developing countries could be so clueless. But then, he thinks, society doesn't require anything more of doctors than the ability to put a round peg in a round hole.

. . . .

"IT'S NOT THAT, SILLY," ANI WOULD SAY, HURLING HERSELF onto his bed. "It's just that you know how everyone's like a character in fiction? Mom's like Gertrude in 'Hamlet.' She just wants everyone to be happy. And people like that tend to smooth things over."

"Like the fact that you married your husband's murderer, and it's driving your son nuts?"

"Precisely," Ani would say, laughing the laugh that would disperse Daniel's clouds. Together they'd lie there, heads touching like the sculptures of the innocent babes in the Met's American Wing.

He put a framed picture of her in her riding costume with their mother on the top shelf of his locker as he undressed for the first race in Denver.

"Who're the chicks?" a husky voice asked behind him. He felt a stab in the gut. Cirio: He'd tangled with him at a junior meet.

"Members of my harem," Daniel said sarcastically.

"You know, Reiner-Kahn, I've been meaning to ask you: If you make the Olympic team, you'd be like the first Jew since Mark Spitz to do that, right?"

"I don't think so," Daniel said, coloring slightly. "Don't know much about history," he sang, even though he planned to study it as a Harvard freshman in the fall.

"'Cause your people aren't usually athletic, are they?" Cirio pressed on. "I mean, the record books aren't exactly littered with the names of great Jewish athletes, are they?"

"Oh, I don't know," said another voice, attached to the sculpted arm suddenly thrown over Daniel's shoulder. "There's Hank Greenberg and my personal favorite, Sandy Koufax. God, that man had such integrity and a gift for concentration. And that baseball player who they said took steroids, but then they overturned the ruling, and then it turned out he did it and was suspended. I can't think of his name."

"Ryan Braun?" Daniel offered, still trying to figure out why this kid he hardly knew was acting all chummy-like.

"That's it. Except his mother is Catholic, although I think he still counts, since his father's Jewish. And anyway, Cirio, anti-Semitism is so last century, isn't it?"

As Cirio walked away, Daniel turned to gaze at a boy who seemed to be backlit by the sun.

"Sorry about that," Dylan said, removing his arm. "But I just can't stand a bully. Dylan Roqué, by the way," he added, extending a hand.

"Daniel Reiner-Kahn," Daniel said, offering his.

"Yeah, I know. We swam against each other in the 200 IM last year. You wouldn't remember me. I finished fifth. But you were awesome. I've been meaning to say hi. I think your dad knew mine at Princeton."

"Oh?" Daniel said, annoyed. Who did this kid think he was, some savior showing support for the poor little Jewish boy? What was he, Googling him? Was he a stalker?

But as the national championships ended—with Daniel and Dylan finishing 1-2 in every race in which they both competed—it was Daniel who felt like the stalker. He couldn't stop thinking about Dylan, couldn't help but admire the ease with which he talked to everyone, couldn't stop smiling at the way Dylan could pick someone out of the crowd on any day and make up a story about him. Mostly, though, Daniel couldn't banish the tingle he felt when they'd embrace after a race.

To "hold eternity in an hour": He could remember his English teacher droning on about the line. Some Romantic poet, William Blake. But Blake didn't understand. It wasn't about holding eternity in an hour. It was about holding it in the nanosecond that decency allowed before love slipped through your watery grasp.

"Such a nice boy," Daniel's mother said to him afterward. "I like him. And the aunt, I'm already in love. Did you know she's the artist Deidre Norquist?"

"As opposed to the ax murderess Deidre Norquist?"

"Don't be smart."

"Yes, Mom. I know his aunt is the painter Dee Dee Norquist, and his mother was the Olympic champ Diana Norquist and his grandmother was the folk singer Debo. His father's some big-shot movie producer who knew Dad in college."

"You don't say. Small world. The brothers are darling, too. Poor things. They couldn't have had it easy. We should all have dinner during the next meet so you and Dylan can get to know each other better."

"Why, Mom, so we can compare personal tragedies?"

"I just meant that he looks like he could use a friend, too."

Daniel's coach, Chuck Mathis, who was not always on the same page as his mother, was all for it.

"Look, this Roqué kid is very gifted, and he doesn't take himself too seriously. He could push you in the water and at the same time help you lighten up out of it. You know the old saying: Keep your friends close and your enemies closer? That, and keep your rivals right where you can use them."

But the more they prodded, the more Daniel resisted. That was usually the way until he caved and discovered they had been right all along. But this time his attraction to Dylan gave him added incentive to resist: He just couldn't trust himself not to betray his feelings around him.

Dylan was no help, of course. He seemed to be there at every turn with a hug, a word of encouragement, a suggestion, a text message, a phone call, a dinner invitation, or an extra concert ticket. Daniel couldn't figure out if he was socially blind, terribly seductive, or both.

Then Dylan traded with Daniel's roommate-to-be at the national training center in Boulder, and Daniel couldn't take it any more.

"Look," he said, "I'm sure you mean well, and you're a really great guy, and you've been through some tough times and all. And I really appreciate your sticking up for me on the anti-Semitism thing. Although since your people probably murdered a lot of my people, it's really only a drop in the bucket. But the thing, is I'm a person who needs his space. And you're all over it. So I'd like you to back off."

"You don't have to be so mean," Dylan said quietly at last. "I get it. I'll be out of here in a minute. It's too late now, but tomorrow I'll switch back with Carter. I'm sure you two will get along just fine. He's a class-A jerk, too."

"Well, you don't have to be a baby about it. Come on, put down your duffel bag."

"Let go of it."

Soon they were tussling over it, wrestling each other to the floor. Daniel pinned Dylan to the ground, his wrists over his head, triumphant. He had won. He always won. Dylan looked up at him with an expression of infinite sorrow and compassion and a mouth that seemed to have been carved out of marble by some ancient Greek or Egyptian sculptor. But Daniel was sure it wasn't cold and hard like marble. Still, he had to find out, to taste it. He kissed him gently at first, sucking the sweetness, the softness from those ripe lips, and then fiercely as if he would devour or at the very least crush them. When he realized what he had done, he rolled off Dylan breathless, like after a hard swim.

"Oh, my God, I'm so sorry. I didn't mean to do that. Please. You can't tell anyone, ever. I beg you."

Dylan didn't move at first, didn't say anything. Then he sprang to his feet, and Daniel, in a panic, thought he was going to call the police or Coach John Walsh, the team's coach, or some other official. Frankly, he didn't know what to think. His mind was racing. But Dylan merely drew the drapes tight and made sure the door was double bolted. Then he turned off the lights and lay down beside Daniel on the floor near one of the twin beds, kissed his cheek, and, wrapping his arms around him, laid his head on his chest.

Daniel exhaled deeply and ran his hand through Dylan's thick curls. After a while, he drew him up, turning on his side to face him.

"Let's snuggle," Dylan said, smiling as he peeled off his T-shirt.

"Have you ever?" Daniel asked, trembling as he discarded his.

"No, no," Dylan said, the blush spreading over his face, neck, and chest. "Never. I'm not sure what to do."

"Neither am I," Daniel said as he unzipped Dylan's jeans. "Maybe we can ride each other like a wave."

After, they lay with their heads together staring at the ceiling. Here at last, Daniel thought, was Blake's eternity—not in an hour or a flower but in a bold freckle, a long eyelash, a tear. He thought of all those years ago when he and Ani would lie in the backyard looking up at the stars. Daniel tried to pretend this was as innocent as those moments, that he and Dylan were really exiles from Eden seeking shelter from the storm in each other's arms. But he knew that they would never be that innocent again.

After a while, they heard footsteps and voices in the hall and a pounding on the door.

Daniel and Dylan clung to each other, hearts beating wildly.

"Reiner-Kahn, Roqué, you in there?" one of their teammates was shouting.

"Shut up," another said.

"Why don't you shut up," the first said.

"Why don't you both shut up," a third said.

"They must be asleep."

"Who goes to sleep at nine on a Friday night? What a pair of losers. They so deserve to be roommates."

"Losers? They're the best swimmers on the team."

"Still losers. Come on, let's see what the girls are up to."

"We have to be careful, baby," Daniel said, holding Dylan as the footsteps receded. "We can't ever tell anyone."

"No, I know," Dylan said, though Daniel thought he looked hurt. Daniel hugged him and kissed his forehead.

"It'll be all right," he said.

. . . .

"IT WILL BE ALL RIGHT": ANI TOLD HIS WEEPING THIRTEEN-year-old self. Even though she was a mere forty-five seconds older than he, she had always been like that, a second mother.

They were listening to their parents talking on the patio beneath Ani's bedroom window in the family's Tudor home in Scarsdale.

"I'm not going to give up one of my children, Ari," Daniella was saying. "Your lawyer may think this is some kind of Solomon-like solution. But I don't."

"You're already getting the house, Daniella, and a fortune I can't afford. I'll be goddamned if I'm going to give up both kids, too."

"So you want your pound of flesh, is that it? Fine. Keep the house. Don't make me help you split up our children."

"It's not that. It's that Arianna has always been mine. You said so when she was born. Whereas Dani was always more your child. He and I wouldn't be any good together. I need this, Daniella, I have to have something, someone who's part of me."

"There, you see," Ani whispered, clinging to her brother. "I'll go live with Daddy, and you'll stay with Mommy. You heard him. Daddy needs me. He doesn't have anyone. You and Mommy have each other. And you'll always have me. I'll always be with you."

At that moment, Daniel had such a sense of foreboding he started shaking and sobbing.

"Shh, don't cry," Arianna said, holding and rocking him, "or I'll start weeping, too. And then there will be a big puddle right on my beautiful pink shag rug."

Daniel started to laugh.

He smiles now at the memory.

. . . .

"SHE WAS SUCH A SWEET GIRL," HIS FATHER IS SAYING.

"Mm?" Daniel murmurs, coming to.

"Your sister: She was such a sweet, sweet child."

The implication, of course, is that Daniel wasn't such a sweet, sweet child. But then, we can't always choose whom we end up with, can we, Daddy? Daniel thinks. Indeed, more often than not, the one we end up with is not the one we loved. That's because the God he doesn't really believe in has a sense of humor, Daniel thinks bitterly.

He and his father are lunching at some restaurant near Wall Street that his father favors though Daniel for the life of him can't understand why since he's complained about everything from the moment he entered. It's one of those father-son get-togethers his mother encourages, also for reasons mystifying, since they're always stilted affairs.

"So," his father says bluntly, "what are you going to do with the rest of your life?"

There's a question to accompany the sole almondine, Daniel thinks.

"I'm swimming. I'm a swimmer."

I'm Daniel Reiner-Kahn, Daniel thinks. I'm the No. 1-ranked swimmer in the world.

"I understand that," his father is saying. "But what are you going to do with your life after the Olympics this summer? I mean, you're not Secretariat. Maybe there's something to being an athlete if you're like an icon. But you need a plan."

"I'm twenty-two, Dad. You don't know what I might accomplish."

"All I'm saying is you went to Harvard. You majored in history. I could get you an entry-level job in my firm."

Ari Kahn, LLP: As far as Daniel is concerned, the company disproves the notion that complex things are automatically fascinating. And yet, Ari thinks of himself as interesting and creative. It always makes Daniel laugh when business people talk about creativity. To Daniel, there's nothing creative about business—innovative perhaps, inventive even, although those are words he applies to the sciences. Perhaps there's something entrepreneurial in using money to make money. But creative? No.

Dylan is creative, Daniel thinks. He sings. He acts. He even draws. Dylan.

"I see you spend a lot of time with that Roqué kid. I knew his father at Princeton. Great guy, Tony Roqué. Jeez, what a shame, huh? Poor Tony."

Poor Tony who used to smack his wife around, then beat Dylan as he tried to protect her and shield the kid brothers, that poor Tony? Daniel wonders.

"Let me tell you something," his father says as if reading his mind. Then he interrupts himself.

"Miss," he says to the waitress, "this coffee is horribly cold. I don't know how you can serve it. Bring me another cup."

Daniel, mortified, tries to catch her eye and smiles. But he sees her cold sulkiness. It's a lost cause.

"You have no idea what it's like to marry someone, live with someone who's crazy," his father says, returning to his theme. "Tony tried. He really tried. He even put her in a couple of his films. But she stunk. The thing about Diana Norquist was that she really was a mermaid— great in the water, lousy on land. But we're not made for the water, Daniel. We're born of earth to be measured in pounds, inches, dollars, bars of gold, and finally dust. That's all there is. That's all there ever will be.

"Look, the whole family was nuts. The grandmother killed herself, too, the folk singer. What was her name?"

"Debo."

"Yeah, Debo. Then there's Dee Dee. She used to be a halfway decent painter. Now she does these little classical figures of men in birdcages, her so-called 'Caged Men Series.' What the hell's that all about? Nowadays, they sell any crap as art."

"Mom likes her. She's even commissioned her to do a series of paintings of goddesses for her new office."

"Well, that's just great. That's typical, isn't it? Your mother's always been one to throw good money after bad causes. I wouldn't be a bit surprised if they were doing each other."

Daniel looks coldly at his father, who remembers whom he's talking to.

"Dad, did you ever actually get to know Dee Dee and Diana?"

"Diana was too busy swimming, mostly on the West Coast. Dee Dee came down from Sarah Lawrence to some dances at Princeton."

And right then and there, Daniel knows that his father was in love with Dee Dee Norquist.

"Look, I know you like this kid," Ari adds. "I'm just saying consider the bloodline."

Shall I tell you now, Daddy, that I love Dee Dee's oldest nephew, that I fuck him every chance I get? Daniel thinks maliciously. Better not.

That night he picks up a key card at the front desk of a boutique hotel in Manhattan's Meatpacking District, slips it into the lock of one of the rooms, and approaches the king-size bed.

"I didn't think you'd be coming tonight," Dylan says, looking up, feverish, naked, and suddenly in Daniel's arms.

Shall I tell you, Daddy, that I've become you, that he's become her, his mother? Best not. Instead he strips and flips Dylan over on his backside. Afterward, they spoon, gasping, and Daniel rests against the cove of his lover's beating heart, floating on a sea of Dylan.

Alex

MYKONOS, A WORLD OF WHITE HUDDLED AGAINST THE SMOKE-blue sea. I am this island, Alexandros Vyranos thought, not merely of it or on it but like it: snug within my own kind, safe, secure, and far from the world.

But Alex was not made for the safety and security of Mykonos. He was destined for great things in the wider world. And that was as good a flaw as you might find in any Greek tragic hero.

· · · ·

"TO MY SON, ALEXANDROS, WHO WILL RESTORE THE GLORY that was Greece."

His father, Spyros, is raising a glass with family and friends after Alex shocks the world—well, at least the tennis world—by winning the US Open at eighteen. His father and mother, Sophia, see this as a sign of their son's destiny, one sealed by his name.

The Vyranoses owe their surname to an ancestor who took it from Lord Byron as he accompanied him on his quest for Greek independence in 1824. Alex's first name, of course, needs no introduction.

"Like the original, you will be 'the Great,'" his father says extravagantly.

Alex doesn't want to remind his father that the ancient Greeks despised Alexander as a Macedonian barbarian and that Lord Byron died before ever setting his clubbed foot on a battlefield. These are trifling details to romantic men and women like his parents, who tend to see the big picture.

The Vyranoses have done well by Greek standards, by any standards, Spyros Vyranos having made a small fortune in shipbuilding when names like Onassis and Niarchos were uttered in tones once reserved for the gods. And like the gods, they have seen their twilight.

"Now the money's all in Russia and China," Spyros would say bitterly.

He feels his country's loss of economic face deeply and sees his child—his golden child, this gift from God and the gods—as the new hope of Greece.

Alex thinks of reminding his father that winning the US Open is not quite the same as conquering Persia or resisting the Ottoman Empire. Indeed, there is only one way in which he resembled his namesakes. And he doesn't dare tell his father this: He has fallen in love with a man. And not just any man, but the No. 1-ranked tennis player in the world, Étienne Alençon.

In a way, Alex thinks, tennis players reflect the countries they come from. Alex has all the liquid sensuousness of the Mediterranean. The new guy, Alí, is as enigmatic and enticing as the spicy, silky East that peers from those dancing, searching eyes. Evan Fallon is as roguishly rough and tumble as the Australian outback. Cracow-born Marius Tsulsa has the Slav's wit and soul. But Étienne—Tenny—is the blue-eyed, golden-haired, chiseled god of Charlemagne, Louis Quatorze, neoclassical myths, and republican dreams.

"He's French," Marius would say. "He's perfect."

"Well, you have to say this," Alex hears John Demerille, old-fogey commentator, remark to Glenna Day Costa, goody-two-shoes tennis goddess-turned-courtside reporter, on the tube. "There's Étienne Alençon and then there's everybody else. I mean, this guy is Secretariat 31½ lengths before the field at Belmont."

This irks Alex no end. Why is Tenny the only one in a class by himself? Why can't he and Tenny together be a breed apart?

So when Étienne suggests that the two practice together, Alex is beside himself. Is there anything more flattering than being chosen by a god? Apparently, Alex thinks later, he remembered nothing of his Greek mythology: Whom the gods would destroy, they first seduce.

At the moment, however, all Alex can think of is Tenny, tennis, and the two of them hitting together and possibly hitting on each other. At least it will sharpen his game.

Demetrius Livanos—Demi, his mother hen of a coach—thinks otherwise.

"Be careful of that one, Alex," he warns. "He bites."

But Alex has no time for such concerns as Étienne runs him ragged 'round the court: back and forth; up and down; in and out; side to side; long rallies; short bursts; changes in direction and tempi, turning on a centime, as it were. Alex stays with him, stroke for stroke under the hot sun of whatever town they're in. After a while, they all look alike. The only constants are him and Tenny. Tenny and him.

"Come on, let's play," Étienne says, smilingly rakishly as he twirls his racket, the black-and-white scorpion pattern dancing dizzyingly from the frame to the decoration over one shoulder on his crisp white shirt.

Alex can't help but notice the flash of ribs as Étienne whips out a 125-mile-an-hour serve, or the moist dark-gold hair shadowing his underarms when he changes his soaked shirts. He's ashamed of what he feels.

So busy is Alex looking and feeling guilty in his furtive glances that he doesn't notice he's being observed—by the new guy, who watches from a careful distance, and by Étienne himself.

Nor does Alex pay any mind to his aching body until he peels off his socks in the locker room and with them, the skin on the top of his bleeding toes. In the shower, the water offers no balm, only a reminder of raw pain, and Alex leans against the shower stall—dizzy, ready to vomit and pass out—seeking comfort in the cool tile.

"Poor feet," Étienne says, throwing him a jar of ointment back in the locker room as Alex wraps his tootsies in gauze. "This will help with the sting. You know, when we get a break from the tour, you must visit me at my apartment in Paris. We can continue our practice there."

Alex wonders what kind of practice can be had in a Parisian apartment. Étienne's place—in a palace on the Avenue Foch in the haute fashionable XVIe arrondissement—is a robin's-egg blue affair right out of the ancien régime, complete with red-chalk Renaissance and neoclassical male nudes on blue paper, clean-limbed furnishings, parquet floors, and superb copies of Empire paintings, like Anne-Louis Girodet's "The sleep of Endymion," with the male figure in the languid pose, one arm overhead, reserved for women of a certain reputation.

First editions stand at attention on mahogany shelves. The baths themselves are works of art, right down to the male gods and putti that float inside the bidets. The huge country kitchen in celadon and blond wood smells of cinnamon, vanilla, and coffee. Hazelnut chocolates fill Murano dishes.

It is, Alex learns, all part of the Étienne-ness of Tenny, which includes the severely beautiful silver-haired Maman, who is France's cultural minister, and the château in the Loire Valley that belonged to an ancestral marquis.

The marquis was not named de Sade, but, as Alex soon learns, he should've been.

"Come in," Étienne says to Alex as the spider to the fly.

They dine on cold curried lamb and a vegetable rice salad that pays tribute to Alex's Greece. They feed each other spoons of chocolate mousse and lament Europe's troubles over espresso and cognac.

After they tuck the salmon- and gold-colored Sèvres china back into its cut-glass cabinets, Étienne says, "Come on, I want to show you something."

Down a spiral staircase, Alex opens the door to a room that is an indoor tennis court. Practice. Of course. Alex laughs. "Don't the other tenants mind?" he asks.

"Not really. My uncle owns the building."

"Naturally."

"Let's work off the mousse, shall we?"

Though the room is cool, they burn up the clay court. Afterward, Alex feels hot and dusty.

"There's a shower in there," Étienne says, motioning to a room off the court.

"Thanks, but I didn't bring a change of clothes."

"I have plenty of gear that's never even been worn. Besides, we're about the same size. Take your shower while I find something for you to wear."

A shower sounds about right to Alex. And he really wants to explore the museum-like bath. It's filled with plush rose and powder-blue towels and black-and-white tiles of young male couples in various stages of lovemaking. Alex wonders if Mme. Alençon knows what her baby boy is into, although given that M. Alençon died of a heart attack in the arms of his mistress and that Madame had invited her to the funeral, Alex assumes she decorated the bathrooms as well.

Does she surmise that Étienne likes to surprise his lovers in these baths, tie them up with Hermès scarves, and whip them lightly with an Hermès belt on the lower back and buttocks, where it will never show on court? Does Alex surmise all along that this is where it will lead?

He doesn't anticipate the whipping, and it's hard to say what frightens him more, the strap or the way it thrills him. Still, after Étienne releases his hands, he collapses on the floor of the shower, trembling. He feels as if he is moving underwater. Étienne gathers him in his arms.

"No," Alex cries, pulling away.

"Oh, don't be such a child. Do you think I would really hurt you? Anyway, I promise the comforting will be exquisite."

And it is. Étienne stretches him out on pale-green 600-thread-count Egyptian cotton sheets that have a faint leaf pattern and rubs him down with a light sandalwood oil, kneading Alex's muscles as if he were Pygmalion molding a male Galatea, committing him to memory. The pleasure has an element of delicious pain just as the pain has had an element of pleasure.

"Forget tennis. You should be a masseur," Alex says dreamily as Étienne's fingers burrow into the pressure points at the base of his skull.

"But I'm afraid, *cher* Alex, my clients would prove too much of a distraction."

Alex can attest to that. He can feel Étienne's insistent erection against his thigh as he strokes his slightly bruised back and purplish wrists.

"We can cover them with wristbands, *mon pauvre*," Étienne whispers into Alex's left ear, kissing his neck.

After, Étienne ties him to the bed's brass railings and slips his cock between his thighs while commanding Alex's with his hand.

"I read somewhere that this is how your ancient Greek ancestors expressed the love between young men."

Alex doesn't have the heart to tell Étienne that from a genetic and linguistic standpoint, the ancient Greeks are no more his ancestors than the Gauls are Étienne's. For Étienne, such a revelation would be, well, Gauling.

Instead, Alex says, "Well, if this is how the ancients did it, it's Greek to me."

They both laugh as they come.

After, Alex nestles in Étienne's arms. He counts this a small triumph. Étienne is usually as cuddly as a cobra.

"Tenny, I've been thinking."

"Why would you want to do that, Alex? You're such a gorgeous player. Thinking is only bound to confound that."

"Yes, well, having a mind, I've been thinking: Why can't we include some of the younger players in our circle?"

"Like that Alí you're so fond of? I don't like his looks. He's so dark."

"I'm dark," Alex says. He raises himself on one side, throwing back his head and running a hand through his thick hair.

Étienne takes the bait, cupping Alex's neck and lifting himself to kiss him.

"You're a big, beautiful European brunet. He's a swarthy, scrawny foreigner."

Alex hesitates to mention that Alí is descended from a race that was using math to divine the stars while Étienne's people were building mud huts. Instead, he says, "I understand Alí's family lives right here in Paris and runs a successful carpet business."

"In a part of the city I'm sure I never frequent," Étienne says.

"Now you're just being a snob."

"Oh, all right. I suppose we could invite Alí and his little friend Evan to join us and do unspeakable adult things to them."

Alex can just imagine sweet, innocent, doe-eyed Alí in Étienne's snare. As for Evan, well, he'd just freak, causing an international incident.

"Yes, well, no," Alex says. "I was thinking more along the lines of practice—real practice—dinner and the occasional football game."

"Oh, Alex, you're so disappointingly straitlaced."

· · · ·

BUT ÉTIENNE MIGHT HAVE ALEX'S SUGGESTION IN MIND WHEN he invites the top players to an exhibition in Monte Carlo to benefit the Alençon Family Foundation. The event is really a weekend of pool parties, models like the American Chloë Miller, hangers-on, and buffets, complete with ice sculptures, fruit boats, and lots of drinking. Yes, Alex thinks, there is nothing quite like the misery of others to make the rich feel saintly in the pursuit of pleasure to help those they would never actually spend any time with. "Wow," Marius says as he reads the program. "I'm impressed. The foundation actually supports real charities. I thought for sure it was dedicated to indigent super-duper models and bad-boy designers exiled from the House of Dior."

"Don't be catty, Marius," Alex says, laughing.

"Meow," Marius purrs. "Here, kitty, kitty."

"Did someone say Hello Kitty?" Petrov Dubrinsky says as he piles his plate with a Matterhorn of food. "I just bought my fiancée Hello Kitty diamond bracelet worth 50,000 US. Fantastic."

"What a waste of diamonds," Alex says as Petrov moves on.

"I've met the fiancée," Marius responds. "What a waste of Hello Kitty."

On the far side of the pool at the Monte Carlo Country Club, Evan squirts Alí with a water pistol, which Alí grabs and turns on him.

"And these are the people you want to include in our circle," Étienne says to Alex, coming up behind him as he sips Champagne. Étienne is wearing a crisp white linen jacket with nary a wrinkle. Everything about Étienne is unwrinkled—well, almost everything.

"At least they look like they're having some fun."

In truth, at twenty-two, Alex is closer in age to Alí and Evan than he is to Étienne, who's twenty-seven. And, he suspects, closer in interests as well. But instead of having a good time, he's relegated to event organizer while Étienne schmoozes with various sponsors, donors, family members, friends, hangers-on, players—all of whom think he's a great guy. When, Alex wonders, did he become the wife?

The centerpiece of the tournament is supposed to be the match between Étienne and Alex, which Étienne wins. Alex considers himself lucky that he hangs with him for three tough sets, given all the running around he was doing off the court as well. But the marquee event actually turns out to be a doubles match between Alençon/Vyranos and Iskandar/Fallon. Marius, who sits courtside throughout, will later say it's the greatest exhibition match he has ever seen. It certainly doesn't start out that way.

In the first set and the first part of the second, Étienne and Alex play so well that it's embarrassing. Alí tries to keep things close, but Evan is his usual racket-abusing, linesman-questioning, umpire-baiting, soliloquizing self.

Étienne enjoys toying with him on-court. Alex can just imagine what he would do to him in the Hermès-draped bedroom. Alí, however, refuses to yield. He keeps chipping away, forcing a second-set tiebreaker with a beautiful cross-court winner that jams Étienne. Alex can tell Étienne is privately seething. But what strikes him most is Alí, this lovely young man—a boy, really—and the way he lowers his long curling lashes and plucks the strings of his racket to calm himself after a point. Alex smiles, thinking how he might soothe him.

What must it have been like for him, all those years playing satellite tournaments and qualifying rounds? Alex has read the *Sportin' Life* magazine profile that says he stayed at the Y and hostels and slept on the floors of friends' apartments, playing with secondhand equipment. Even now, with his meteoric rise in the rankings since reaching the semis of Wimbledon last year, he calls a small, sparsely furnished apartment in Washington, DC, home, preferring to send much of his winnings to his family in Paris. This stirs in Alex an emotion he rarely feels for any of the guys on the tour. He recognizes it as compassion.

That is off the court. On-court, Alex is piqued and fascinated by the way Alí digs in, dragging Evan kicking and screaming along with him. Soon Evan is raging no longer but having fun. Maybe not goofy water-pistol fun but fun nonetheless. And why not? The two win the second set, go up a break in the third, and are high-fiving each other all over the place as the crowd, always a sucker for an underdog, gets into it. That's when Alex realizes that Alí will do whatever it takes, fight as long as required, sacrifice his very self to win, to be loved really. And that fills Alex with a real sense of dread. For if Alí does that, what's to stop him from leapfrogging over Alex to become No. 1?

Will it never be Alex's turn? He realizes he's going to have to fight for it.

His breakthrough comes a month after the exhibition, at the French Open, where he stuns Étienne in straight sets. They spend a long time hugging at the net, but Alex knows something is different. Something has changed. The power center has shifted.

"What a display of friendship between these two magnificent champions," commentator John Demerille gushes courtside.

What bull. Alex knows he'll pay for it later.

He can barely watch himself in the mirror of Étienne's bedroom, writhing, his arms behind Étienne's neck as Étienne takes him roughly from behind, raking his hands down his rippling belly as he pulls his cock.

"The more you win, the more you lose," Étienne hisses. "The more I lose, the more I win."

Étienne bends him over the dresser then, slamming him into the mahogany top as he finishes the job and Alex cries out.

He wonders why he takes it, how much longer it can last. Is it fueling his run to the top?

Alex doesn't have to wait long. As he inches closer to the No. 1 ranking, Étienne announces that their "training sessions" are over.

"You're dumping me?"

"Let us say that it is time for us to move on to other pursuits: you to a boyfriend your own age and me to Victorine Moreau."

Alex recognizes the jewel-like name of the billionaire heiress who was Étienne's childhood friend. He wonders how she looks in Hermès.

That night, Alex weeps in the shower. He has been seduced, abused, and abandoned. Then he realizes that this describes some opera heroine and that he's relished the entire ride. And, anyway, had Étienne not ended it, he would've had to. This way he can appear to be aggrieved at no cost to himself.

. . . .

A WEEK LATER, HE BEAT ALÍ IN STRAIGHT SETS AT A TOURNA-ment in Washington. Afterward as they collected their gear and themselves courtside, Alex reflected on the strange journey that had brought him to this moment. Alí pulled two crisp red Gala apples from his bag and offered Alex one.

He felt much better.

Dylan

IF OUR FAMILY WERE A COUNTRY, DYLAN THINKS, WE'D BE AN island nation, surrounded by water and none of it to drink.

Dylan's people, the Roqués and the Norquists, are among the 1 percenters. And yet, every dollar is a struggle, tied up in a Gordian knot of trusts, fought over by a deathless legion of lawyers: for Grandma Debo's and his mother's estates; for his father, who is seeking to regain custody of Austin, the only one of his sons who is still a minor; and for Grandma Debo's former business manager, who insists he really wrote her songs.

We're *Bleak House* without Dickens, Dylan thinks bitterly. Apparently, God isn't such a great novelist after all.

Dylan helps his brothers and Aunt Dee Dee as much as he can with money earned from his acting gigs. He loves acting, loves exploring and escaping into a character. He loves the way filming commercials and TV episodes fits into his day job, swimming, although he'd prefer doing theater and movies, which would require a longer commitment. He loves the way acting connects him to his great-grandfather Declan Norquist, a swimmer who would've been an Olympian and a Hollywood star but for World War II. Great-grandpa Declan is a reminder that acting, like swimming, is in his blood, as it was in his mother's. The only difference is that he has the talent for both.

"Let's try again, Mama," Dylan would say. "Close your eyes, take a deep breath and try to see the character and the lines before you, like the pool."

"It's no use, Dylan," she'd say, taking another sip of Chablis. "I can't remember the damn lines, and then I get all confused, and the director starts yelling at me, and then your father starts yelling at me and says I'm embarrassing him and costing his pictures money. I'm not like you. What must it be like to be you? You're so brilliant and beautiful, my Dylie."

"I am, Mama, what you made me. Maybe if you didn't drink so much. Anyway, let's give it another go."

Dylan is always letter-perfect, on time, at once intuitive and analytical, magnetic, a potential star. But he knows it isn't enough, knows, too, that being Diana Norquist and Tony Roqué's son—and thus an object of curiosity, pity, gossip, and whispers among casting agents—will only get him in the door. It won't keep him there. For that he'll need luck, the kind that says, You were born to this; this is your place in the universe, your destiny. If something's meant for you, Dylan reasons, nothing or no one can take it away from you. And if it isn't, well, nothing you do will enable you to achieve it.

It's still not clear to Dylan, then, whether he'll ever be more than Disaffected Student No. 2 or Murder Victim No. 3 in an episode of the latest hit cop series or the best friend of the boyfriend of the juvenile lead or the kid who enthusiastically serves breakfast burritos in a fast-food commercial.

"To succeed as an actor—as anything—you must be single-minded, work at your craft constantly, apply yourself every waking moment of every day," says Tamara Alcott, his acting teacher. "There are two kinds of people in this world, young Mr. Roqué: successful and lazy."

Tall and severe in dark, unadorned Armani, her straight dark bob falling in angles around her owl eyes and skeptical expressions, Tamara Alcott is a "girl" after Cotton Mather's own heart. When she isn't pressing down on Dylan's head to emphasize in class the pressure Hamlet feels as he hears the Ghost's words, she's disapproving of the way he introduces himself. He longs to tell her that though you can dedicate yourself night and day to an art or a sport, if you lack the talent or opportunity, it doesn't matter.

"All that matters is the will," Tamara says.

Or so the Nazis thought, Dylan says to himself. But really, his coach, John Walsh, says as much.

"You're never gonna beat Reiner-Kahn this way," he bellows as Dylan loses focus at the USC pool where he trains.

Walsh paces along the edge, hands on hips, emphasizing the slight paunch under his navy polo shirt. He sports a brush-cut, a whistle, a stopwatch, a clipboard, and a perpetual scowl.

"Not good enough," he says, looking at Dylan's split times. "Come on, Roqué, get your head in the game."

It's not always easy when his phone is pinging with messages and texts from his brothers.

"She just doesn't get it," Jordan says in one of Dylan's weekly conferences with his brothers on Skype. "Austin wanted a pair of sneakers, a lousy pair of sneakers. So she goes out and buys him sneakers. Are they the sneakers he wants? Of course not."

"They're really dorky sneakers," Austin says. "I'm embarrassed to wear them."

"Uh-huh," Dylan says. "Well, how much are the ones you want?"

"Two hundred dollars."

"Two hundred dollars?" Dylan says. "Don't you think that's a bit much?"

"Mom would've bought them without giving it another thought," Jordan says.

"Well, Jordie," Dylan says, "Mom's gone. Aunt Dee Dee's house, Aunt Dee Dee's rules."

"I'm not a kid, Dyl," says Jordan, a junior at Stanford. "And Austin's more than half-grown. I don't see why we can't live with you in LA."

"In a studio apartment? You know the deal: You guys stay based with Aunt Dee Dee in San Fran till you finish school. I train here, look for acting jobs, and save as much as I can so I can get a big enough place, and someday we can all be together again. Remember, it's not easy for Aunt Dee Dee, either. She was never a wife and mother like Mom."

"I don't get it. I just don't get it," Jordan says. "Why, Dyl? Why did you have to take her side in the custody hearing? We could've all been living in Malibu with Dad. Now he waits till the last minute to send the child support and pay the tuition."

"Yeah, well, money was always the currency of love in our family," Dylan says. "When he withholds cash, he figures he's withholding love."

"Maybe if you call him, Dylie, he'd take us back," Austin says.

How can he explain why he can't when he made it a condition of his testimony against his father that his brothers would never know the extent of the truth?

"Keep them out of it," he had warned Aunt Dee Dee's lawyer.

It was bad enough that his father's lawyer had dragged Aunt Dee Dee through the mud, implying—somewhat improbably and contradictorily, Dylan thought—that she was at once a lesbian and had an unnatural relationship with him, thereby unduly influencing him. ("Hey, it's nothing personal, kid," the lawyer—straight out of central casting for the role of the devil's advocate—had told him in the hallway of the courthouse one afternoon, daring to put a hand on his arm. "Just doing my job. No hard feelings, right?")

Ah, but the Norquists and the Roqués are the Houses of Hard Feelings. He doesn't want his brothers to know just how much abuse he took from their father to spare their mother and them.

"Look, someday we'll all be back together," he says, pausing as he chokes up. "For now, your job is to stay in school and mine is to swim and try to make some dough. I love you, guys. I always will."

He keeps his brothers' faces before him when he auditions, because auditioning can be dispiriting work.

"You're too—" Here, Dylan thinks, you can fill in any adjective you want—tall, short, young, old, white, ethnic, etc.—"for the part."

Sometimes the rejection is creative.

"You don't look like a physics student," one director says.

Really? Dylan thinks, despite having had a 4.0 average at Stanford? Must be the jock thing.

"What's a jock doing studying classics?" his classmates would sneer.

"I'm a theater major," Dylan would say softly.

"Oh, a theatah major. Wow. That's gonna serve you well on reality TV."

Dylan had blushed. He wishes he didn't flush in moments of extreme emo, even though Daniel loves to touch it, kiss it, spreading his fingers over what he calls his sex flush.

He flushes now as his picks up his duffel bag and tries to exit from yet another rejection with as much dignity as he can muster. But the director follows him outside.

"I'm sorry to be so hard on you," he says. "I think you have something special."

Dylan's heart leaps. How can he be this naïve?

"Look, a friend of mine is casting a film in the Valley I'd think you'd be perfect for."

Dylan knows all about "the Valley," that ripe, innocuous suburbia where sad, seedy films are made by sadder, seedier people. His friend Eric Rennert—friend may be too strong a word—is always trying to get him into porn. At St. Sebastian's Prep, Eric was three years ahead of him. Back then, he was considered a more talented swimmer than Daniel and Dylan combined. Unfortunately, he already had a taste for anything he could sip, snort, inhale, or inject.

Now he hangs around USC, spending more time out of the pool than in it, bumming smokes, weed, beer, a buck, talking trash about a comeback that will never be and trying to influence a whole new generation of guys who don't need to be like him, a twitchy addict.

"I know a guy—"

Eric always knows a guy.

"I know a guy who can score us some good blow."

"I know a guy who'll pay $1,000 for a blow job."

"I know a guy who's shooting this film in the Valley."

"Why would I want to add to life's challenges?" Dylan asks, trying to walk a fine line between compassion and exasperation.

"Look, Dyl," Eric says, not one to recognize generosity when it's offered. "You're not as talented as Reiner-Kahn, and you're no Johnny Depp. So take the job, close your eyes and learn to swallow."

Dylan thinks of Eric as the director cups his neck. He removes the offending hand with enough force to break it. "I don't like to be touched," he tells him.

Except by my lover, except by my lover, except by my lover.

"Why do you hang out with that douche Eric?" Daniel asks.

He's making a rare West Coast appearance to do promos for some vitamin water, though at the moment he's nuzzling Dylan and fondling his cock and balls as they lie on the pull-out sofa in Dylan's apartment.

"I don't hang out with him, not really. But just because he's made some bad choices doesn't mean he isn't worthy of kindness."

"Christ, you're amazing," Daniel says, in admiration and annoyance. "I mean, look at this place."

Dylan raises himself on his elbows and tries to see his apartment through Daniel's eyes. It's modest, to be sure. But Dylan has turned it into his own little beach house, right down to the pastel walls, an Aunt Dee Dee seascape over the TV, and the mermaid cookie jar that holds his mother's ashes and occupies pride of place on the white bookshelves.

"Come on," Dylan says, almost apologetically. "You know it's convenient to USC and Hollywood. Besides, I don't have as many endorsements as you, and I'm saving for a place where my brothers and I can be together again."

"But that's just it," Daniel says. "I can help you get it now. I have a trust fund. No one need ever know."

This irks Dylan as much as it pleases him. He loves Daniel's generosity. But he doesn't want to be a kept man. And secretly, he's annoyed that Daniel thinks he's not as rich. His people have as much money as Daniel's. It's just not as liquid.

"I need to do this for my family by myself, Dani."

• • • •

"I NEED TO DO THIS BY MYSELF." HE IS TALKING TO HIS GRAND-mother, Adeline Roqué, over tea at her home in Hancock Park. "Grand-mère," as she is known, is an elegant woman of French descent dressed in black, her still thick, dark hair swept into a serpentine chignon. Only the black lace-up Oxfords that encase her arthritic feet betray any hint of imperfection. Her dustless—airless—Tudor home is filled with antiques.

"Touch nothing," his mother would hiss, stubbing out a cigarette before steeling herself and her brood for dinner at Grand-mère's.

The antiques are a mélange of Chinese export porcelain,

Greco-Roman busts, and eighteenth-century botanicals. What has always fascinated Dylan most, though, is a gold-leaf niche that holds a Byzantine icon of the Virgin and Child before a burbling fountain. Flanking the icon are pictures of Dylan and his brothers; Aunt Trixie, Maria Beatriz, Grand-mère's only daughter, who is a diplomat in Lisbon; and Roberto, Grand-mère's eldest child, a soldier who was killed in Vietnam. Conspicuously absent are any pictures of Grandpa Roqué and Dylan's own father.

"I told your father not to marry your mother," Grand-mère is saying. "I told him the Norquists were crazy and that he didn't have the temperament to withstand madness. But your mother got pregnant with you and . . ." Grand-mère shrugs. "I want to make it up to you. I could've been nicer to her. I could've been more to you and your brothers. I want you to have this."

She presses a check into his hands.

"Grand-mère, I can't."

"Please."

"No, no, I can't. I have to do this myself. I have to try."

She shrugs again and leans back in a fan-shaped, natural-colored wicker chair in her plant-filled conservatory.

"You don't take it now, you'll take it later. I have settled everything on you, your brothers, and your Aunt Trixie in my will. Your father will get nothing for the way he treated his wife and children and the disgrace he has brought on this family."

So here I am, Dylan thinks, the richest poor man in America, impaled like an insect and frozen in the aspic of the choices I have made and the ones made by others long ago.

He is so exhausted from his workout, so hungry and in such pain that every fiber in his being seems to burn, and he has to pull over on the way home and vomit. Once there, he hurls himself onto the couch, dizzy and still nauseated. He has swum twelve miles today and even Coach Walsh is impressed with his times. He has done a scene in his workshop that has moved Tamara.

"Where did you get all this?" she wonders.

This I have lived, he thinks.

And he's aced an audition for an episode of a cable cop show, in which he'll play a rape victim. The director insisted on the scene being acted out, right down to Dylan's shirt being ripped off.

"That was nice," he leered.

Dylan tents his eyes with his left arm. His right reaches for his phone as it pings with a series of texts.

From Jordan: "Call me."

From Daniel: "Don't 4 get what I said re: Eric."

There are messages from his agent, Aunt Dee Dee's lawyer, Grandma Debo's lawyer, and, lastly, Eric.

"Hey, dude. Ric here. You haven't answered any of my texts. Anyway, I know this guy who—"

Dylan doesn't wait for the rest. He presses delete.

Instead he hears the voice in his head:

Submit.

Yield.

Surrender.

Not yet, he answers. Not yet.

Alí

MORNINGS, ALÍ AWOKE ERECT AND GUILTY, CAUGHT BETWEEN his desire and his shame. He told himself his desire was normal, part of being a healthy young man. He told himself to accept it, revel in it even. But how could he savor something most males did without thinking when sex and his body were for him tangled up not only in Catholic expectations but also in childhood brutality?

Try as he might, he could never shake the feeling that he was somehow responsible for what his guardian had done to him. Certainly, his guardian's family—whom he suspected knew without knowing—never let him forget that he was an interloper, less than human even, someone to be relegated to the elegant cage of a bedroom in the finished blue and white basement of the family's model home in Arlington, Virginia.

"You don't belong here," his "new brother," Greg, shrieks at him, forcing him downstairs to the basement bedroom, where Alí spends all his time, save for the hours at school, on the practice court, and at church.

Alí would be happy to remain down there, away from the sad-eyed gaze of his guardian's wife; the cold hatred of Greggy; the pinches of his "sister," Stacy; and the charade of Sunday masses and brunches, when they all pretend to be a family.

Why doesn't he run? Why doesn't he stand up and scream that he is being held captive and abused? Why doesn't he try to contact his family beyond the supervised emails and phone calls, always conducted in English? Is he afraid he won't be believed? So much has already been written about what his guardian and his family have done for him, he hardly believes the reality himself. He moves as if in a dream.

But then, there is the crack of the basement door, the creak of heavy footsteps on the stairs, the click of his bedroom lock, and illusion is rent like a veil. I must be very wicked to deserve this, he thinks as he lies still and tries to bury his mind, heart, and soul deep within himself.

This makes no sense, of course, for what childlike sin would merit such hell? Very little about what is happening to him is rational. The only way to make sense of it is to study hard, play well, and pray for deliverance. That is why he stays, keeps quiet. That is why he has endured all he endures. School and the tennis court become his salvation until the day three years later when deliverance arrives in the most unexpected of ways: His guardian is driving home on the Beltway from a meeting at the Pentagon when he apparently suffers a massive heart attack and his car hits an oil tanker, igniting both.

Alí remembers exactly what he feels when he hears the news—savage glee as thick as gore and blood lust. He hopes the death has been slow and unbelievably painful. He smiles secretly throughout the funeral, knowing that he is now free, and there isn't a damn thing his guardian's family can do about it.

"Poor thing, you must be lost without him," mourners offer.

But all Alí returns is a cold, enigmatic smile. He imagines his guardian's family will be forced to give him a one-way ticket to his family in Paris. But here life takes a surprising turn again.

The night of the funeral, his guardian's wife calls him into the family study. She is a big woman—bigger than her husband had been—with a sloping pear shape that is not flattered by the Peter Pan–collared blouses and denim pinafores she favors. She wears heavy woolen stockings and black flats with ankle straps. Her craggy features are shorn of makeup, and she smells of sweat and sweet cologne. Her only beauty lies in her elaborately coiffed hair and her squared-off French-manicured nails, which jut out from her stubby fingers and fat palms like the implements in a Swiss Army knife. Alí has always found it fascinating how people can be so slovenly, even contemptuous about every aspect of their lives, save one. It's as if all the love she has denied her children, her despising and despicable husband, her cold, colorless modern home, and her own doughy ugliness has been poured into that incongruous coiffure and those improbable nails.

She gazes coldly at Alí and shoves a black checkbook across the desk at him. He opens it to see a JP Morgan Chase account bearing $500,000 and his name alone.

"You are to pack your things at once," she says, "and to wait outside for a car that will deliver you to a studio apartment in Washington, DC, where the rent has been paid for the first two months. What you do with it and the money is entirely up to you. But you are never, ever to return here or mention this family, except in the most glowing of terms. Should I find that you have revealed anything you imagine happened here to anyone, I will call the police, accuse you of blackmail, and have you thrown in jail where whatever you think you have suffered here will be visited on you a thousand times daily. Do you understand?"

"Yes," is all Alí says. He packs in a fever and exits just as a car pulls up to deliver him to his new life. But not before Greggy offers the final insult: "And stay out," he says with all the petulant absurdity of the weak.

Alí looks him in the eye and gazes at the house as if memorizing every detail. He spits at them both and hoists his duffel over his shoulder. He pats the checkbook inside his jacket pocket.

I earned this, he says to himself.

The next day, he takes off from school, goes to the bank, and invests all the money but six months' expenses. He hires a lawyer to have himself declared an emancipated minor and to ensure he has no visa problems until he can become a citizen. He returns to Maria Goretti Academy in Washington, DC, where he is a junior, and posts signs hiring himself out as a tennis coach.

Now comes the hard part: He calls his family to tell them his guardian has died.

"Oh, Alí, I am so sorry for you," his father says. "Our family will pray for his sainted soul."

"Yes, Papa, why don't you," Alí offers, imagining the "sainted soul" roiling in Hell. "His family has asked me to stay on, to help them sort through his belongings."

"Naturally, and soon you'll be looking at colleges."

But Alí has no intention of looking at colleges. He intends to graduate high school early, set himself up with college courses online, and play every tournament he can to claw his way up the rankings. He travels by train and bus, hitches rides with some of the players he meets, sleeps in motel rooms and on couches and floors, and washes his few tennis outfits and practice clothes at local Laundromats.

His efficiency apartment in the modest Brownsville section of DC, not far from Catholic University, has few furnishings and fewer comforts, besides his books and the cross he hangs over his bed. But Alí likes it this way. It's almost monk-like, allowing him to concentrate, to think of what he knows he must do next: He must find Michael.

Easier said than done. Washington, he has discovered, is a vast, colorless bureaucracy that exists only to perpetuate itself. Helping its citizens is its last mandate. So he turns to the Internet and, when that fails, the *Washington Post*, whose reporters remember the little boy who so charmed the Army. It isn't long before he is standing outside a house in Bucks County, Pennsylvania. If the prospect of ringing the doorbell doesn't sink his heart, the place itself does. It is the kind of place he has seen on the news a thousand times before, a brick and white-clapboard ranch-style house with a red wood deck in a nondescript wooded landscape. The lawn is pitted and brown, the bushes full of holes. Garish plastic toys stand out from the drabness without improving it. Next door, a dog bays.

Alí stands poised on the stoop, sensing that once he rings the bell, his life will somehow change forever. His heart is beating like the wings of a caged bird that knows it cannot flee but would like to do nothing else.

He rings the bell, and a pretty, heavy-set platinum blonde in a pink T-shirt and khaki capri pants answers.

"Mrs. Smeaton?"

She looks weary. "Come in," she says, holding the screen door for him.

She motions to a kitchen that is as cluttered, dirty, and unorganized as the rooms they pass through. Alí is torn between compassion and trying to reconcile the kind-hearted soldier he knew with this mess. She motions for him to sit down at the kitchen table, which is filled with a laptop, a pile of unpaid bills, and a child's craft project. A cuckoo clock ticks heavily.

"Would you like something to drink?"

He thinks it impolite to refuse. "Tea, please."

She presents two pink Hello Kitty mugs of orange pekoe tea and a chipped plate bearing chocolate-covered peanut butter Girl Scout cookies. Alí takes one.

A little girl with curly blond hair and a chocolate-smudged mouth dressed in a soiled sherbet-colored sundress bounds into the kitchen. She looks at Alí shyly. He recognizes Michael's curious blue eyes and loving smile.

"Michaela, this young man knew Daddy," her mother says, kissing her. "Can you say hi?"

"Hi," Michaela says, dancing away.

"Can I ask you something?"

"Anything," Alí says, wishing he hadn't.

"How old are you?"

"Seventeen."

"Seventeen," Kathy says in wonder. "Michael met you when you were nine. All those years. He wrote me about you. He said he hoped the baby would grow up to be just like you, full of life and spirit. Can I tell you something?"

Alí nods though he wishes he could say no.

"For a long time, I hated you, hated the Iraqi people, hated the war, hated the old men who send young men and women to die."

Alí longs to tell her that his country did not ask to be invaded, to be rescued, that while much good was done, much harm came with it, the one canceling the other.

Instead, he says, "My people and I are grateful for the service of men like your husband. I only wish I could've thanked him myself."

She nods, warming her hands with her mug though the season is spring and the day is humid.

"When they flew him back to Walter Reed, he was gone. I mean half of him was gone. I told myself to be prepared. Nothing prepares you for that. I mean, on the court he was so beautiful, not that he ever played at a country club. He only ever played on a public court. But still, he moved so well. Could he have been a pro? I don't know. It's one thing to practice and play for fun, another to be ready in the moment.

"Maybe if we had been born into another circle, you know, better off or lucky like you, then he would've been a club pro and never gone to Iraq and got his legs blown off.

"When the infection set in, taking the rest of him—God forgive me—but I was relieved, relieved and almost happy. I was. Oh, God. I can't talk about it. I can't think. I loved him. I did. But I didn't want him that way. I didn't want him that way."

She starts sobbing and Alí puts his hand on hers, patting her fleshy arm. He glances into the living room where Michaela plays, oblivious. On a nicked sideboard stands Michael and Kathy's wedding photo, framed in silver and crowned with a relief of two intertwined bells. They were such a lovely, lithe young couple, Alí thinks. What must they have been like before the war tore him in half and set her adrift?

"I must blog about this later," she says, drying her eyes.

Alí wonders if she would not be better off shaping up the house and herself and taking care of her child. But perhaps her passions are writing and her husband, and, having lost the one, she clings to the other.

"Take me to him," is all Alí says.

. . . .

HE STANDS BEFORE THE GRAVE IN A CEMETERY MARKED WITH similar graves and planted flags. Michael's is next to that of his fire-fighter-brother, Timmy, who has lived in Alí's mind through Michael's words and songs. Now he thinks of when the first bombs rained down on Baghdad, killing their neighbor.

"Papa, I feel so bad for him," Alí said. "What can we do now?"

"Alí, you best honor the dead," his father said, "by serving the living."

I will honor you all the days of my life, Alí prays before the grave. I will help your family and watch over your child like the angel you saw in me. I will become the tennis player you wanted me to be, for what has all this been for if not for that moment?

Back at the house, Alí takes his leave, placing an envelope wordlessly on a stack of mail atop a metal table in the foyer. Inside is a check for

$10,000. There will be more where that came from, Alí thinks. But how to make more?

. . . .

THE ANSWER COMES IN THE FORM OF A SPIKY-HAIRED, BLACK-clad English gentleman who approaches him in the National Gallery on a Wednesday afternoon. "Excuse me, but have you ever done any modeling?"

Alí must've given him a look to turn flesh into stone for he says, "I'm not some kook, or worse. I'm Elliott Gardener. Here's my card. If you're interested, call me."

Alí thinks nothing of it, but he doesn't throw the card away either. On such seemingly insignificant things does life turn—a weekday museum visit, a card thrust deep into a pocket.

His call to Elliott leads to a modeling agency and a photo shoot for a shampoo in a New York building that's basically a hot white cube. There are lots of cables snaking around the floor, quickly sidestepped by sour-faced young people dressed in black with Bluetooth headsets and clipboards who want you to know they are very important. Perhaps they would feel more secure if they consumed something beyond bottled water, Alí thinks, polishing off one of the peanut butter and jelly sandwiches on whole wheat he keeps in his duffel bag precisely for such moments.

There's a photography book on the table that Alí recognizes from a visit to the Museum of Modern Art. Oh, that Elliott Gardener, he thinks.

"Ah, there you are," Elliott says. "Now, Alí, you understand that this is a print campaign for men's Lust-rous shampoo. It's like acting. It's all about illusion. You'll be in the shower but you won't be nude, though I can imagine that will be something of a disappointment to the ladies and some of the gentlemen present. You'll be wearing swimming jammers, and you'll be photographed only from the waist up, so it will look like you're naked. Right. Let's get to work, people."

Some female assistants make sure he is fluffed, buffed, and made up with waterproof products. He is less embarrassed than he thought he would be. It is, he keeps reminding himself, a means to an end.

Once he gets in the "shower"—an open set of shimmering blue-green and gold tile—he doesn't have to wash his hair. Apparently, selling the product doesn't mean actually using the product. Instead, he is instructed to revel in the water and he does so, giving himself over to it as if it were a lover.

"Turn your back to us," Elliott commands, "reach up the wall with one arm and with the other hand run your fingers through your hair."

Alí hesitates. Will they see the scar?

"That's quite a tattoo," Elliott says.

"We can Photoshop it out?" a male assistant asks hesitantly.

"No need," Elliott says. "The water will blur it, and I rather like it. It gives him an edge. Other camera. OK, here we go, people. And hold it. Yes, yes. Beautiful. You're beautiful, Alí."

"It would be better if he lost the jammers," the assistant says.

"We're not doing porn, Christian, or even erotica," Elliott says. "We're selling shampoo to ladies who are buying a male fantasy."

"That's what I mean," Christian persists.

"Forget it," Elliott says.

Nonetheless, he adds to Alí, "If you could roll the top down just a bit, yes, like that, perfect, stunning, absolutely stunning."

Alí doesn't mind. No one he knows will see the ad, probably, or his face, he hopes. What's a little bit of flesh on camera? And anyway, hasn't he already prostituted himself? How many nights did his guardian say, "Why do you make me do these things to you?"

Why didn't he run? But where and to whom? Baghdad was yesterday. Paris wasn't home. America could be home, if only he had the courage to try. He remembers a TV report about dogs rescued from puppy mills. All they've ever known is a cage. Freed, they confine themselves to small spaces. I am like those dogs, Alí thinks.

Off camera, he dresses in jeans—not too snug, not too loose— T-shirts, and hoodies and tries to make himself as inconspicuous as possible, particularly as he makes his way up the rankings and begins traveling by plane, where his darkling beauty and Middle Eastern name attract attention. The hoodie, he soon realizes, doesn't help. Nor does his newfound friendship with Evan Conor Fallon, even though Alí cherishes it and him. Already Australia's top-ranked player at twenty-one, Alí's age, Evan is the whitest white person Alí has ever seen. His face is paler than moonlight; his hair, eyes, and temper, darker than sin.

"Evan is really a Bolshevik in search of a revolution," Marius once observes in the locker room as he and Alí watch Evan lose his cool and then a match in which he was up 5-0, having won the first set.

"Tough loss" is all Alí says as he heads for his semifinal in the ExxonMobil Classic.

"Thanks, mate" is all Evan says before he bursts into tears, sobbing on Alí's shoulder.

"It's OK," Alí says.

He's careful not to be overly familiar. He knows Evan has a girl-friend, Brigid, back in Queensland whom he's been engaged to since they were twelve, it seems. When Alí meets Bridge, she treats him like a long-lost brother, and Alí is relieved, as he misses Miriam and Birka, his older sisters, and Mikyal and Makmud, his younger brothers, terribly.

Family, of course, has its price, even when it's one of your own choosing, as Alí discovers on a flight from Pittsburgh to Cincinnati for another interminable tournament sponsored by yet another face-less American corporation that nonetheless provides Alí with sufficient prize money and perks to help Kathy and his family and thus requires major sucking up.

Alí is seated between Evan and a rather large man, who sighs with every exhalation on the crowded flight, which Alí is sure is a preview of Hell. He's in desperate need of the men's room but doesn't dare get up for fear that that fanny-packing grandmother who's holding a delightfully shrieking baby and has been glancing his way every so often will report him as "the bathroom bomber" to the flight attendant in their area.

Perhaps it is the baby. Or perhaps the flight attendant, a woman in her sixties with a scull-cap hairdo that flatters neither her age nor her long face, has simply flown with one too many jerks. But when Evan, often in a low blood sugar tizzy, asks her for another package of nuts, she refuses.

"You've had yours, and that's all you're going to get," the flight attendant, Marta, says in her best prison-matron approximation.

"You can have mine," Alí says, beginning to sweat and feel slightly nauseated as he does whenever he has an anxiety attack.

"It's OK, Alí," Evan says in a voice loud enough to be heard in the cockpit. "Marta here is determined to be as nasty and controlling as she is fat, ugly, and stupid."

It's no surprise to Alí that when the plane lands, they are taken into custody by the TSA. If there is one thing Alí has learned during his short time as an American citizen and frequent flier, it's that you don't mess with the Transportation Safety Administration.

"Please, Evan, please, don't show these people any emotion," Alí begs. "And for God's sake, don't say anything more."

But Evan is now in full on-court Evan mode, somewhere between Achilles dragging Hector's corpse around the Trojan citadel and the Incredible Hulk. Yet it is Alí who is drawing the fish-eye and calls to Homeland Security describing "a situation."

Alí begins imagining deportation, jail, or worse, the schadenfreude of his guardian's family, and the dismay of his own family as the incident mushrooms in the press.

"Tennis bad boys Evan Conor Fallon and Tariq Alí Iskandar were detained in Cincinnati tonight after an altercation on board an Eagles Airline flight turned violent," an anchorwoman intones on the TV that is the only source of diversion in the airless cinderblock room in which a pacing, muttering Evan and a trembling Alí are being held.

Tennis bad boys? Two seconds of mouthing off, and they're already desperadoes? And what violence? She should've given him the damn nuts, Alí thinks miserably, realizing that the flight was only the first circle of Hell. The TSA detention room is the second.

And they're about to meet the third in the person of a well-suited, lightly cologned man with a briefcase and sweeping blond hair who sets off Alí's gaydar.

"I see we are already off to a bad start here, so let me get right to the point. My name is Andrew Baines Harrington V, and I have been retained by one Alexandros Vyranos to act on your behalf. My acquaintances and business associates call me Drew. My family and friends call me Quentin. You are to call me Mr. Harrington and to keep your mouths shut from here on in unless otherwise instructed, do I make myself perfectly clear?"

To the guard, Quentin says, "I wish to see your supervisor immediately."

To the supervisor, he says, "You are to bring these young men something to eat and allow them to use the restroom instantly. Forthwith, we will be bringing suit against both the airline and the TSA not only for harassment and defamation, but for endangering the lives of these two upstanding young athletes who suffer from a prediabetic condition."

Prediabetic? Alí wonders. Whatever. At the Quentin-arranged press conference, Alí and Evan express their personal (memorized) regrets, Marta is portrayed as an airborne Jezebel, and the airline, a flying deathtrap. The depiction is backed by some of the passengers.

"Frankly," Mrs. Irma Smedley of Boca Raton, Florida, tells a TV reporter while en route from one set of grandchildren to another, "the darker boy was actually very nice. It was the other one, also very handsome, who caused the trouble. But they were just hungry. Poor things. They both look like they could use a good meal. And to think I thought they might be nice for my granddaughters. Well, I still think so."

Thank you, Mrs. Smedley—I think, Alí says to himself.

Still, there is someone who is not appeased.

"What has happened to you, Alí?" his father is shouting over his cell. "You have grown so wild. I blame these new friends. Why can't you conduct yourself like Étienne Alençon? That is someone to look up to, not this Evan. Really, Alí, I am surprised. You bring shame on your two families and your two countries."

"Yes, Papa. I'm sorry, Papa," Alí says, when he really wants to scream, Shame? You want to know what shame is? "May I speak to Mama?"

"Alí, I know you are a good boy," she says. "I believe in you."

He puts the phone to his lips and kisses it. Someone else believes in him, too.

"They are part of the tour," Alex is telling reporters in Athens, where he is playing in a tournament for UNICEF. "Evan and Alí are our players, our brothers. What is this 'bad boys' nonsense? We are all good boys trying to do the best for God, our countries, our families, and our sport."

That night, Alí has a dream. He is in the shower with Elliott and his camera crew, facing the wall. An arm wraps around his nude waist. "Shh," a voice whispers. He feels the warmth of the body attached to the voice as it holds him, washing his back and carefully brushing his scar.

"It's all right now," Alex says. Alí leans back into his embrace as Alex gently kisses his neck.

What must it be like? Alí wondered in the morning, to be touched intimately without brutality, to be touched by him?

He reached under the covers, touched himself instead, and, arching in a gesture of ecstasy and despair, wept.

Daniel

IN HIS DREAMS, IT'S ALWAYS WINTER. NOT THE SENTIMENTAL
season of Currier and Ives prints or box office tearjerkers—framed and
contained—but the real deal that traps you in an icy vise on a dark,
blinding road that vanishes before you.

"Come with me, Dani," she says in memory and in those dreams.
"I'll let you ride Criterion."

"I don't want to, Ani," he says, burying himself beneath his com-
forter on a Saturday morning as she waits by his bedroom door. "I
don't like riding, and I especially don't like riding Criterion. Besides,
it's going to snow."

"It's not going to snow, silly. It's only the end of October."

"It's going to snow. They said so on TV. A big, fat nor'easter is moving up the coast."

"Well, even if it does, October snow is like April snow. It never
lasts."

"No, but it can be pretty treacherous while it does."

"What a wuss. You're not very in tune with nature. You have to
surrender to the elements. Is that why you don't like swimming in the
ocean?"

"I don't like swimming in the ocean, because I swim six hours a day
in a pool."

"But that isn't the ocean any more than a garden is a forest."

"Doesn't matter. I won't be doing much swimming of any kind
today, because, oh wait, it's going to snow."

"Well, Clyde's coming to pick me up any minute, and we're going
to go up to the farm. If the weather holds, I'll take Criterion out for

some exercise. And if it doesn't, well, I'll check on him and the others for a bit and be back. I've just got to get out, Dani. With the divorce and all, I just need something that takes me out of myself for a while, you know?"

Daniel does know. With the final nail in the coffin that was their parents' marriage, he can't stand to be home either. Their father has long since moved into a Manhattan apartment, but the movers are an ever-present reminder of him as the boxes of his stuff—as well as the golf clubs he never uses that were a Father's Day gift from all of them—make their way out of the house. Their mother tries to compensate with a little too much of the survivor's "making lemonade out of lemons" spirit: redecorating the house; reorganizing her finances; signing up for yoga and a course in the Talmud (good God, Daniel thinks); and, of course, recommitting herself to what matters most, her twins and her efforts to improve women's health.

Nothing, however, can stave off the reality that Ani will be moving in with their father and then once high school is over in December, heading to the A circuit in Wellington, Florida, while Daniel takes early decision next year at Harvard. In Florida, Ani will live at the house their father built ostensibly as a family winter retreat and a place to entertain clients. But it's really a shrine to his baby girl and her riding career. "The princess palace," Ani calls it. In any event, the family, and especially the twins, will be separated forever.

"You can ride Jezzy. She's nice and mild. Or Mariner. He's gentle," Ani says.

"That's because he's been cut," Daniel responds.

"There's nothing cut about Criterion," she teases.

A big, black, raw-boned stallion, Criterion is proof of what happens when you romanticize nature. Daniel and their mother think he's a devil; Ani and their father, a noble soul. But Criterion is neither good nor bad. He's part of nature. And nature is what it is. It's we who ascribe motives to it, Daniel thinks. After all, a lion doesn't think it's being evil when it kills a zebra. It's just hungry. It's just being a lion.

Nonetheless, their mother offers, "I don't think Criterion's a practical horse for a young girl."

"He's not safe," Daniel puts it more bluntly.

"Nonsense," says their father, who always wanted to own a race-horse and sees Ani's budding career as an equestrian as the next best thing. "Look at them."

It is, Daniel has to admit, a classic girl-and-her-horse story. No matter how feisty he is, Criterion calms the moment Ani comes on the scene. The one time Daniel gets on him, Criterion throws him.

"You're all wet, aren't you, boy?" his father says then, somewhat maliciously, Daniel thinks. "You weren't made to be a landlubber."

While it's not entirely true that he's all fins on land, Ani can play any sport. But it's on the back of a horse that she shines. Her carriage, her command, even the elegant roll of her chignon or the crisp turn of the collar of her riding costume are perfection.

Oh, God—the God he doesn't believe in—let him not dwell on it.

. . . .

THAT WAS WHY HE WAS ON THE PLANE, TO ESCAPE HIS WINTER dreams and fly to where it always seemed to be spring: LA and Dylan.

"I just need this," he said to Coach Mathis. "Just a few days on the West Coast to do some promotions, film some commercials, raise some funds for the Olympic team. I promise to keep up with my practice. And once I get back, no distractions. It's nothing but swimming through the Olympic Trials and the New York Games."

"I know. I know you'll practice. It's more who you'll be practicing with I'm concerned about."

"Shouldn't it be 'whom you'll be practicing with,' Coach?"

"Don't be a smart-ass. I'm talking about Roqué. Initially, I thought this was a good thing. Now I'm not so sure. I don't want him discovering all your moves."

"What about his moves?"

"Just make sure you get more out of the relationship than you give, will you?"

Daniel had an ulterior motive for his West Coast jaunt. Dylan had proposed driving up the coast and spending a few days with Dee Dee and his brothers, and Daniel couldn't resist the thought of getting up close and personal with the woman he was sure had once broken his father's heart.

Besides, Daniel's birthday was approaching—and Ani's. So he had to go. Because that's what his family did when there was anything unpleasant or painful. They ran. His mother, too, was off.

"I hate to be in Geneva and miss your special day."

"Go, Mom. The Women's Health Project needs you. I mean, women in Africa being raped and mutilated. Do you think my twenty-third birthday can compete with that?"

"Well, to me it's the most important day in my life, the day you and Ani were born."

And now, Daniel thought, a day to bury as much as to remember.

"Go, have a good time on the West Coast," his mother said. "We'll celebrate when we're back in New York. Anyway, I feel better knowing you'll be spending a bit of time with Dee Dee. She's so wonderful and capable. Did I tell you she designed the poster for the conference? Wouldn't take a cent. What a treasure."

Her treasure of a nephew was waiting for Daniel at LAX.

"Welcome," Dylan said, excited as a schoolboy as they hugged.

"I can't wait to taste you again," Daniel whispered in his ear.

Dylan blushed as he pulled back.

"I missed you, too," he said.

They drove up the coast in a mint-condition red 1990 Acura Integra that Dylan insisted was one of the most aerodynamically efficient cars ever made.

"Look at the back window, a perfect isosceles trapezoid. And only ninety thousand miles. It's a cream puff. I bought it for just $1,500."

"From a little old lady in Pasadena."

"I never understood that joke."

As they zipped through the serpentine hills, the ocean followed, glistening, beckoning.

"Down there. That's where our home is. Well, was. My father still lives there with his new girlfriend. The boys say she's young, nice. I mean, I don't know."

For a moment, sadness washed over Dylan. Daniel reached over and began massaging his crotch.

"Hey, not while I'm driving. You'll distract me."

"Is that so bad?"

"Yes. Then we'll crash and we'll miss stopping at this great roadside diner for lunch. They have these banana-and-chocolate chip pancakes that are to die for, although they're not as good as Aunt Dee Dee's. Still, we wouldn't want to miss them."

Being on the road with Dylan reminded Daniel of the only happy times with his family—on the way to Great Aunt Tessie and Great Uncle Louie's summer house in Long Branch—he and Ani in the back seat, his mother and father in the front, chatting almost amiably, the old water tower spied through the lush mystery of summer signaling that they were near their destination. Whenever Daniel thought of it, he was filled with a sense of freedom and overwhelming joy.

"OK," Daniel said. "Pancakes it is."

He gave Dylan's crotch a squeeze before removing his hand. "This later."

They rolled into San Francisco around dinnertime. The sky was periwinkle, pink, and orange sherbet, the colors of sunset on the Jersey shore. It was his favorite time of day, flooding him with a longing for he knew not what. If he knew, maybe he wouldn't long for it.

Dylan parked on Cole in the Haight-Ashbury district, a street so steep that Daniel wondered if he should put the emergency brake on.

"Relax, man, it's cool."

They were outside one of the famous painted ladies, this one on a corner lot, a pink double-width Victorian with turrets, gables, and sky-blue shutters. The pastel palette was underscored by the array of potted flowering plants that hung on the gingerbread wraparound porch, with its white wicker furniture. Dylan's family had gathered there in anticipation of their arrival.

"Dani, it's so good to have you with us," Dee Dee said, hugging him even before she greeted her nephew with a "Hello, kiddo." "You know Jordan and Austin, of course. And this is Rosa, our housekeeper, without whom none of us would survive. The Collies are Fred and Ginger. Ginger is fine. Fred, settle down. You guys must be famished and exhausted. Jordie, take the bags up to your room. Austie, let the dogs out into the garden. I'll show you where you can wash up. Dinner's almost ready."

Dinner turned out to be crisp, succulent roast chicken, sweet potatoes and other vegetables, and chocolate cake for dessert. They ate at a big round table in the pale yellow and earth-toned kitchen. Rosa joined them for coffee. Dee Dee cleared.

"No," she said, patting Daniel's hand as he and Dylan rose to help. "Sit with the boys. You're a guest."

Daniel's guest status allowed him to spend a lot of time listening and drinking in chez Norquist. The house had once been Debo's, a haven for the Haight-Ashbury scene in the sixties: hippies, artists, protesters, politicians, druggies, and dealers.

"The rooms were painted black, forest green, and brown then," Dylan said later, pulling out a photo album containing pictures of Debo and her friends in what Daniel recognized from the fireplace was the living room, which had sparse furnishings and posters on the wall. Everyone was smiling except the naked child Debo held in her arms. Daniel assumed it was Dee Dee.

Time really is another country, Daniel thought. For where was that dark miasma in this place of light? The rooms were airy and brilliant with pastel and jeweled colors, intricate white moldings, gleaming hardwood floors, and French doors that opened onto other rooms— each more delightful than the previous—until at last the eye arrived at a courtyard garden teeming with cherry blossoms, dogwoods, azaleas, tulips, and daffodils.

Inside, hundreds of books stood at attention in white carved book-cases or rested on cushions or under tables, like proprietary cats. Music of all kinds wafted from a sound system topped by an old-fashioned gramophone or a piano that had once belonged to Debo and that, it seemed, everyone could play. The air was redolent with cinnamon, lavender, vanilla, gardenias, and jasmine.

Fred and Ginger were let back in for the cake and café latte portion of the meal, served in the living room, which had once been a front par-lor. Ginger rested her head on Daniel's knee, which he took as a compliment. Fred lay down at a wary distance, looked at Daniel between his front paws and emitted a low growl.

"Fred," Dee Dee said sharply. "Honestly, I don't know what's wrong with him. He's not as bright as Ginger. But he is pretty."

Fred and Ginger slept in Austin's room in the finished attic across from Jordie's room, which Daniel and Dylan would share.

"I don't know why I had to give up my room," Jordie grumbled.

"Well," Dee Dee said, "I don't think any of you guys want my pale pink boudoir. Rosa's room has only a twin bed, while your room and Austie's have nice full-size beds. So it was either you let Austin and the dogs bunk with you, or you bunk with Austie and give up your room for a few days."

"Ugh, I don't want dog hair all over my stuff."

"Well, that settles it then."

Jordan's room was a spare, pale blue lean-to with posters of babes and a few lads' magazines hidden among his textbooks, a real hetero guy's guy cave. The irony wasn't lost on Daniel.

"Do you think Dee Dee knows? You know, about us?" Daniel asked when they were alone there.

"No, no way."

"'Cause this might be her way of acknowledging what she doesn't want to confront."

"Listen, don't let that feminist, artist stuff fool you. There's a part of Aunt Dee Dee that's a disciplined, devout Roman Catholic."

"Hard to figure that, given her hippie upbringing in this house."

"Not really. You see this place now. Even her paintbrushes are bright-eyed and bushy-tailed. It's her attempt to order what must've been a chaotic childhood with Grandma Debo. Believe it: If your name were Danielle instead of Daniel, we wouldn't be sharing this bed."

"Then flying under the gaydar has its advantages," Daniel said, grinning.

"It certainly does," Dylan said as he sat down on Jordie's bed and patted the space beside him.

Daniel never knew lovemaking could be so quiet, so still. But what choice did they have, with Jordan and Austin in the room across the hall and Dee Dee on the floor below?

Daniel lay on top of Dylan inside him, barely moving for fear of making the bed creak. The pleasure-pain was intense, almost unbearable. As Dylan arched and began to moan, Daniel covered his mouth with his own, thrusting his tongue in to meet Dylan's. He thought they'd drown in each other. Finally, when he could stand it no longer, Daniel moved slightly, igniting a chain of come. He buried his face in the side of his lover's graceful neck, licking the damp curls that had not yet been shorn, kissing the flesh to reassure him as Dylan wept.

"We'll have to take the garbage with us," Daniel said in the morning as they woke early for a quickie. "You know, the used condoms."

"You should really work for the CIA. Would you stop being so paranoid? Aunt Dee Dee's not going to be going through the trash looking for erotic clues."

"What about Jordie? What if there's a stain on the sheets?"

"Oh, please. I hate to think of what he's done in this bed. I'm sure Aunt Dee Dee would, too."

Just then, Herself knocked on the door.

"Dylie, Dani, you guys up?"

"In more ways than one," Dylan whispered to Daniel.

"Shh, stop."

"Coming, Aunt Dee Dee."

"God."

Dylan and Daniel muffled their laughs in the pillows.

"Jordie, Austie, rise and shine. Your brother and Dani have practice. Jordie, you have finals; Austie, class. Come on. Chocolate-chip pancakes for all. Dani, Dylie, yours will be ready when you get back. For now, there's fruit and cereal. Let's greet the day so we can all go out later."

. . . .

DYLAN HAD ARRANGED FOR THEM TO PRACTICE AT STANFORD, his alma mater, a forty-minute drive south, although the way Dylan drove they made it in a half-hour. Daniel, who liked being famous, nevertheless sometimes forgot the effect he had on others. Students nodded and whispered as the two got into the pool.

Unless they were in a relay, Daniel and Dylan never talked swimming. Now each did his thing, going through his paces, tweaking his strokes and times, yet acutely aware of the other. At some point, Dylan proposed they race "for fun." Daniel looked up to see students gathered on either side of the pool, as if this was what they had been waiting for all along.

"Sure, why not?"

"I'll be timekeeper," a girl in horizontal pink and orange stripes yelled. "Ready, set, go."

Daniel started out ahead in the butterfly, exploding on the surface like a stealth weapon. Dylan had a slight advantage in the backstroke. They were about even on the breaststroke. It all came down to the freestyle, with the throng shouting for both of them.

Dylan out-touched Daniel by a finger.

"That was unreal," Dylan said, panting as if from their lovemaking. "No one's going to be able to touch us."

But Daniel wasn't thinking of that. He was wondering how he could've allowed himself to be shown up on someone else's turf, especially Dylan's.

"What's wrong?"

"Nothing," Daniel said. "Congrats."

"Hey, it's just practice."

"That's right. It's no indication of what we'll do when the pressure is really on."

On the ride back, Daniel was quiet and annoyed. Why did it matter that he had lost a stupid makeshift practice race? Except that it did. God, he was so weak. Fortunately, Dee Dee's pancakes broke the spell.

"Everything all right?" she asked.

"I think I was just having a low blood sugar moment," Daniel said.

"Good, well, eat up. I have a great afternoon of sightseeing planned for us."

Dee Dee had put together an itinerary based on the places in Alfred Hitchcock's movie *Vertigo*, which Daniel soon learned was something of an obsession with her. They went to the Palace of the Legion of Honor; the Palace of Fine Arts; Fort Point, under the Golden Gate Bridge; and the old Mission Dolores, capping the day with dinner at Ernie's.

Poor Dee Dee, Daniel thought. She was a San Francisco blonde haunted by the past and the spirits of two blond madwomen: her mother, Debo, and her sister, Diana. No wonder she was obsessed with

Hitchcock's film. And like his heroine, she, too, clung to the watery city that was itself just a little bit in love with death. There was something nostalgic, louche, and decaying about San Francisco that reminded him of Venice and their first Olympics four years before when Dylan was twenty and Daniel nineteen. What a friggin' disaster.

. . . .

IT HAS BEEN A SEASON IN WHICH THE RAIN FOLLOWS SUMMER everywhere. From their hotel in the Olympic Village it looks as if they are on the deck of a great ocean liner, about to be submerged in water. And then "Pool-gate"—as it is known in the "gate"-challenged press— breaks. It seems one of the members of the US men's water polo team has, depending on whose account you believe, dated/seduced/raped an underage Italian fan. The press and public are calling for his arrest, and things take another ugly turn as the American basketball team loses to the Italians in overtime, a shocking defeat that sends fans, seats, and players flying.

When the members of Team USA aren't in the pool or on the court, track, or field, they're in lockdown. The incessant rain under-scores the mood.

"Jesus Christ," Daniel grumbles. "I can't stand guys who can't keep it in their pants on the road."

"Not everyone is as lucky as we are to have found someone," Dylan says.

Why do such sentiments make Daniel uncomfortable? He presses on: "And you know what? I don't think water polo players are even very good swimmers."

"Oh, come on," Dylan says, flipping through his phone messages. "Are you listening to yourself? Can you imagine how hard that must be? It's like playing soccer and swimming at the same time. Could you do that? I'm not that coordinated."

Daniel flashes on himself falling off Criterion.

"Frankly, I feel for the guy. Although if he did what they say he did, he deserves to be punished."

"Damn right. It's just that it puts more pressure on the rest of us."

"Here's a text from Aunt Dee Dee and one from your mom: 'Are you guys OK?' 'Yes,'" Dylan types. "'Don't worry. See you after the race.'"

There's a knock on the door. Daniel and Dylan eye each other and the twin beds they have pushed together.

"Just a minute," Daniel yells in the flurry to get the room back to its original chaste state.

He tries to look nonchalant, flipping through a magazine in a chair by the window as Dylan opens the door to Coach Walsh, who coaches the swim team as well as Dylan.

"What the hell are you guys doing in here that it takes so long to answer the door? Tell me that you don't have women in here and are not doing drugs."

"We don't have women in here, and we're not doing drugs," Dylan says as innocently as possible.

"Good," Coach Walsh says, sighing, "because I don't think my nerves can take any more. As long as you're not sleeping with under-age girls or doing meth, anything else, I don't care. Listen, you two need your rest so I'll make this brief: I wanted to talk to you about the finals of the 4 x 100 freestyle relay tomorrow. Normally, I don't like to put pressure on athletes, but the literally fucking water polo team and those prima donna basketball players leave me no choice. I've just come from a meeting of all the coaches with the head of the USOC. This is not playing well back home. I need you guys to go out there tomorrow, get a big lead, and then hang on. I do not want to lose, do you hear? I want that gold medal."

"Understood" is all Daniel says.

Dylan's large gray eyes grow larger the way they do when he's worried, and he swallows hard, his Adam's apple bobbing. So when Coach Walsh leaves, Daniel says, "We're going to win."

But when he, Dylan, Carter Cabrera, and Boyd Algren step onto the deck the next day, holding hands for the introduction, he can feel himself trembling. The crowd—a real bullfight bunch—scents blood and is in no mood to be appeased. The throng boos as Daniel and company are introduced and raise their joined hands. He and Dylan, ever the actor, smile almost defiantly. Showtime, but they know it's going to be an uphill fight at best.

Dylan crosses himself and prays, "Be with me Mom. Give me your love, your courage, and your strength."

"Do you really think she's here?" Daniel asks.

"I know she is, just as I know Ani is watching over you. And we'll see them again some day. I believe that. I have to."

What Daniel believes is that he and Dylan are at their best in adversity. There's something about having a coldly critical father (his) or a hotly brutal one (Dylan's) that gives them a distinct competitive advantage. They don't shrink from a challenge, having learned early to turn inward to dig deep. (This comes with a steep price: How many nights has Daniel comforted Dylan as he whimpers in his dreams with the words "I have you, fatherless child.")

Now Daniel trains his laser focus on the pool, which seems lit from within. As he hits the water, he stays beneath its surface as long as he can, gliding effortlessly, offering little resistance and thus receiving less. It would seem counterintuitive but the calmer he is, the less he does, the faster he moves.

He hits the wall in record time and gets out quickly to watch Dylan swim his leg. It occurs to him, then, that Dylan is not merely a great swimmer but that rarity, a natural. In the dive off the deck, his body is one exquisite line, fingers touching, toes pointed. He stays underwater even longer than Daniel, traveling farther faster. When he comes to the surface, his strokes are the minimum he needs to get the job done, the sculpted head—made sleekly glamorous by the dark cap and superhero reflecting goggles—tilts to the right, the chiseled left arm rising, carving arcs in the air. The head tilts left, the right arm rises, same height, same motion. Centered, devoid of thought, just unconscious grace, power, and efficiency, like Ani on Criterion or a great white in its own habitat. Perfection.

Daniel feels sick. Why should this affect him so? Even if Dylan is a more natural swimmer, it doesn't really make him a better or greater one. He doesn't have Daniel's single-mindedness, the thing that makes a winner. There are just too many distractions in his life and too many interests. But Daniel realizes that if Dylan can tune them out and recognize how good he is, everything will change, and Daniel can't bear it.

Dylan's out of the water now, having added to their lead, which gives Daniel an excuse to touch him, hold him in public, if ever so briefly. There's a part of Daniel that would like to throw him right down on the pool deck, rip off his suit, and take him right there for all the world to see.

Boyd's in the water now. He's tightening up and so is the race. The Aussies, the French, the Chinese, the Japanese, the Russians—they're all still in the mix, and damn if the Italians aren't coming on. The crowd is going wild. Not good, Daniel thinks. Who names their kid Boyd anyway?

Daniel must be thinking out loud again, because Dylan answers, "His real name is Leslie. Boyd is his middle name."

"Come on, Boyd!" they scream.

Carter's about to get in. Big and fast, he's probably the best sprinter on the team. But he's also a few floors short of an observation deck, Daniel thinks. Dylan puts a hand on Carter's shoulder.

"Look," he whispers. "Just do your best. That's all anyone can ask. Whatever happens is what was meant to happen. The trick is to want what happens as if you planned it all along."

Daniel, who thinks whatever happens is what you make happen, is annoyed with this pep talk. Still, they need to cheer Carter on. The Italians are closing in, but in the last 50 meters, Carter seems to have found another gear. He's eating the pool. He just out-touches the Italians.

Shouts, hollers, whoops. Daniel slams into Dylan's body, engulfing Boyd and Carter in an embrace, arms linked, damp heads touching.

"I'm so proud of you guys," Daniel says. "This is one to remember."

They come out of the huddle and raise their arms in triumph. Daniel scans the stands. He catches sight of his mother, whose parents were born in this country and lost everything and everyone to the Fascists. She touches her hand to her heart and lips, sobbing. Daniel chokes up then. Dylan puts an arm around him.

"Look, it's your mom with Aunt Dee Dee."

Dee Dee has an arm around Daniella. She is smiling, laughing, saying something to Austin and Jordan, who are clapping.

. . . .

DANIEL WAS WIDE-AWAKE AT 5 A.M. IT WAS STILL DARK OUTSIDE, AND the air through the open window had a chill. Dylan was awake, too.

"Happy birthday to you, happy birthday to you. Happy birthday, Mr. President. Happy birthday to you," he sang.

"Your Marilyn could use a little work," Daniel said, "you nut."

"Speaking of nuts," Dylan said. He flipped back the covers and began kissing his way down Daniel's lightly furry plumb line. When he arrived at his lover's treasure, he took it almost reverently in his hands. Daniel held his breath. He shut his eyes as he felt the tip of Dylan's tongue against the tip of his cock. He didn't want to speak but felt he must.

"There are condoms—"

"Shh," Dylan said. "It's your special day. I want nothing between us."

Dylan sucked his cock the way he swam: expertly, with just enough pace, tracing the pulsing vein underneath, brushing the balls and then when Daniel felt he couldn't get any harder, taking him entirely in his mouth, and gulping his come. He licked him clean, and, coming up to rest beside Daniel, thrust his tongue into his mouth so he could taste himself.

"Now you truly live inside me," Dylan said, "even if only for a moment."

Daniel didn't know quite what to make of it all. He wondered if Dylan had been practicing his "strokes" in another pool, so to speak. He didn't trust Eric, who was always sniffing around Dylan, trying to get him into porn. That outraged Daniel even as it aroused him.

But he was also worried about what Dylan meant, "Now you live in me." What were they really? Rivals, to be sure. Friends and lovers, yes. But husbands, eternal soul mates? Or just two guys having a momentary good time?

"Not quite," Daniel said aloud as he left Dylan's mouth. He made his way down to his lover's cock, parting his legs, nibbling at the flesh as he did. Dylan had the loveliest cock, long and thick with a perfect arrowhead, and his balls were like two ripe figs nestled in a tree.

But Daniel wasn't interested in paying homage to classic beauty. He wanted Dylan to know who was No. 1 in and out of the pool. He took him roughly, scraping his teeth against his scrotum, sucking him hard and dry. After Dylan came, Daniel touched the tip of his hypersensitive cock, heard him moan and watched him arch and clutch the sheets. He had such beautiful swimmer's hands—long fingers and lots of webbing.

Daniel lay down beside him and took the trembling Dylan in his arms.

"It's OK," Dylan said, burying his face in his lover's shoulder. "You can be as rough with me as you want. I can take it. I'm used to it."

"Has someone done something to you, baby?" Daniel said, pulling Dylan's head back and peering into his eyes.

"No, Dani, no. There's never been anyone but you. That first time, when we were teenagers, I said to myself, This is our wedding night."

Daniel kissed Dylan savagely then and held him so tightly he thought his ribs would crack. What am I doing? Daniel wondered.

"You decent in there?" Dee Dee yelled.

"Not yet, Aunt Dee Dee," Dylan said as they scrambled to part and find some clothes.

"OK, well, up and at 'em. Time for the pool. Come on, it's Daniel's special day. We don't want to waste a minute of it."

Dee Dee had prepared Daniel's favorite brunch—strawberry-stuffed challah bread French toast with cinnamon, powdered sugar, and maple syrup, and turkey bacon, sliced melon, and latte.

"I have a candle in my French toast," Daniel said.

"Ooh, lucky you," Dylan said, as he brought a tiny triangle of toast to his lips, rather seductively, Daniel thought.

"Everyone gets a candle on his special day," Dee Dee said.

After practice, Daniel and Dylan got tattoos, circular leaf patterns with interlocking Ds—Dylan's present to him.

"We can tell everyone the initials are ours and our moms'. Only we will know they're really about us."

Daniel chose an armband style; Dylan, a bracelet style over his right shoulder. The tattoo artist was a friend of Dee Dee's.

"I think it's so sweet you guys want to honor your moms this way,"

Dee Dee said as she distractedly thrust a paintbrush into her upswept curls.

Daniel wondered if they were fooling the less distracted tattoo artist. As Dylan lay there with his shirt off wincing as the artist worked on him, Daniel had all he could do to hide his erection.

"There's a big surprise with dinner," Dylan said as they left, mouthing, And more after.

Dinner featured more Daniel faves—chicken parmigiana, spaghetti, garlic bread, and mesclun salad, with red velvet cake for dessert.

"My, it's just an orgy of carbs, isn't it?" Dee Dee said.

As she and Rosa laid out the feast, the doorbell rang. Fred and Ginger were on the case.

"Austie, put the dogs out in the garden for now. Jordie, get that."

Daniel wasn't expecting his mother.

"God, what are you doing here?" he said, rising to hug her tightly.

"You are surprised: I can see it by the look on your face. Did you think I'd be anywhere but with you on this day? We shared it twenty-three years ago. I haven't missed it since."

"It's the perfect present, Mom. Thanks."

"Don't thank me. Thank Dee Dee and Dylan. They arranged it."

Dylan looked sheepish as he raised a Coke to Daniel. Daniel felt like a heel for not treating him better.

Afterward, they went onto the screened-in porch to watch a new DVD remix of Debo's last concert, in San Francisco. Daniel looked for her in her descendants, who were watching with varying degrees of interest. They all had the thick Norquist curls, molded beauty, and large eyes, though only Dee Dee and Austin could be described as Norquist blonds. Still, none had Debo's silvery blond mane or faraway, almost otherworldly look, which Daniel decided was a good thing. There was something unnerving about Debo, as if she were one of those silkies she was always singing about.

One of her encores was also a Debo signature, "Wind and Rain."

"OK, is it me, or is this one of the stupidest songs ever?" Jordan grumbled.

"It's you," Austin said, not bothering to look up from his iPad.

"No, check it out. This is a song about rivals, two sisters after the same guy. Of course, the brunette is the less attractive, evil one who pushes the pretty, goody-two-shoes blonde into the river to drown, because, as we all know, brunettes aren't as nice as blondes."

Poor Jordan, Daniel thought with brunet sympathy, always the underappreciated mid-kid, even if he were the greatest beauty among the Roqué brothers.

"But here's the clincher: A guy fishes her dead body out of the river. Does he give her a decent burial or try to find her folks? No, no. He makes a long fiddle bow out of her long, yellow hair, and a fiddle out of her bones. Tell me that this is not the most grotesque thing you've ever heard. I mean, why did Grandma Debo even sing this song? What was the point?"

"The point, my dear," Dee Dee said, "is that though life is short, art is long. And the fact that you don't grasp that after almost four years at Stanford, is, well, goodness gracious, great balls of fire."

"'You shake my nerves, and you rattle my brain,'" Austin sang, pretending to be Jerry Lee Lewis.

"No, we're singing with Grandma Debo tonight," Dee Dee said, laughing.

"'Oh, the dreadful wind and rain,'" Austin sang, pointing to Dylan. The next time the chorus came up, he sang the line, handing it off to Daniel, who sat next to him, and so on. Even everyone's favorite contrarian, Jordan, got into the act, pounding it out on the piano in the next room.

After Daniella went back to her hotel to work on a paper she would be presenting in Chicago and Rosa retired, the boys said good night.

"I think there's one more present for you upstairs," Dylan said.

"Well, why don't you get it out," Daniel said with as straight a face as possible, "and I'll be up in a minute."

He sought Dee Dee out in her pale yellow studio. It faced the northern light and was really as much an old-fashioned library as it was a studio. It was there that she graded papers for the art history class she taught at Berkeley, planned exhibits and lectures, and did her artwork. She was sketching a portrait of Diana and the boys when they were young. Above the desk hung a painting of her, Debo, and Diana as diaphanous, silvery sea nymphs, their backs to a dreamy sea.

"Now I know the secret of your success," Daniel said. "You never sleep."

"You know what Teddy Roosevelt said?"

"'Black care rarely follows a restless rider?'"

She smiled: "Exactly."

"I just wanted to thank you for everything—my party, this long weekend."

"You're welcome. But it was all Dylan. I'm glad he has a friend. I worry that he takes on too much responsibility. But you didn't come in here just to say thanks. You want to know if your father and I were ever lovers. It's all right. I anticipated that you'd get around to asking."

"And were you?"

"Ari Kahn was the loveliest boy, with big, beautiful hazel eyes. And he was a wonderful dancer. He wanted to be a math teacher in the inner city. Did you know that? I bet you didn't."

"Why'd you let him go, Dee Dee?"

"Your father wanted a Jewish wife to give him Jewish children. I wouldn't give up my religion. When I was growing up, the nuns were the one thing that gave my life stability, order. I couldn't turn my back on that."

"So because of stupid, meaningless religion—"

"Oh, honey, life is so much more complicated than that. The war had changed everything. It robbed your father of his extended family, just as it robbed Grandpa Declan of his mind."

She pointed to a photograph of a smiling young man in a scoop-necked, 1930s-style swimsuit, who looked just like Dylan, save for his blond hair.

"Grandpa Declan was a swimmer with dreams of being an Olympian and a Hollywood actor. Then the war came, and he was sent to Okinawa. My mother said the only time he spoke about it, he said they had to smoke the Japanese out of the caves on the island. I later learned the Japanese would cut off the genitals of the American POWs and shove them down their throats. After the war, Grandpa came home to San Francisco, married Grandma Rosemary, started a very successful insurance business, and they had my mother.

"Then one day he went out to the tool shed to clean his service revolver and it went off, killing him. He had been an expert marksman in the war.

"Our choices are reactions to the choices made by others. Now time for bed. But Daniel, when you see your father, give him my best and try to have some compassion for him. He's lost so much of what he loved."

That night Daniel dreamt of his sister. He imagines her lying on the path, her neck broken, the snow bloodied, Criterion fleeing wildly. He hears his mother say, "Oh my baby. You were my baby." He sees his father weep as they pray the kaddish.

Two weeks after Ani dies, Criterion is dead, in the same place, in the same way.

. . . .

DANIEL WOKE TO THE LIGHT STREAMING ONTO THE BED, CUT-ting a lemon wedge across the room. Its warmth brought the scent of spring. He rose and wrapped a cotton blanket around himself as Dylan stirred.

Soon it will be summer, time for the Olympics in New York. And winter is just a dream, he thought as he looked out a small gabled window at the glittering bay.

Alex

WHENEVER SPORTSWRITERS PORTRAYED ALEX—AS KEN RANSOM did for a cover piece in the current *Sportin' Life* magazine, profiling athletes to watch at the upcoming New York Olympics—they invariably referred to his sense of irony.

"He has the most delicious, ironic wit," Étienne told Ransom when reached on his honeymoon on the French Riviera. (No doubt Étienne must've been thinking of the Hermès scarf I sent his bride as a wedding gift, Alex thought.)

"An ironic wit and a wicked backhand," Evan texted Ransom from his home in Melbourne.

"Ironic?" Marius mused. "Yes, of course, he is. He'd have to be, wouldn't he? After all, he's Greek. He knows all about tragedy."

. . . .

ALEX DID INDEED KNOW ALL ABOUT IT. HE WAS BORN TO IT. How many times as a small child has he peered at the grave marked with his own name, his own birthday?

His mother, Sofia, kneeling beside him and filling his head with the scent of her Chanel No. 5, shows him how to make the sign of the cross—right to left in the Eastern tradition—and brings his pudgy fingers to his bow-shaped mouth.

"Now kiss the stone, Alex," she whispers. "Kiss your baby brother and say, 'I love you, baby brother, and I pray every day for your sweet soul.'"

The baby who lies cold and decaying in the grave is actually Alex's older brother, Alexandros Philippos Vyranos, born and dead one year to the day Alex was born.

"They gave you his name and his birthday," his sister, Eleni, says when they visit the spot, under an olive tree in Athens, as older children. She rests a hand on Alex's shoulder. "Poor you."

But Alex doesn't feel sorry for himself at all. Peering at the grave is like peering at another self. It's a quality that will stand him in good stead as he watches himself weather life's painful moments, of which Étienne's little S&M games aren't the half of it.

When he is five, his parents decide to hire a relative who has had much success coaching athletes, his mother's cousin Stavros. His parents, who believe their son is a child of destiny sent by God to assuage the loss of their firstborn, nonetheless don't want to push too hard. Stavros understands.

Except that when Alex's parents aren't around, they play by Stavros's rules. And Stavros's rules are brutally simple: For every ball Alex misses hitting over the net, he has to stand there while Stavros hits one into his back with a real whoop that knocks the wind out of him. Cry, complain, or express any displeasure—not to mention any hint of telling Mama and Papa—and it's two balls, whoop, whoop.

Alex quickly learns not to miss any serves or returns. Still, he's not perfect, and many days he leaves the court with no other thought than hiding the welts.

"I'm telling," Eleni sobs when she catches sight of his back. "I'm telling Mama and Papa, and the police will come and take cousin Stavros away."

"And what good will that do except to upset everyone. Let me handle it."

Over the years, Alex watches his self take and take the abuse until the time when he is big and strong and fast and smart and successful enough to ram the ball down Stavros's throat. Instead, he informs him that his services will no longer be required and that he should think twice before taking on any other students.

Whereupon Alex hires good, kind, lovable Demetrius Livanos—Demi to all—who is more Sancho Panza to his Don Quixote than coach. But Alex figures he has earned the right to coast as far as a coach is concerned.

It is, Alex thinks, ironic.

. . . .

SUCH THOUGHTS GIVE HIM DISTANCE, PERSPECTIVE. THEY PRO-tect his heart, which he's in danger of losing to a certain young man with wide, nutmeg eyes and long, curling lashes that veil his soul. Alex longs to kiss the lids, which flutter like butterflies in their cocoons, and set that soul free. Where is his famous ironic detachment now?

Alí has touched something in his heart and stirred something in his own soul, something that he thought lay buried with his baby brother. So when he sees Alí on TV after he and Evan are escorted off the plane during "Nutgate," looking so thin and fragile in his hoodie, Alex knows he has to act.

"Papa," he says, "your company has a team of international lawyers. I'm sure you have someone in Washington who can help my friends, who are in trouble."

"I hear, Alex, that these boys are very wild."

"No, no, Papa. They are good, family-minded, church-going boys. Frankly, I think the airline overreacted."

"It's the Americans. They've been like that since 9/11."

Alex knows his father's just bitter about the bailout in Greece, which comes with austerity strings that he thinks are attached by the Americans. Best not to bring that up now.

"Yes, well, Papa, I'm sure you have an interesting geopolitical point there. But that doesn't solve the problem at hand, does it? Can you help?"

Spyros leads to his company's law firm, which leads to Quentin, which leads Alí to send Alex a gorgeously woven basket filled with Gala apples. Not since Eve tempted Adam with one has fruit been so fraught with meaning.

The basket is accompanied by a handwritten note, which reads in part: "I only wish I knew how to repay you for rescuing Evan and me."

Alex can think of a thousand ways and none of them involve him and Alí being clothed.

"Just glad I could help," Alex texts.

After, they flirt with each other at a distance, a mating dance conducted over many tournaments in which Alí finishes no better than the quarterfinals or semis. Alex longs for him to break through, if only so they can meet regularly in the finals, and Alex can know the rippling pleasure of embracing that taut, sweaty body at the net, lingering there for all the world to see. He gets his wish at last year's US Open when Alí stuns Étienne and the New York audience with a 6–7, 6–7, 7–6, 6–3, 6–4 victory.

Alex, who has defeated the hotheaded Evan in the first semifinal—hardly an accomplishment, Alex thinks, as Evan has a way of defeating himself—hangs around the locker room to watch the second semifinal and is as shocked (and, he suspects, as secretly pleased) as everyone else at Arthur Ashe Stadium to see Alí, down two sets, battle back to take the match. For Alex, the irony is doubly exquisite: Here is his supercilious former love deposed by his potential love, a man Étienne has no use for.

What happens after, though, elevates the extraordinary to the transcendent. Courtside reporter Glenna Day Costa, the former women's No. 1-turned-TV's golden girl du jour, asks Alí if there's anything special he'd like to say.

"Yes," he says. "I owe my career above all to one person, Private First Class Michael A. Smeaton, who died of injuries received in Iraq. He taught me many things, including this song, which they sang at the funeral of his brother, Timmy, a firefighter who died in the Twin Towers on 9/11. Michael loved his brother. He loved tennis. And he loved this country. I promised him that if I ever got to the finals of the US Open, I would sing it for him. So I sing it now as we approach the 9/11 anniversary for everything that has been lost and still remains."

In a limpid tenor he began:

> The minstrel boy to the war is gone,
> In the ranks of death ye will find him;
> His father's sword he hath girded on,
> And his wild harp slung behind him;

'Land of Song!' said the warrior bard,
'Tho' all the world betray thee,
One sword, at least, thy rights shall guard,
One faithful harp shall praise thee!'
The minstrel fell! But the foeman's chain
Could not bring his proud soul under;
The harp he lov'd ne'er spoke again,
For he tore its chord asunder;
And said, 'No chains shall sully thee,
Thou soul of love and bravery!
Thy songs were made for the pure and free
They shall never sound in slavery!'

When Alí finishes, the throng is silent. Glenna is silent. Alex sits alone in the locker room silent, weeping.

"God bless the United States of America, my adopted country," Alí says softly. "God bless Iraq, my native land. God grant the whole world peace."

The crowd rises, erupting in applause. Even Mme. Alençon—seated in one of the premium boxes with Étienne's other guests, including his fiancée, Victorine Moreau, and her friend, the model Chloë Miller—is on her feet, brushing away a tear.

"Where did you learn to sing like that?" Glenna asks.

"My mother is a music teacher in Paris," Alí says proudly, then adds, blowing a kiss to the air, "*Je vous aime, Maman. Je vous remercie.*"

He waves and exits the stadium, having won the match, the crowd, and the YouTube moment.

"I think," Glenna says, "we've just been treated to a clinic on all kinds of grace."

Alex stalls in the locker room through the interminable press conference playing out on the TV screens there. He just wants to size up his opponent, congratulate him, he tells himself. But whom is he kidding? He's much too smart to lie to himself.

He waits until he and Alí are alone in the locker room.

"That," Alex says, "was magic."

"Thanks. Coming from you, that means . . . that means everything."

Alí's nutmeg gaze meets Alex's cognac one before he lowers the curtain of sable lashes and laughs. There's a beat, a continental divide of a space. OK, awkward, Alex thinks, very awkward. Oh, what the hell. Take the plunge.

Alex's mouth is on Alí's as he presses him against the lockers. They are alike and yet not so, about the same height, 6 foot, 2 inches, but not the same build, and Alex wonders if he's crushing his beloved as he grinds his sculpted muscles into Alí's sinewy frame. There is, however, no mistaking the equal hardness of their wet groins, the liquid warmth of their release.

Then just as suddenly, it's over. Alex is on the other side of the locker room as a parade of coaches, reporters, officials, and linesmen comes through. He watches furtively while Alí undresses quickly and heads to the shower. Alex is annoyed he can't join him. How he'd love to lather the sweat off him and take him for real without the impediment of clothing.

After he manages to get rid of the sponsors, well-wishers, and autograph-seekers, Alex heads back to the locker room to find Alí dressing alone, rubbing his eyes periodically with his sleeve.

"Sorry about before," Alex says. "I mean, I heard voices. We can't be too careful. What's the matter? Why are you crying, angel? Oh my God, are you a virgin?"

Alí says nothing, just sits there trembling.

"It's OK," Alex says, putting an arm around his shoulder and kissing his forehead. "It's lovely. You're lovely."

"Tell you what: Let me give you a proper date. My suite at seven, dinner, then dessert."

For Alex, the next few hours pass in a flurry of blind preparation. He texts Demi and his team that he will be going to bed early, which he has every intention of doing, he thinks with a wicked grin. He plumps the plush, leopard-print pillows and cushions in his jeweled-tone, penthouse hotel suite. With its Abstract Expressionist prints, bold bird of paradise arrangements, and floor-to-ceiling views of the East River, it's vibrant, virile, and exotic, though never more so than Alex himself, who is showered, buffed, blow-dried, cologned, and clad only in leopard-print pajama bottoms and a short, open black silk robe. Don Juan himself couldn't have staged a better seduction scene.

Alex has timed it so the meal arrives at 6:50 p.m., with the waiter, ecstatic at the size of the tip, departing before Alí's arrival. And yet for all the care Alex has lavished on the moment—has he ever prepared for a tournament so painstakingly?—he has not really thought it through. He's about to embark on a love affair with a man he must play in tomorrow's final and who is likely to be his rival for the foreseeable future, someone capable of great passion.

Will passion trump irony? Where is the sense in it all? Isn't it madness?

Alex doesn't know, and he doesn't care. All he knows is that when the knock on the door comes, he throws it open, pulls Alí into the suite, presses him against a wall, and covers his mouth with kisses. It takes him a minute to realize that maybe his soon-to-be lover would like to take things more slowly.

"Oh, sorry," Alex says, stepping back to consider the bashful smile at play on lips lightly shadowed by stubble. He draws back Alí's hoodie then, slowly, gently, as if lifting a bridal veil. Alí laughs and tries to pat his hair into place. His thick, straight brown locks seem to head charmingly in every direction. They're a shade or two darker than Alex's own. Who knew such a drab color as brown had so many rich variations? Alex thinks. He smooths Alí's hair.

"That's better. Let's see you," he says, unzipping the hoodie to expose the fine bones of Alí's throat and the start of his manscape. He catches the glint of the gold cross Alí always wears and pats it affectionately. For Alex, there is no contradiction here, no irony, only love, and God is love.

"Come," Alex says smiling, taking Alí by the hand. "Let me show you something."

He leads him to the room-service table, which he has set up by the French doors that open onto a terrace. Alex has ordered a fig salad with a balsamic-gorgonzola vinaigrette, filet mignon with wild-mushroom ravioli smothered in mascarpone cream, Dom Perignon, espresso, and chocolate-boysenberry torte. It only occurs to him now that perhaps his would-be inamarato is: a) vegetarian, b) lactose-intolerant, c) diabetic, or d) otherwise allergic. Then he thinks back to the peanut butter and jelly sandwiches and apples Alí carries in his duffel bag and realizes that this is probably the most food he has ever seen. Suddenly, Alex is feeling something he's rarely used to feeling, a sense of shame.

"Wow," Alí says, bringing his hands to his mouth. "What a feast. But how will we ever play the final tomorrow? Maybe we should just apply this to our arteries directly and die now."

"We're never going to play," Alex says, holding up the forecast on his iPhone. "See? Hurricane Inez is going to skirt the coast, bringing heavy rain."

"Well," Alí says, "that is a shame."

"Yes, it is," Alex says, raising a glass. "To rainy days."

They sit side-by-side, Alex, a righty, to the right of Alí, a lefty, so there are no awkward bumps. They hold hands and Alex feeds Alí bits of fig, meat, and ravioli.

"More," Alí says.

Alex cuts a tiny triangle of torte and places it in Alí's mouth, letting him lick his fingers. He kisses him then, sucking the sweetness from his lover, longing to eat and be consumed by him. And Alí responds like a drowning man clinging to a lifeline.

"I choose this. I choose it. I choose you," he gasps when he breaks off.

"Of course, you do," Alex says, somewhat baffled, "and I choose you."

Only later, when it's too late, does he understand the full import of Alí's words. For now, all he says is, "Choice gives life meaning, Alí. It's the only thing that does.

"For instance, by choosing room service, we can wheel the table into the hall, and voilà! we're finished with the cleanup. Now for the real dessert."

Alex had forgotten what it's like to have a lover for whom it's all new—for whom he is new. His own first time, at age fifteen, consisted of cousin Stavros walking in on him in the bath, ripping the towel from around his waist, and inspecting him. A hurried, hushed call to his father led to a hastily arranged visit to the apartment of a much older woman, who tied him to her bed and took his virginity while Stavros and his friends laughed and played cards in the next room. He wonders how Alí would fare in such an environment. Not well, he imagines.

Alex sits next to him on the bed and slowly removes his hoodie. He tugs at the waistband of Alí's matching pearl-gray sweats, pleased to see that he's wearing nothing underneath.

"I didn't know what to wear. I wasn't sure what, I never—" Alí began.

"Shh," Alex says, taking his face in his hands, kissing his forehead, his nose, and each eyelid. "It's easy. All easy."

He slips his robe off his shoulders and, kissing Alí's hands, guides them there. Alí touches him like a blind man marveling before a work of art, reverently exploring the rounded muscles and caramel skin. For the first time in a long time, Alex understands just how beautiful he himself is.

Alí is lovely in a whole other way—nervy, jangling, spiky, still a man-child, really—even though they are barely a year apart on the birth certificate, so dear in his vulnerability.

"So sweet, so innocent," Alex teases as he slips off his own pajama bottoms. "So unsuspecting."

"Do you want me to—" Alí offers, shaking as he turns over on his stomach.

"No, no, it's too soon for that," Alex says, tenderly turning him over to face him.

As they lie side-by-side, Alex strokes the pulsing vein beneath Alí's long, erect cock and gently draws back the hood. Alí shudders.

"I know, angel. It's very sensitive. That's why we're going to take things nice and slow."

He places a condom on Alí's member and then one on his own. He takes Alí's hand and, guiding him, shows him how to mimic his touch.

"See? Easy," Alex says, running his free hand down Alí's spine. "So easy."

After a while, there is nothing but their breath as their lovemaking mirrors the music of their matches: long, deep rallies dazzling in their shifts of tempi and direction that open and close the space between them, the rhythm punctuated at long last by orgasmic winners that leave them panting. Alí nestles near Alex's heart, waiting to be held and kissed.

Later in the veiled light of a tear-streaked day, Alex wonders if he hasn't romanticized Alí's fragility into something it isn't. Somewhere in the middle of the night, Alex has been awakened by a shriek that sets his heart to beating like the wings of a bird he once saw crashing against a white-washed steeple on Mykonos.

"Alí, what is it? Wake up. You're dreaming."

But Alí is awake, staring wide-eyed straight ahead.

"The city's burning," he cries. "They're all dead."

Is he back on 9/11? Baghdad? What happened to him there? Alex doesn't know. And perhaps more terrifying, he realizes he doesn't know him.

He longs to tell him that old men send young ones off to die, as if that truism will be any comfort.

Instead, he says, "It's all right, angel. It's all in the past. And the past can't hurt you anymore."

But he knows that's a lie, knows the past is the floating country that can sink like Atlantis only to resurface when you least expect it, near the borderland of grief.

Alí isn't listening anyway. He's hyperventilating, and Alex, frantic, scrambles to find a paper bag for him to breathe into.

"That's right, slow and steady," Alex says, holding it in front of Alí's face with one hand and cupping the back of his head with the other.

When Alí's breathing returns to normal, the sobbing begins.

"Shh," Alex says, kissing his forehead as he rocks him in his arms. "There's nothing here in the dark but you and me. See only me."

After a while, they lie back on the bed, Alí's head on his chest, and Alex begins to stroke him.

"It's OK, nothing to be afraid of. It's only love."

Soon Alí falls asleep, but Alex lies awake for a long while, thinking. It must be the Iraq War. Yes, that's it. Yet even as Alex thinks it, he knows that isn't it, that there's something darker, even more evil than war itself. And it scares Alex, scares him like when he was a child and his father told him the story of Theseus and Ariadne going into the maze to slay the beastly Minotaur. What will he find at the end of this labyrinth?

When they finally wake, Alí seems none the worse for wear, but Alex is an exhausted wreck, though one with no time to think about fatigue. There is an insistent banging on the door, and a day begun badly is about to get a whole lot worse.

"Vyranos, open up," an official shouts. "Drug test."

"Just a minute," Alex yells back.

"Now."

"Alí, come on. They're doing drug tests."

When it comes to drug tests, tennis officials are like General Custer: They attack at dawn without warning. Better than being swimmers, Alex thinks. They have to pee in front of their officials. Gross. Still, the banging at the door is one way to get the old ticker pumping—though not the preferred way.

"I'll get out," Alí says.

"No, no time," Alex says. "Stay in the bedroom. Lock the door. I'll tell him I'm entertaining someone. Where's my cell? Wait five minutes, then text me. It doesn't matter what. I'll tell him that you're on your way back to the hotel from the gym now and that you're running late for our breakfast meeting. When he leaves here, you sneak upstairs."

"The gym, a breakfast meeting with my opponent on the day of a final, really? In what world, Alex, does that make sense?"

Alí looks at him expectantly, and the terrors of the night vaporize, along with Alex's fatigue.

"We're meeting at a sponsor's request. Listen, Alí, it doesn't matter what's true. It only matters what you can persuade people to believe might be true. Besides, we won't be playing today. Remember the hurricane? Afterward, you sneak back down here, and I'll have breakfast waiting. Blueberry pancakes."

Alí grins: "You better get going."

"I'm so sorry to keep you waiting," Alex says, running a hand through his cloud of thick, dark hair. "My companion was reluctant to let me go."

The geezer of an official in his crested blazer is still enough of a man to leer but not enough to be distracted.

"Let's move it along. I've still got Iskandar on my list."

Just then Alex's phone pings.

"Speak of the devil. I'm supposed to be meeting him in a bit. These sponsors can be so tedious with their breakfast meetings. Anyway, he's on his way back from the gym, running late. I'll be done in a minute."

"Don't you dare let him know I'm on my way up to his room," the official says as Alex hands him a sealed bag with the sample vial.

"Oh, I wouldn't dream of it," Alex says, smiling.

He waits till he hears the elevator close then zips up Alí's hoodie and ushers him out with a kiss. He heads back to bed, inhaling his lover's scent on the sheets. He hugs his pillow as he watches the rain bead on the windows, luxuriating in the thought of a tennis-free, Alí-full day. When the phone rings, his heart sings. But it's only Demi.

"You up early."

"Drug testing."

"Sleep well?"

"Like a baby," Alex lies.

"Good. Rest a bit more. You play later."

"What? It's raining."

"They say it clear."

"But the hurricane."

"Change course. Out to sea."

"But it can't. Hurricanes don't just change courses."

"Alexandros, you like a little boy who does not want school so he pray for snow. God no answer those prayers."

"Those cheap bastards, Demi. They don't care who they hurt so long as they get their final in and make money."

"Is a business, Alex, your job. You lucky you paid so well to do something you love, something you so good at."

"I know, I know. I'll be ready at 1:30. Pick me up then."

"Good boy. And don't forget church. You can pray for something real, like a win."

Alex's phone pings again.

"Coast clear. Breakfast?" Alí's text reads.

"Better not. We play later," comes Alex's response.

He waits for Alí to reply, and in that eternity of a minute, that void of a blank iPhone screen, he feels all the disappointment of Alí's heart and his own.

It's not going to work, Alex thinks, except that it must, because I want him.

"Understand," Alí writes. "Is OK. Good luck."

Alex pauses, uncertain of what to say.

"Late-nite celebration? Win or lose, no matter what?"

"No matter what," Alí replies.

Except, of course, that Alex has no intention of losing. No, he intends to win the US Open, and not only to win but to cement his No. 1-ranking, with Alí in his old spot as the new No. 2. That is what he prays for at the Church of St. Sophia. He doesn't need Demi to tell him that God doesn't answer such prayers either.

. . . .

THEY HARDLY TALK AS THEY WAIT TO WALK OUT ONTO THE court of Arthur Ashe Stadium amid a drizzle and a torrent of applause. And though Alex will ultimately prevail 7–5, 4–6, 6–3, 6–7, 7–6, Alí stays with him for more than five hours of play. Alex has never been so proud and so conflicted about anyone else. What did he expect, that Alí would roll over, the way he did in bed? Instead, in the deathless rallies, he matches endurance for endurance, waiting for his moment to seize the tenor of the match and dictate shots worthy of a pool hustler.

It's then that Alex knows that he is in the presence not merely of a player possessed of great athletic gifts but one who can see time in space, anticipating Alex's shots as they leave his racket. And something else, Alex knows: He is now inextricably linked to someone who sees tennis as another vehicle for love. And that chills him more than any 125-mile-an-hour serve.

"Will you sing for us tonight?" Glenna asks Alí at the trophy presentation.

"Not tonight. The night belongs to the champion and the people of New York. Congratulations to Alex, his entire team, and his family for a job well done."

And on that disquieting note the day comes full circle. What is Glenna doing, asking Alí to sing, Alex wonders, more than miffed. It's his moment, isn't it? Alí has recognized as much. Why hasn't Glenna?

Or the rest of the media, for that matter. On the morning shows the next day, all everyone wants to ask him about is Alí: What does Alex think of his recording "The Minstrel Boy" for a 9/11 charity? What is he like? Are the rivals good friends?

Oh, yeah, Alex thought almost a year later as he flipped Alí over on his stomach during their Martha's Vineyard break before the New York Games, real good.

Dylan

WITH THE NEW YORK GAMES SET TO BEGIN, DYLAN AND THE rest of the team are putting the finishing touches on their practices at a facility outside the city. This is the time Dylan loves best: no more cross-training, well, not much; no more dryland workouts; just pure swimming, he and Daniel and the team and the water and several thousand screaming fans. OK, so it isn't so Zen. But if he focuses, he can pretend it's just him and the water, because that's all he can control, really. And Dylan is all about control, since his life thus far has been so out of it.

. . . .

"LOOK, DYLIE, LOOK AT THE OCEAN," HIS MOTHER WAS SAYING to his three-year-old self. "Pacific means 'calm.' But the ocean is anything but today. Feel it, baby, feel the water between your toes."

She began to sing: "'There were two sisters came walking by the stream. Oh, the wind and rain. Older one pushed the younger one in. Oh, the dreadful wind and rain.'"

"Diana, what are you doing?"

"I'm teaching Dylie to swim."

"In this weather? Are you crazy? Come back up to the house."

"No."

"Diana—"

"Stay away from me."

"Diana, listen to me: You're six months pregnant. You're not thinking clearly. It's going to storm. Give me the boy and get out of the water."

"No."

"Give me my son."

Whereupon Dylan started shrieking as his father tore him from his mother's arms, and she, tripping through the waves, struggled to beat his father with her fists.

"Let go of him. Let go of my child."

"Mama, Mama," Dylan cried, wriggling to try to set himself free.

"You wait, Diana. You wait till you drop this second one. I'm going to commit you so fast, your crazy head will spin."

"No, Tony, please. I'll be good. I promise. Just give me my child. Give him to me now."

. . . .

HE IS STANDING IN THE GUEST ROOM OF DANIEL'S HOME IN Scarsdale. The room is slate blue with Delft-print curtains. Except for the painting of the girl and horse over the bed—one of Dee Dee's works—you'd never know this had been Ani's bedroom.

Dylan can't help but glance at the canvas as he places his wallet and sunglasses in his black sports jacket. Here she is, he thinks, framed by the past, frozen in time, so blond and pretty, like Daniella, Aunt Dee Dee, and his mother.

"She was lovely, wasn't she," Daniella says.

She stands in the doorway, looking lithe and lightly tanned in a sleeveless electric-blue, cowl-neck dress and black sling-backs.

"Yes, she was. She looked like you, Daniella. Daniel, I take it, looks like Ari."

"Well, you'll see for yourself tonight, won't you?"

"I wish you were coming with us."

Daniella straightens the lapels of Dylan's jacket and smiles.

"That's very sweet. But I have a date, of sorts, with a proctologist." She rolls her eyes. "We're working on a paper."

"Besides, you'll do fine with Ari. It's my son I'm worried about."

Her son says little as they whiz down the West Side Highway in his fire-engine red MG. Daniel's always less chatty when they're about to face off in competition, and now they're about to go head-to-head in the biggest competition of all. But there's the added stress of dinner with D.O.D.—Dear Old Dad, the great Ari Kahn, whom Dylan secretly thinks of as his father-in-law. It gives him the giggles to think of Ari that way. He's sure Ari would not be amused.

Ari has suggested they meet first at the headquarters of Ari Kahn, LLP, not far from Wall Street and the Olympic Village in lower Manhattan, before they head out to dinner at Jade's in Chinatown. Dylan is well aware that this is no mere generous gesture. This is Ari's chance to size up Deidre Norquist's oldest nephew. And Dylan is as ready for the encounter as he is for the 400 IM.

Ari Kahn may know money, but Dylan Roqué knows people. He has learned the hard way.

Still, Ari Kahn, LLP is just a teensy bit intimidating: thirty floors of wall-to-wall glass, climbing orchids, fish tanks, tickers announcing the news of the day—including a fat football contract—sleek gray furnishings, and sleeker young people clad in black and bustling about in a pleasantly self-satisfied way. A terrace filled with silver furniture gleams as the sun dazzles above the Hudson River and New York Harbor, casting shards of light over the water.

The gold letters in the slate-gray lobby announce the names of Ari Kahn Financial, Ari Kahn Global, and Ari Kahn Industries. About the only personal touch is a large framed photograph with a fresh bouquet of pale pink roses and stargazer lilies. Beneath the photo is the name "Arianna Reiner-Kahn" and the dates of a life too brief. Next to the photo is the name of The Ani Foundation and the list of its contributors. Dylan recognizes the names of some of the country's biggest movers and shakers, including his own father.

"What do all these companies do?" Dylan wonders.

"I have no idea," Daniel says.

"Perhaps, I can answer that. I'm Ari Kahn. It's a pleasure to meet you."

Ari is an older, handsome version of his stunning son: perfectly coiffed—and, Dylan assumes, expertly dyed—dark-brown hair; hazel eyes tending toward green; an aquiline nose; a well-shaped mouth; and lightly tanned skin that had triumphed over an early battle with acne.

His still-trim physique is offset by an impeccably tailored dark-blue suit that stops just so at his highly polished black lace-up shoes, a custom-made pale pink shirt with French cuffs and gold studded cuff links, a purplish tie, and a pocket hanky that is actually tiny squares of pink in every shade.

Dylan thinks he looks like a man who has everything a man could want and thus is very pleased with himself.

"Well, shall we take the fifty-cent tour before heading out? Katrina," he calls to a severe blonde dressed in black with clear hose. "Ring for David. We'll take the new silver Jag so the boys don't have to drive."

Dylan wonders whom the full-court press is really for. Certainly not for the son who glowers through most of a meal that features shrimp with Chinese broccoli and Peking duck pancakes in hoisin sauce. Nor, Dylan suspects, is it really for the benefit of himself. No, he imagines that Ari is in a way auditioning for a casting director who's not there and a role he actually lost a long time ago. It takes Ari a while—or maybe he's just waiting for enough time to elapse after the duck—but he finally gets around to his material point.

"So you are Tony Roqué and Diana Norquist's oldest son?"

"That's right, sir."

"Dreadful business."

"Dad," Daniel admonishes, trying to intercept the conversation.

"Poor Tony. How is your dad?"

"You'd probably know better than I, sir. I see his name up on the wall with the other big donors to The Ani Foundation."

"Yes, Tony's been remarkably generous, though it's been a while since we talked. Yet I know if I need anything, I have only to call. That's the kind of roommate he was, that's the kind of friend he is."

"His friends have always spoken highly of him, sir. That his family can speak as glowingly is another matter."

"And, of course, that makes you Deidre Norquist's nephew. How is Dee Dee? Still making those images of naked men in birdcages? What the hell is that all about?"

"Give it a rest, Dad. Dylan's not an art critic."

"No, it's all right, Dani. I think Aunt Dee Dee's trying to get at the way men are trapped by their expectations of themselves. But I think she's moved on from those. In any event, we're enormously proud of her work."

"I take it she'll be coming to see you swim."

"Yes, she and my brothers will be arriving in a couple of days, in time for the opening ceremonies."

"Must be hard, being so wrapped up in her work."

"Well, no more than you are in yours, sir. But Aunt Dee Dee's always been involved in our lives. Even when we were young, Mom—may she rest in peace—my brothers, and I would go to Aunt Dee Dee's in Frisco, or she'd come stay with us in Malibu. We've always been close."

"She still lives in that big house?"

"She does."

"It was your grandmother's, wasn't it?"

"It was."

"And then she killed herself, just like your great-grandfather and your mother."

"Dad, really, enough. This isn't an interview or an interrogation."

"No, it's fine, really. There isn't a day goes by that I don't think of them and pray for their souls."

"So you're a practicing Catholic?"

"Well," Dylan says, laughing, "perhaps more observant in the spirit than in the letter of the law."

Even Ari has to laugh then. Dylan takes it as an opening.

"Will we see you at the games?"

"Oh, God, no. I mean, I went to Ani's equestrian events. Those were something. She was something, magic. Swimming is like watching fish in a tank—soothing but not particularly thrilling."

"That's too bad, because Daniel and I and the whole team, we're something, too. We can really light up a pool."

"How does that work?"

"Sorry?"

"I mean, you and my son are rivals, and yet, you room together, you're staying at my ex-wife's place for a couple of days, Daniel's been to Dee Dee's. I don't get it."

"Well, we're rivals of sorts, sure. But we're also teammates and friends. Don't forget rivalry is a lot like friendship: common cause, complementary temperaments. I'm sure you're friends with some of your rivals."

Ari gives him a hard look.

"I'm friends with none of my competitors.

"Daniel, that reminds me. My office—and I'm sure your mother and Dee Dee have experienced the same thing—has just been inundated with requests for interviews. I've deferred these to your mother's office. One reporter even wanted to talk about—get this—being the dad of an 'Olympic hero.' I mean, can you imagine? Hero? You guys are hardly fighting in Afghanistan or curing cancer."

"Well, sir, don't you think there's something heroic in the pursuit of excellence, whether you're swimming, steering a steed, or running Ari Kahn, LLP?"

"Daniel, I can see you have your hands full."

"What's that supposed to mean?" Daniel shoots back, alarmed.

Ari is taken aback.

"I only meant that he's a sharp competitor. I'd watch my back if I were you."

After, Ari insists on a quick stop to see his penthouse in Battery Park City before David drops them back at Daniel's car. The place, at the tip of Manhattan Island, with the harbor splintered silver in the moonlight, is like the prow of a ship and is designed accordingly. It's all teak wood and paintings of marine scenes, horses, and dogs, the epitome of commanding masculinity. Indeed, there are no feminine touches save for two surprising photos, one of Daniella and Ani on what appears to be Mother's Day, judging from the old-fashioned orchid corsage Daniella wears, and one of Ari and Tony as young men and two young women whose blond curls tumble about their shoulders, Dee Dee and Diana.

"Where was this taken?" Dylan asks, unable to resist the urge to pick up the photo and examine it closely.

"Sarah Lawrence. Tony and I came up from Princeton to see Dee

Dee and Diana, who was visiting. That was the spring before she won five gold medals in the Olympics."

"Aunt Dee Dee says back then you were planning to teach math in the inner city. What made you go into finance?"

"You know what Willy Sutton said when they asked him why he robbed banks?"

"'Cause that's where the money is?"

"I like this guy," Ari says to Daniel, who looks just miserable.

On the way back to Scarsdale, Daniel says nothing, and Dylan can't help but think he's done something wrong. Tomorrow, they'll be moving into the Olympic Village, where they'll be under such scrutiny there won't be a moment for any intimacy, and he can't stand the gulf that has risen between them.

When they get into the house, Dylan sees Daniella isn't home yet.

"What's wrong?"

"Nothing," Daniel says.

"No, something has to be wrong. You sulked like Achilles in his tent through dinner. You gave me the silent treatment all the way home. Now you won't even look at me. So let's have it. What the hell did I do?"

"Well, for starters, you didn't have to suck up to him. Calling him 'sir' and asking all those questions about his business. Understand, Dylan: There's nothing in it. My father thinks your whole family, apart from your father, is nuts. And he'll never forgive Dee Dee for dumping him. If he knew what we really are to each other, well, you would feel Ari Kahn rain down on you like a New York hurricane."

Dylan looks at Daniel sadly.

"I wasn't trying to 'suck up to him,' as you put it. I was merely being kind. And trust me, Daniel, if your father ever found out what we were doing, we wouldn't have to fear his wrath and the potential loss of our sponsors, certain fans, and our 'hero status,' because my father would kill us both. I remember one time he pulled me from my mother's arms with such force it knocked the wind out of me. You have no idea what he's capable of."

Daniel takes him in his arms then in a great wavelike rush, pressing him against the wall of the guest bedroom. Dylan catches sight of his aunt's painting of Ani planting a kiss on Criterion's nose, the epitome of innocence, as her brother tears off Dylan's shirt and rips open his pants.

"What if he killed you?" Daniel rasps. "What if he tore you limb from limb, crucified you like your God, gouged your eyes out and castrated you, all because of me?"

Dylan hears the door then and Daniella's footsteps.

"I wouldn't care," comes Dylan's urgent whisper. "I don't care."

Alí

THE PROSPECT OF THE NEW YORK GAMES FILLED ALÍ WITH A delicious sense of anticipation as well as dread. He had worked for this moment, sacrificed his very self. It was his destiny. But he feared what the press might dredge up. Already, Alex and his family had been hounded by reporters, eager to spin the story of a young man who'd be playing for the baby brother he had lost.

Huh? Alex was many things. A sentimentalist was not among them. If he were playing for the brother who might've had his life, he would hardly tell Alí, let alone the media. That poor dead baby: Why did they have to drag him into the picture?

And if reporters had ferreted that out, what would they do with his story? Alí thought. Fortunately, his former guardian's family had issued a preemptive salvo: "It has been an honor to see Alí Iskandar grow into a fine champion and an even finer young man. And we'll be rooting for him as he represents our country at the New York Games."

With that, the family refused further comment, to Alí's relief. How he longed for the day he could repay the $500,000, with interest. For those reporters who kept prying, Alí had an unexpected counter-check—Michael's wife, Kathy.

She turned out to have an untapped gift for public relations, filtering Alí's story through her late husband's and in the process reinventing herself as the author of *A Widow's Tale* and the blog of the same name.

Kathy had lost some weight, restyled her hair and makeup, and reorganized her house and life, but not so much as to alienate the women who were her base. Clad in black slacks and sweater sets, with a pretty Michaela, now thirteen, by her side, she was catnip to soccer moms in

Peoria and sob-sister interviewers like Angela Fong of the International News Network's (INN's) morning show *Here and Now.*

Hair hastily arranged in a twist held in place by a clip, which caused her to tuck the loose strands behind her ears constantly, Angie Fong had the air of a woman trying to get in on the joke before she became the butt of it. Sifting through her notes endlessly, touching her sympathetic subjects, or waving a finger in front of the unrepentant ones, Angie never let viewers forget how noble she was in bringing them stories like Kathy's.

"It must've been so difficult for you," Angie intoned, clutching Kathy's arm, eyes glistening.

"Wow," Kathy said, completely taken aback, "imagine if you had actually lived it."

"Touché," Alex said, laughing. "I can't stand journos who take someone's story and make it their moment. Brava, Kathy. She's magnificent."

"Magnificent," Alí repeated dreamily. He clasped Alex's hand as he lay face down on the bed, and his lover moved over him. The wind blowing off the Atlantic onto Martha's Vineyard whipped the white lace curtains and shades in the bedroom, creating a lapping sound that echoed Alex's thrusts and the pair's ragged breathing. Alí rested with his head on two pillows placed at the foot of the bed as if in a trance, listening to Kathy's voice on the tube, the whirring ceiling fan, and the snapping shades. This was heaven, a few days' respite in a contemporary colonial courtesy of an associate of Alex's father, who rarely used the place; a pale blue and white bedroom; a raised mahogany bed, imported from India that required you to climb a polished step-stool to reach it; crisp white sheets; and an expert lover who drew him up to himself so that he came so intensely his cries drowned out the plaintive sighs of the gulls, the murmur of the waves, and even Angela Fong's bleating.

Panting, Alí and Alex lay side by side then, spent. Usually, this was reassuring cuddle time, with Alex drawing the creamy quilted coverlet tenderly about his lover. Instead, they lay with their damp, sun-kissed skin exposed to the humid air. Alex traced the ropy landscape of Alí's body, as if exploring it for the first time and committing it to memory. He fingered the cross-shaped scar as he held Alí by the back of the neck and kissed him.

"I know a tattoo artist who can turn this into something beautiful."
Alí shook his head.

"It's fine as it is."

"What brutes."

"They were children who had been brutalized themselves."

"And so they chose to brutalize another child."

Alex paused before asking, "Did they touch you, angel, when they did this to you?"

Alí flashed on his guardian, licking his scar as he molested him. He drew back, gazing into Alex's eyes.

"No one has ever loved me like you, and no one ever will."

"Well, then," Alex said, grinning. "Shall we have another go at it?"

After, Alí felt only sadness. Why was it that at a moment of pure happiness, he should feel only its fleeting nature? Perhaps because he knew it wasn't long before the Games would begin, and he and Alex would be forced to part amid family arrivals and the world's scrutiny. Neither set of parents would be attending. They were just too nervous to watch their talented progeny. But Eleni would be coming to New York with her shipping magnate–fiancé, Georgios Andropolis, nicknamed Geo, while Alí's four siblings would be seeing him play for the first time in America.

He went to Kennedy Airport to meet them, and they rushed into his waiting arms like children who had found a long-lost father. Which was only right, Alí thought. Though he was the middle of the siblings, he had always been the big brother—sending them money and gifts, texting jokes and encouragement, shielding them from the high price he had paid for his success.

As they stood in the terminal in a huddle, arms linked, heads touching, he felt it had all been worth it. To have Birka and Miriam attend the Sorbonne and become doctors while Makmud studied business and textile design in southern France and Mikyal planned to enroll at the École des Beaux Arts, well, Alí couldn't have been prouder. But there was a part of him that worried about how to balance this family visit with the Olympics's professional demands (and his hard-won private life).

"You leave that to me," Kathy said. "I'll take care of the family. You just concentrate on tennis."

And she did, shuttling the sibs to the USTA Billie Jean King National Tennis Center, where the tennis events were being held, escorting them to sites about town, and generally serving as a big sister, with Michaela, the adored and adoring little sister, in tow.

Left to the game and the Games, Alí soon realized that the Olympic experience was not quite what he imagined: from the highly symbolic and somewhat pompous opening ceremony, this one taking a Cook's tour through American and New York history, complete with a chorus line of Statues of Liberty; to the too-small rooms at the Olympic Village that required you to roll over the bed to get to the other side, a running joke among the athletes, who dubbed it an extra event; to the crushing expectations. In tennis, even the Slams, you won, you lost, sometimes triumphantly, sometimes bitterly, but you moved on. In the Olympics, you could go from hero to goat—as opposed to GOAT, greatest of all time—in a matter of hours, and the sweetness or sting went on forever. Magnifying the lens under which victory and defeat were inspected were people like roomie and doubles partner, up-and-comer Ryan Kovacs, for whom no hurdle—be it a scraped elbow, a missed line call, the traffic going to the stadium—was safe from hyperbole.

With the family and Kathy off enjoying themselves and Alex ensconced in the Greek House in the Olympic Village, concentrating on his own singles and doubles performances, there was nothing for Alí to do but stretch, play, shower, eat, sleep, and listen to Ryan complain about everything everywhere. Not even Alí's books and music offered a refuge from the heartbreak of Ryan's sinus problems in the New York humidity or the failure of Ryan's family to secure adjoining suites at the Four Seasons. He made Evan look like a Zen master.

"How's it going?" Alex texted.

"Oh fantastic," Alí wrote back. "U?"

"Uh, same. Miss U."

"Me 2."

Alí and Alex were on course to meet not only in the singles final but the doubles as well, thanks to a little heart-to-heart with Ryan, in which Alí suggested that they put aside the tragedy of Ryan's ingrown toenail for the good of God and country. Wherein Ryan—who was wildly talented, emphasis on the wild—started playing better. And though they were seeded eighth, they found themselves in the finals against Alex and Dmitri Constantin. The match contained some sparkling play at the net, the ball pinging among the quartet as if attached by invisible rubber bands.

Alí, though, had all he could do to keep his mind on the match and not on his longing for his ravishing lover. He loved to watch Alex serve in particular, loved the way his shaggy hair and the tail ends of his blue-and-white head scarf trailed down his back as he arched in a slight twist to meet the ball, loved the way the trickle of man fur peeked out from the waistbands of his shorts and undies as his shirt rode up, loved the way he stalked the base line like a panther. Alí's long fingers fiddled with the strings of his racket between points. It helped him to concentrate, to soothe himself, to keep from hurling himself into his lover's arms.

In the end, Alex and Dmitri—well, mostly Alex—were too much as they prevailed 7–6, 6–4, 6–7, 6–7, 6–4. Ryan's last forehand went wide, and he was on the verge of crumbling into tears when Alí grabbed him by the scruff of the neck and hugged him.

"You did a great job," Alí said. "They simply played better."

Alí shook hands with Dmitri first.

"Too good," he said as he offered a hand to Alex, who embraced him.

"I'd like to suck you right here," Alex whispered.

He stepped back, adding, "Now off you go to the press conference with that thought in your head and that blush on your cheek."

"What did he say?" Ryan asked as they made their way to the post-match interviews.

"Oh, he just wanted to congratulate us on winning the silver medal in doubles."

The singles final was a different story. For seven hours, Alí and Alex slugged it out from the base line, chasing down seemingly irretrievable shots, each refusing to yield to the other as they did so often in bed. Alí saved at least three match points, or was it four? He lost track of the score, the time, the number of shirts he changed. He must've sweated off ten pounds. His doubled socks were soaked with perspiration and blood.

As an unbearably hot afternoon gave way to a sticky evening, he was only aware of the need to stay entirely within the moment and play the ball, the point before him. The lover who so gently drew the covers around his shoulders, saying, "You're shivering, angel. Let me warm you," now glared at him across the net, as if he would devour him whole, leaving only Alí's long, fine bones.

But Alí didn't flinch. As much as he wanted Alex, he wanted this, too, for himself; his family, who shouted encouragement from the stands; for his two countries; for all the bombs that had been dropped and lives lost; for the nights he had suffered at the cruel hands of his tormentor. When Alex netted the last return, and the crowd screamed—as much in relief as in disbelief—Alí dropped to his knees and kissed the ground. He pounded it with one outstretched fist as he sobbed in both joy and sorrow.

At the net, Alex waited, ashen, shaken, dazed, lost. Alí had seen that look many times in Iraq. He held him for what seemed like an eternity, burying his long, exquisite profile in Alex's sculpted shoulder, drinking in his ripe, spicy scent. Slowly, Alex embraced him with one arm. But the other, which held his racket, went limp. And in that gesture, Alí realized that more had changed than the pecking order in tennis, that something had been gained and lost, that they were separated not only by a net but also by the border of their own ambitions. They were real rivals now. Their relationship would never be the same.

What Alí would take from that Olympics was not the thrill of watching Alex lead the Parade of Nations as the Greek flag-bearer; or his siblings standing and cheering for him, waving the American and Iraqi flags; or Kathy, wiping tears from her eyes; or himself, atop the podium, clutching two tiny American and Iraqi flags and a nosegay, singing "The Star-Spangled Banner" through his tears; but the image of himself, captured by a photographer, with his face pressed against his lover's right shoulder, and Alex's racket arm caught somewhere between passive resistance and death.

Daniel

DANIEL WAS ANNOYED. NO, THAT WASN'T QUITE THE RIGHT word for it. Pissed. Beside himself. Angry at the world. Disheartened. Depressed. Frightened. Sick. He was getting closer. Disenchanted: That was it. Daniel was disenchanted.

He had come to the Olympics with certain expectations. He and Dylan had forgone the opening ceremonies—always a heavy-handed affair, save for the Parade of Nations—ostensibly to rest for the 400 IM the next night but actually to fuck as many times as they could before any of their rowdy teammates returned to their suite.

"Wow," Dylan said as they lay naked, breathless and glistening, "if hot sex were an Olympic event, we'd so medal."

"We'd go gold every time," Daniel added, kissing his lover's ripped belly.

The Olympics, though, had a way of tarnishing golden dreams. Not that Daniel hadn't done well. He had done very well, winning the 400 IM—his signature event, and let's face it, the one that established the best overall swimmer—as well as the 100- and 200-meter butterfly. But he had finished second, second, third, and fourth to Dylan in the 200 IM, the 100- and 200-meter backstroke, and the 200-meter free-style. They had teamed to help crush the opposition in the 4 × 100- and 4 × 200-meter freestyle relays and the 4 × 100 medley. So Daniel had finished with six golds to Dylan's seven.

And Dylan had earned all silvers in Daniel's winning events. So Dylan had come out ahead. Plus, the way the organizers stacked the events it seemed as if Daniel faded while Dylan got stronger as the week went on.

Daniel knew he should've been happy. He was brilliant, beautiful, and even without the endorsements and offers that always easily came his way, rich beyond most people's dreams. And he shared his life with someone who was as accomplished, maybe more so.

And therein lay the problem. He wasn't the dominant swimmer anymore. He was coequal of a real rival. The context had shifted. And, as Daniel knew, context drove perception, which was everything.

Maybe it was the media coverage, with him and Dylan back-to-back on magazine covers or facing, cupping each other's medals. Did the publishers have any idea how gay that was?

He didn't know: Maybe it was the smart-ass bloggers, taking sides with their snarky remarks.

"Why do you even read that stuff?" Coach Mathis said. "You know it's written by a bunch of fat guys with long ponytails in greasy black T-shirts who sit around all day jacking off to porn and feeling superior to the athletes they see when they channel surf."

"Just because they didn't go to Harvard—"

"Go to Harvard? They couldn't drive to Harvard. Tune 'em out."

There was, however, one critic he couldn't.

"Congratulations," began his father's email. "But I told you that Roqué kid bore watching. Still, a good effort though not quite as good as his."

What did it matter? He and Dylan were young, healthy, in love, and Olympic champions. Daniel should've been ecstatic. That he wasn't only deepened his unhappiness. How could he be so selfish, so jealous when there was real misery in the world? he thought as he and Dylan watched the medal ceremony for Alí Iskandar.

"Do you know this guy's story?" Dylan asked. "Absolutely incredible. I mean, to survive all he did in Iraq and come here to train and live with a foster family thousands of miles from home when he was still a kid. I'd like to shake his hand."

"Me, too," Daniel said. "Although I feel bad for Alex Vyranos. I always thought he was amazing."

Daniel thought Alex looked as miserable with his silver medal as he himself felt. He had to do something. Achievement had always been his antidote for unhappiness. At Harvard, he'd study and swim to the point of exhaustion. Too restless to sit reading in the Olympic Village, he took off to the one place he knew could restore his spirit, Central Park. I'll just walk, he thought. Soon, however, he was not just walking briskly but running. He didn't know why. It wasn't like he ran regularly. He had always thought he had two left feet on land. Maybe he wanted to prove something, tire himself to the point of oblivion. Or maybe if he ran far and fast enough, he could escape everything.

But the park was a loop that doubled back on itself, a pattern within a pattern. "The pattern of my life," Paul Simon sang on his iPod. "And the puzzle that is me."

The song was jangling and modal. It suited his mood and his thinking. It didn't matter what you did. Like Simon's "rat in a maze," you had to follow your strand in the pattern of the universe. His and Dylan's strands were bound—for now.

Another runner was approaching. Daniel recognized him immediately as Alex Vyranos. He turned around to run alongside him.

"Hey, I don't want to spoil your run. Just want to say congratulations. The championship match was amazing."

"Thanks, same to you."

"Dani."

"Alex."

"Uh, I think we kind of know each other."

Alex laughed. "Yeah, I guess we do."

"Look, I won't keep you, but I'm having a party. Actually, my father's having a party, tomorrow night for some of the Olympians. I'll send an invite over to the Greek House."

"May I bring a friend?"

"You may bring as many as you like."

Daniel ran in place, watching Alex run on, admiring his beautiful form.

The prospect of seeing Alex again was about Daniel's only reason for going to the party, even though he was technically the cohost. Daniel wasn't really a people person like Dylan, though he had to admit that when he was out with them, he generally had a good time. Psyching himself up for it was a different matter. He usually had to turn some aspect of it into a game. Tonight's game was Six Degrees of Separation from Alex Vyranos.

There were Geo Andropolis and his fiancée, Eleni, Alex's lovely sister, chatting up Daniel's father, who had some business dealings with the Andropolis family. God, the couple looked so much in love, Daniel thought. He was happy to see that the conversation appeared to be agreeable. But then, Ari was very nice to people with money. Rich people always were.

More surprising was how gracious his father was to Makmud Iskandar, the elder of the two younger brothers of Alí Iskandar, Alex's friendly rival. Daniel had read that the Iskandars ran a Middle Eastern carpet emporium on Paris's Left Bank. They were nicely situated yet hardly in Ari Kahn's league. And yet, there was Ari, all fatherly concern, listening to Makmud, who was dressed, despite the August heat and humidity, in a pinstriped suit, as if on a job interview. Hell, Daniel thought, maybe he was. Ari touched his arm and produced a business card. No doubt his father, who seemed to know everything about everyone, didn't want to dis the brother of America's new Olympic hero.

And then there were Makmud and Alí's sisters, Birka and Miriam, already deep in conversation with Daniel's mother. It figured that the three doctors in the room—there were probably more—would huddle together. At least you knew where to turn if someone choked on the scrumptious fried salmon and cream cheese dumplings that were making the rounds but had somehow eluded Daniel, who was too busy meeting and greeting for even a sip of Champagne. That was one of the prices for playing Six Degrees of Separation from Alex. His father had others in mind.

"I expect you to be attentive to all our guests tonight," he had said earlier to Daniel, gripping him by the elbow, "but especially Chloë Miller, Stan Miller's daughter. He's a great guy and a business associate who . . ."

Daniel was too busy seething to hear the rest. He got it: His father, who fancied himself something of a Lorenzo de' Medici, had already picked out his future wife, someone whose family was Jewish, went to the same schools, produced a similar income, and belonged to the same clubs. Daniel was mildly interested, however, when he realized she was the BFF of Victorine Moreau Alençon, newly minted bride of tennis legend Étienne Alençon, friend and rival to Alex.

The Alençons were ensconced in one corner of Ari Kahn, LLP's three-story lobby/atrium, looking more pleased with themselves than their surroundings. Why did Daniel suddenly feel as if he were a male Elizabeth Bennet?

Any hopes he had for a diverting conversation with Chloë Miller were dashed by his introduction to Chloë herself. She intercepted him as he was making his way to the other side of the room to greet members of the triumphant US swim team, including Caroline Quinnick, nicknamed Caro, the top female swimmer in the world and a good friend to Dylan and himself.

Chloë was almost as tall as he, pencil-thin, with a pretty, square-cut face, passable skin, devouring blue eyes, and long, straight brown hair that she wore in a bun on one side of her head. She was dressed in a sleeveless black mini and incongruous matching boots with minimal makeup and no jewelry—no doubt an affectation of the beautiful, Daniel thought.

His father had said she was some sort of model, though given the way she tripped not once but twice up the freestanding frosted glass spiral staircase, Daniel guessed she wasn't made for the runway. Still photography must be her thing, he thought maliciously.

"I just have to say how much I admire what you did at the Olympics," she said, her small, pointy white teeth gleaming between poppy-stained lips as she placed an unmanicured hand flirtatiously at her throat.

"Thanks."

"And your friend, what's his name, Dylan Roché?"

"Roqué."

"Dylan Roqué. He seems oh-so-sweet and yet über-sexy, totally."

She turned to wave to Dylan, chatting with Alex and Alí, who all waved back in a We-don't-really-know-you-but-we're-gracious manner. Dylan shot Daniel a Who-is-this? shrug, to which Daniel responded with an I'll-tell-you-all-about-it-later nod.

That Dylan was already talking to the only two people Daniel wanted to spend time with furthered his annoyance.

"I have a friend," Chloë was nattering on, "who would just die to meet him. May I be so bold as to suggest that we two hook them up?"

Daniel smiled icily.

"There's a thought, but here's another: I happen to know that he's hot and heavy with someone, a real babe."

"Oh, that's too bad."

"Yes, well, there it is."

"He's just so attractive and so talented. You know, I watched all those Olympic profiles, and I was so moved to hear about his mom and her death and his closeness to her. So, so, so sad."

"Yes, it certainly was. Well, let me not keep you from your friends—"

"Daniel," here Chloë paused—for effect, for control, for some passive-aggressive reason he knew not what. She was a slow, slow talker, a cross between a character passing through a "Seinfeld" rerun and one of those Henry James/Edith Wharton heroines whose demureness hides an unconquerable will. When Jesus said the meek shall inherit the earth, he had Chloë Miller in mind.

"Daniel, I hope you don't think it would be too forward of me to give you a call. Your father took the liberty of giving me your cell number. Perhaps we might arrange a play-date?"

"Read much Edith Wharton or Henry James?"

"Excuse me?"

"Nothing. Sure, Chloë. Why not? You obviously know how to find me."

Daniel was making a beeline for Dylan, relieved to be free at last of Chloë and furious at his father, when he was intercepted again, this time by his mother.

"Jeez, can't a guy just get across the room?"

"I won't keep you but a moment: How did it go?"

"How did what go?"

"You know, with her?"

"Oh, swimmingly."

"Really? She seems very nice."

"Yes, but then, vampires are often well-mannered. That's how they reel you in."

"Oh, stop it. Would it be so wrong for someone your age to meet a nice young woman? And if it so happens that she's also the daughter of a business associate of your father's and she happens to be Jewish—"

"Oh, I see where all this is going."

"Where what is going?"

"Do you have the temple already picked out? The reception hall? The names of the kids and grandkids?"

"It's only natural that you should one day settle down now that you've fulfilled your Olympic dreams."

"I haven't fulfilled my athletic dreams, not by a long shot. I didn't become a swimmer to be No. 2 to Dylan Roqué."

"Is that why you've been such a grumpy-puss lately? How can you be jealous of a friend who loves you so and has suffered so much in his young life already? Look around you: There he is talking to that Alí Iskandar. I've just met his wonderful sisters. They're going to join the Women's Health Project. What that family has been through. What he's been through. When I saw him on that podium, clutching the American and Iraqi flags, I cried."

"Yeah, I know, I started tearing up myself."

"God has given you so much."

"I don't believe in him."

"You see, the very fact that you say you don't believe in him proves he exists. You can't not believe in nothing."

"OK, Mom, that sentence contains a triple negative."

"I don't care, and I don't care if you don't believe in God. Believe in yourself. You owe it to those whose lives were snuffed out, to the sister who loved you more than she loved herself, to me and yes, even to your father, to use all your talents to give back to the world. But I fear, my darling boy, that it's going to take some big heartache to make you realize that."

"Yeah, not exactly cocktail-party conversation, Mom."

"You're right. You're right. Go, play, have a good time. You earned it. I'm headed uptown. Dee Dee's being honored at MoMA, and some of us should be there to support her."

"I don't see why we can't all go."

"Because your place is here. Your father threw this party for you. He may not always show it, but he's proud of you."

Finally, Daniel reached the goal line. He felt like a quarterback who'd been sacked twenty times on his way to the end zone.

"Sorry, it's been hard to get away."

"No apologies necessary," Alex said. "Daniel Reiner-Kahn, Tariq Alí Iskandar."

"A pleasure," Alí said. "I can't thank you enough for inviting my family and friends. And your father: He was so kind to offer advice and help to my brother Makmud."

"He really is a thoughtful man," Dylan said.

"Yeah, he's a great guy," Daniel said, feeling somewhat defeated and more than a little bit sorry for himself. He perked up, though, as he turned his attention back to friends old and new. It was like a four-way mirror. He looked with excitement at Alex, who in turn met his gaze with interest and glanced appreciatively at Dylan, who bumped shoulders with Alí, who smiled shyly at Daniel.

Never had he experienced anything like it—four people who just clicked. Maybe they should be a relay. Or doubles teams. It certainly gave new meaning to round-robin and preliminary heats.

"Look," Daniel said, "what do you say we get out of here and get ourselves some real food and drinks?"

He thought Alí seemed hesitant.

"I wouldn't want to abandon my family during one of their last nights in America."

Alex was looking at his phone. "I just got a text from Eleni. She and Geo are taking Kathy and your brothers and sisters out to dinner."

"And," Dylan added, "Dee Dee texted me that she's headed out with Daniel's mom and my brothers after the MoMA gig."

"But what about our host?" Alí asked.

"Oh, I wouldn't worry about him," Daniel said. "He has everything a man could want. It's settled then. I know a place in the Meatpacking District where the drinks are strong, the bodies beautiful, the clothes tight, and the dancing goes on forever. I'll call for my father's driver."

Daniel could see it now: the Page Six photos, the captions, the Four Musketeers, somewhat smashed, heads close together, arms around one another, laughing.

Here's to new friends and new adventures, Daniel thought. Here's to being young, beautiful, alive, and in love. But above all else, here's to escapes.

As his father and Chloë made their way down the staircase, arm in arm, they called to Daniel.

But the quartet, with other music to play, had already ventured triumphantly into the night.

Alex

ALEX WOKE ON MYKONOS TO A SUN-KISSED SKY, THE PLAY OF soft air on his cool skin and a free week that fanned out before him like the open sea. He smiled and stretched lazily, naked in the big white canopy bed that had been his since childhood. Soon his guests would be arriving—Alí, Daniel, and Dylan—and there would be nothing but "fishing," as in sex, relaxing, drinking and, well, sex.

"I so deserve this," he said to himself as he threw back the covers, letting the breeze from the ceiling fan caress his body.

It had been a tough year, though it had started promisingly enough. He had won the Australian Open, the French Open, and Wimbledon, the gold medal in doubles with Dmitri at the Olympics, plus the silver medal in the singles competition. Anyone else would've been ecstatic. But Alí's win in that memorable marathon singles contest, followed by his victory in the US Open, had cemented him as the coming player. That impression was confirmed by the US victory over Greece in the semifinals of the Davis Cup, in which Alí had beaten Alex not once but twice. It was only a matter of time before Alí became the No.-1-ranked-player in the world.

Alex tried to view this with his famously ironic detachment. He told himself he was happy for Alí, that a netted ball here, a missed serve there, were all the difference in the rankings.

Yet whom was he kidding? Certainly not himself. Alí was tennis's new It Boy, and Alex suddenly understood how Étienne felt. He felt old, like the toy a child loves beyond reason and then just as irrationally discards.

Yet how could he be angry with the lover who, having arrived by boat and scaled the Vyranoses' hilltop retreat, threw himself into his arms? Alex breathed in Alí's sandalwood scent, marveling at the way their bodies just fit, their washboard abs locking into one another like the pieces of a jigsaw puzzle.

Alí buried his face in Alex's shoulder as Alex stroked the small of his back.

"I've ached for your touch," Alí said. "I ache so much it makes me sick."

Alex grinned. "We'll have to see what we can do about that."

Spending time alone with Alí—Dylan and Daniel weren't due for another couple of days—gave Alex insight into what it would be like if they were a real couple. He had to admit it was surprisingly easy, natural even. Alí was the type who liked to leave a small carbon footprint. He tidied up after himself, anticipated the need to help, ate whatever was set before him, and was willing to try anything you suggested. He was the perfect houseguest, which Alex knew was different from being the perfect mate. Still, as Alí sat before him and a chessboard in the evenings, sipping Cognac, biting his lower lip as he waited for Alex to make his move, just as he did when he readied himself to pounce on his serve, Alex thought, "This is bliss, and it will never be mine again."

Later in the clamminess of an early-fall night, they surrendered to the fullest expression of their passions with only the moon and the sea as their witnesses. Alex thought of it as but a delectable appetizer for the meal to come. But it was one thing to hit it off with another "couple" at a party. It was another to spend an intimate week with two virtual strangers.

Alex's fears were renewed the moment Daniel and Dylan arrived at the Vyranoses' private dock. Daniel seemed tense—well, he was a bit more tightly wound than most, anyway—but certainly tenser than the charmer Alex had met in New York a few months before. He had the look of the star footballer who marries a supermodel, only to find her fame has eclipsed his. Alex knew that look. It was like gazing in a mirror. Not exactly what you want to be reminded of on your precious vacation.

"Welcome," Alex said, giving Daniel and Dylan a discreet kiss on each cheek, European-style. Not so Alí: He embraced Dylan and Daniel wholeheartedly all at once.

"We're so glad you guys could make it," he said.

He grabbed the bags with Dylan, and the two started talking as they made their way up the steep stone steps to the house. Not even the climb could stop their conversation. At one point, Alex thought he heard Dylan say to Alí in French, "I told Daniel there was nothing to worry about. He tends to overthink."

"Alí really is quite the chatterbox, isn't he?" Daniel said to Alex as they brought up the rear, huffing and puffing.

"And he can chatter away in any number of languages: English, French, Spanish, Italian, German, Arabic, and Farsi. Iskandar is actually a Persian name, the family having emigrated from Iran to Iraq hundreds of years ago and then at some point in the nineteenth century married into a French family, which is how they became Catholics. Dylan?"

"He speaks fluent French and Portuguese," Daniel said, "which he gets from his father's side, and he knows Gaelic and Norwegian on his mother's. He studied classics at Stanford so he can curse easily in Greek and Latin. You?"

"I can get by in all the Romance languages as well as English," Alex says. "And you?"

"Apart from the Hebrew I learned for my bar mitzvah, I speak passable Italian. My mother grew up in Italy, and I took a few classes in it at Harvard."

They had reached the top.

"Well, that was certainly worth it," Daniel said. "Would you look at this place."

There was nothing quite like seeing something you had—especially your home—through the eyes of your guests. Alex marveled at the way his parents' jewel gleamed in the Mykonos sun, as if it had been carved out of soapstone, its rainbow-colored touches—on seat cushions, awnings, rugs, and umbrellas—giving off flashes of another kind of brilliance. It was a simple house, large and rough-hewn, with icons on spare white walls, thin rugs on scrubbed hardwood floors, and terraced gardens cradling a clay court and an Olympic-size pool.

"It's wonderful," Daniel said, putting an arm around Alex. "You'll have to come to my mother's place. It's not like this. But it's pretty special."

"Thanks," Alex said, patting him. "Right, then. Let me show you to your rooms, where you can relax and refresh yourselves for a bit. Let's meet in the living room in a half-hour or so."

No sooner had the group assembled than the guests voted to play a few sets, followed by some brisk laps. Of course, Alex thought, why should vacation be any different?

"I'll take Alí, you take Daniel," Dylan said to Alex.

"Let's toss to see who serves," Daniel said.

He and Alex lost the coin toss but got to serve anyway as Dylan and Alí elected to return. Which was smart, Alex thought, since Alí had the best return in the men's game, and Dylan was a remarkably good player, especially for a swimmer, with superb hand-eye coordination. Daniel was, too, for someone who always protested that he was all fins on land. But Dylan and Alí soon got the upper hand in the match.

"Break point," Dylan yelled.

"I can keep score, too," Daniel said.

The team of Iskandar/Roqué beat that of Vyranos/Reiner-Kahn 6–4, 6–3.

"Good match," Dylan said as they shook hands at the net.

"We'll get you tomorrow," Daniel promised.

"Why don't we all cool off with a swim?" Alex offered.

But once they got into the pool, things heated up.

"We can play water polo," Alí suggested.

"Why don't we race?" Daniel countered. "Let's make it interest-ing—same teams. I'll swim the first two legs against Dylan. Alí, Alex, you'll swim the last two against each other."

It couldn't have been more exciting, Alex thought, than if they were at the Olympics again. He and Alí screamed encouragement as Daniel and Dylan raced each other to a virtual draw. Alex was determined not to let Daniel down. But Alí just out-touched him at the end.

"We're two for two," Dylan said, high-fiving Alí.

Alex smiled at them.

"Why don't we shower and head into town?"

Indeed, it would be hard to compete there, or so Alex thought. Just lunch, shopping, and sightseeing in one of the most picturesque places on earth. The tourists had long since discovered that, making it one of the most expensive, too, even this late in the season. Still, Alex loved the place he thought of as his own private island, where the Titans once battled the gods for the right to rule Olympus; loved the white-washed windmills, even though they lured birds to their deaths and terrified him so as a child; loved the way the light bled into the narrow, mosaic stone streets and wooden balconies of Little Venice.

"It's enchanting," Daniel said, walking alongside him as they watched Dylan and Alí snap photos up ahead. "So many galleries."

"It's a very artistic place," Alex said with a proud smile.

"And, I understand, so many gay bars, too," Daniel added, sotto voice. "Do you ever?"

"Never," Alex said.

"Kind of ironic."

"You could say that."

Just then a wrinkled old woman dressed top to toe in black came up, grabbed Alex's hand and kissed it as if he were a Mafia don. She said something to him in Greek. He laughed and responded. A couple of middle-aged men on a balcony yelled to her, but she waved them off, bowed to Alex, and hurried off.

"She told me she had a granddaughter—unattached, of course—she'd like me to meet," Alex said to Daniel. "I told her with such a gracious offer, how could I resist? When you asked me why I never visited certain places—"

"You don't have to explain. I know why."

"I wonder if you do. America is such a large, diverse country. Here we are smaller, more alike. The Greeks have an ancient saying: 'My power is the love of my people.' I couldn't hurt them that way."

"Even if it means living a lie?"

"How is it a lie to live our lives in private and have a public face, too? We are all actors, Dani, wearing several masks."

A young female passerby stopped them. "I was so sorry you lost the gold medal," she said to Alex.

"Blame him," he said, as he gestured to Alí up ahead.

"Is that?"

"It is."

"Do you think he would mind giving me an autograph?"

Alex had to laugh: She was sorry he lost the gold medal until she realized she could meet the gold medalist.

"Why don't you ask him?" Alex offered. "I'm sure he won't mind."

The young woman ran up to introduce herself to Alí and Dylan, who were only too happy to oblige her with autographs, pictures, and what seemed to be an in-depth conversation. Dylan and Alí were really very much alike, Alex thought; lively and social, though Alí had to overcome a bit of initial shyness. And they were both delighted to race ahead, so to speak, leaving Alex and Daniel in the dust.

"Dani, check it out," Dylan yelled back. "This gallery has some of Aunt Dee Dee's prints and a picture of me with my gold medals."

Alex looked at Daniel: "Well, then, we'll have to go in."

It was one of the first of many artistic stops where the four bought gifts for their families and one another.

"Good thing we brought the car," Alí said as they struggled with canvases, shopping bags, and even statuary.

"OK, I'm going to have to eat," Daniel said, "or I'll turn into the Incredible Hulk."

"Me, too," Dylan said.

Alex suggested Divo's, a Greco-Italian place on the beach where they could indulge their passion for card games. They settled on a few hands of bridge, which Dylan and Alí won.

"You two are definitely on a roll," Alex said.

"And you are so paying for lunch," Daniel said. "Dinner, however, is on me."

Afterward, Alex steered them to the one place he was sure there'd be no need to compete: Panagia Paraportiani, perhaps the most celebrated of Mykonos's many churches, in the oldest section of town. Even if you weren't a believer, Alex thought, it would be hard not to be moved by the red, green, and gold icons that soared to the ceiling of one of the ground-floor chapels. Alex genuflected, crossed himself right to left in the Eastern manner, and sat in a back pew, watching Alí take photos while Dylan sketched impressions. The two stopped a young priest to ask about one of the icons. Before long, he was posing for pictures, taking photos of them, and leading them on an impromptu tour.

"They're really amazing," Daniel said, brochure in hand, coming to rest beside Alex.

"They certainly are."

"Do you ever think about it?"

"What?"

"The contradiction: I mean, here you are a gay man in a religion that despises homosexuality. Do you ever feel like a hypocrite?"

Alex shook his head.

"It's only love. And God is love, my friend. Or at least, he ought to be."

Or was it only lust? Alex thought as he watched Dylan and Alí on the dance floor of Thaïs, two young women slithering around them as he longed to do himself.

He and Daniel were sipping Scotch on a balcony overlooking the shimmering peacock-blue club, which had an air of fin de siècle decadence owing to the crimson private room that beckoned upstairs.

"Do you ever wonder," Daniel asked, "what it would be like to still be on top?"

Alex leered: "Who says I'm not?"

"You know what I mean."

Alex watched Alí and Dylan make their way to the bandstand. It was warm and humid in the club, and their almost-matching pale pink shirts were open, their chests glistening. God, they were so hot, Alex thought.

"When Alí beat me for the gold medal, I thought, OK, he deserves it. He was better than me today. But when he beat me at the Open in the same place a few weeks later and then in the Davis Cup semifinals, a part of me died inside. Then I thought of all the Alís to come after him, beating not just me but him, too. And then I thought that someday we'll be retired and maybe all we'll remember is the passion that brought us together in the first place. Can you hold on, Dani, until that day when you remember only love?"

"I don't know," Daniel said. "It's partly what I came here to find out."

Alí and Dylan weren't making it any easier, Alex thought. They were on the bandstand now, ready to try out for Thaïs's peculiar variation on *American Idol*. You picked a song title out of a fishbowl. If you didn't know it, well, you could try to bluff and make a fool of yourself. If you knew it, you could try to sing it and still make a fool of yourself. Or you might succeed and live to sing another day. But if you chose to pass, it was all over.

Alí thrust his hand deep into the fishbowl, looking away, then shared the paper with Dylan. They agreed to sing Bruce Springsteen's "Because the Night."

Alex had to allow that Alí was a real singer. He sang with a bell-like tenor that could turn attractively dusky in the lower register. More important, he had the true performer's gift for connecting with the audience, holding out the mike to the crowd on the phrase "because the night." That was a nice Springsteenian touch.

Dylan backed him admirably, content to let Alí have the spotlight and thus shining himself in the process. Dylan was much like the sun, which shone not because of what it did but because of what it was.

"What sign is Dylan?" Alex asked Daniel over the Dionysian singing and applause.

"Leo."

"I thought so. He's just a little sun king, isn't he, sharing his light."

"What about Alí?"

"Gemini. I think that's why he's so fascinated by doubles."

"He's a good doubles player, isn't he?"

Alex smiled: "Not as good as me."

Just then a man passing by the table did a double take.

"Alex? Daniel?"

It was *Sportin' Life* magazine's Ken Ransom. What a prick, Alex thought. He hadn't forgotten that psychoanalytical cover story Ransom did, equating Alex's sense of irony with the death of the sibling he was meant to replace. God, he hated these journalists who vivisected your life and said, "Oh, I was just doing my job," and then came sniffing around for more, like chums. More like chumps.

"I didn't realize you two were bros?" Ken said, smiling.

Here's the serve, Alex thought.

"We hit it off at the Olympics and Alex suggested a fishing trip."

And there's the volley, Alex thought.

"Uh-huh," Ken said, distracted. "Is that who I think it is onstage?"

Ooh, sneaky backhand, Alex thought. He could see the journalistic wheels and gears clicking in Ken's tiny brain. He was onto something. But what it was he couldn't quite make out. He was about to say something when Daniel said, "Is that your girlfriend waving at you from the bar? Kind of young, isn't she, Ken?"

And there's the cross-court winner, Alex thought.

"Yeah, well, great to see you guys, but I gotta run. My best to Alí and Dylan."

Game, set, and match.

The songbirds were making their way from the bandstand back to the table amid applause and admiring pats from well-wishers when two well-dressed, middle-aged women stopped them. It was obvious to Alex that the women were trying to pick them up. Alí and Dylan talked to them for several minutes before reaching the table.

"God, what a rush," Dylan said, his face and chest beautifully flushed, Alex thought.

"Did you see us?" Alí asked, his bright eyes the color of Frangelico in firelight.

"Yes, yes," Alex said, adding as the waiter approached, "another round of Scotches."

"And?" Alí said.

"You two were positively, absolutely not bad," Daniel said.

"Oh, that's what my brother Jordie always says to me," Dylan told Alí. "What did you think, Alex?"

"No, no, very good. Good projection and enunciation."

"Ugh," Dylan said. "You sound like the nuns I had in grammar school. Well, someone thought we were pretty damned good. Those two ladies told us they were agents looking for new talent."

"Oh, I bet they were," Daniel said with a snicker. "They were just flattering you to get in your pants."

"Maybe. Anyway, I told them we were student badminton players at the University of Slovenia and had to get back to our team."

Alex and Daniel looked at Dylan.

"Student badminton players at the University of Slovenia?" Daniel wondered. "Why in the name of the God I don't believe in would you tell them that?"

"I don't know. It was the first thing that came into my head."

"Clever, no?" Alí said.

"You don't even know where Slovenia is," Daniel said to Dylan.

"Yes, I do. It was part of the former Yugoslavia. I did have a 4.0 average at Stanford, you know," Dylan reminded Daniel.

"Which would be a 3.5 at Harvard," Daniel said.

"I wouldn't know," Alex interjected. "I never went to university. I'm what you would call an autodidact, a good Greek word. Alí, though, has a degree in psychology and music from some online university and is working toward a master's in music therapy, which isn't the same as going to Harvard either."

"No," Alí said, "but that doesn't make it any less of an accomplishment."

The four sat quietly with their drinks until Alex said, "Well, I think it's time this badminton team headed home."

They wound up in the master suite, where Alex had imagined them the first night they met in New York. The four were quiet still, perhaps sensing that this was where they were meant to be from the beginning, that something profound was about to take place. Finally, Dylan said, "I don't know, your parents' bedroom?"

"They never stay here," Alex said. "When they're here, they sleep downstairs in Grandma and Grandpa's old room. It helps them feel close to them."

Daniel began unbuttoning his shirt with Alex following suit. Dylan shrugged and joined in. Only Alí seemed hesitant, lowering his long lashes just as he did, Alex thought, whenever he wanted to veil his thoughts on the tennis court.

Alex kissed the shaded peepers.

"My sweet innocent," he said, laughing, "come out from behind there."

"Here, I'll help," Dylan said. Patiently, he undressed Alí, talking to him as he went along, looking at him, kissing him deeply. For a while, they lay on the bed, facing each other, caressing only lightly, their brown-gray gaze a stormy sea.

Finally, Dylan traced a hand down Alí's manscape till he held his cock, drawing back the hood, and eliciting a gasp. He waited before guiding Alí to his own member. Alex, in bed behind Alí, watched in fascination, nibbling on his neck and shoulders, motioning to Daniel to do the same to Dylan. His cock was as lovely as Alí's, Alex thought, though in a whole different way, like a long, thick arrow with a perfect mushroom head, while Alí's was more like a nice long sausage in a bun. (He really had to stop thinking of food during sex.)

"It's beautiful," Alex said as he trailed a hand down Alí's raised right hip. "You're both so beautiful."

Their breath and their gestures quickened then, subsiding at last into a shudder.

Sated, they smiled at each other and reached out to cuddle.

"OK, floor show's over," Daniel said, clapping.

He turned Dylan roughly to face him.

"Did you forget who brung you to this dance?" he asked, before thrusting his tongue into his mouth.

Alí reached out to Dylan, confused.

"No, no, angel," Alex said, mounting him. "Shh, it's OK. It's not too soon."

Alex was surprised by the rawness with which Daniel made love to Dylan. But he soon realized Daniel's "performance" wasn't for Dylan alone. It was a challenge to Alex, who had always treated Alí with kid gloves. Now he drew up his legs and, raising himself up, placed one hand on the headboard for leverage as he thrust into him wildly, alternately looking into Alí's mystified eyes and glaring at Daniel. They were like two racers eyeballing each other in the water, matching each other stroke for stroke. They came almost simultaneously, each collapsing on the side of his beloved in laughing wonderment.

Alex drifted off immediately, waking a short time later to Alí's soft whimpering and Dylan's comforting.

"Don't cry," Dylan whispered. "It's the price we pay for being so greatly loved. Besides, we can take it, because we're the stronger."

A short while later, having fallen asleep again, Alex woke with a start to the sound of Alí's voice. He was sitting up in bed, wide-eyed, gasping for breath. Dylan woke with a jolt, too.

"I'm sorry," Alex said. "He's like this sometimes. The fucking war."

"Yes, that must be it," Dylan said, sounding as unconvinced as Alex felt.

"I hope he doesn't wake Daniel," Alex said.

"Are you kidding? He could sleep through a nuclear attack. You go back to sleep. I got this."

"You sure?"

"Trust me. I have a lot of experience. My mom used to hallucinate all the time. Sometimes, I even had to sleep in her bed. We do what we have to do."

"If you stroke him—"

"Alex, just rest. I'll deal with it."

"It's OK, Alí," Dylan said, stroking his back. He clasped Dylan's shoulder as if clinging to a rock on shore.

"We're going to take slow, deep breaths, in and out, just like the tide, ebb and flow. You're here on Mykonos with Alex, Daniel, and me. We're your friends, and we're not going to let anything happen to you. That's right, slow, deep breaths. There's nothing here but you, me, our friends, the ebb and flow of the breath-tide, and the sound of my voice. Hear only me."

After a while, they lay back and Alí, now calmed, nestled in Dylan's arms.

"I'm so tired," he said.

"Me, too," Dylan said. "I could sleep forever. Soon but not yet."

Before Alex could ponder what he meant, he fell asleep.

The next morning, Alex woke to find Daniel up in more ways than one, licking Dylan, who lay curled up with Alí. Alex grinned at him.

"Let the sleeping beauties rest. They earned it. I have a better idea for you and me."

He ran naked to the bath, motioning to Daniel to follow him, barely turning on the shower faucets before their mouths collided. Daniel was nothing like Étienne or Alí, neither mentor nor baby bro. He was a real equal: fierce, electric, challenging, intent on finding that spot beneath Alex's balls that was the intersection of pain and pleasure.

"Pain is part of pleasure," Daniel rasped as Alex mirrored his movements, and they stood transfixed between needing to continue and wanting to stop. When Alex came, his orgasm reached all the way down to his toes. He watched the soapy water follow it, mingling with their come. It looked like the foam swimmers trail.

"I have wanted you since the moment I met you in Central Park. Thank you for this."

"You're welcome for this," Daniel said as they rested, panting against a nautical navy and white tile wall.

"Come on, let's finish up and make some breakfast for the SBs."

Alex was a good-enough cook when he put his mind to it.

"If you did things with the passion you have for tennis," Eleni would say to him, "you'd be—"

"I know, a Leonardo," Alex would respond.

"I was going to say a half-way decent cook."

Ah, Eleni: Way to debone an ego.

Still, she would be proud of him now. In no time, with Daniel's expert assistance as sous-chef, he prepared freshly squeezed orange juice; thick, strong Greek coffee; fluffy egg-white omelets with spinach and feta cheese; grilled lamb chops; and fruit salad.

Together they set the terrace table with blue-, red-, and orange-print ceramics.

"Perfection," Alex said. "We make quite a team."

"Now if the sleepyheads would just get up."

"I have a feeling that they are up and already doing what we've been doing."

Soon the pair appeared, dressed in complementary tennis outfits: Dylan's a blue shirt with white shorts; Alí's a white shirt with blue shorts. Their hair was damp; their faces, wreathed in conspiratorial smiles.

"What have you two minxes been up to?" Alex asked.

"Laundry," Dylan said as Alí giggled. "This lamb is divine. What for today?"

"I thought we'd have a stress-free, tennis-free, swim-free day and sail to Delos."

Alí and Dylan were as excited as kids, Alex thought.

"Oh, the amphitheater," Dylan said.

"We can take a picnic," Alí said.

"Daniel?" Alex asked.

"Sounds great," he sighed, sipping coffee and scrolling through his iPad.

"Ooh, let's not forget to bring our cameras and sketchbooks," Dylan said to Alí.

"Good thing we don't have to go back to Thaïs till tomorrow for the semifinals," Alí said.

He and Dylan exchanged high-fives and continued eating as if Alí had just said, "The sun is shining."

"Semifinals of what?" Daniel asked.

"The semifinals of Wimbledon," Dylan said sarcastically. "The semifinals of the singing contest."

"You two made the semifinals?" Daniel said, incredulous.

"The band thinks we have a good chance of winning," Alí said.

"Well, isn't that something," Alex said, clapping.

After, Daniel helped Alex clean up and pack a lunch of cold lamb sandwiches, hummus, grapes, honey-dipped filo dough, Coca-Cola, and Dom Perignon. Daniel loaded the dishwasher and slammed it shut.

"Tell me in what universe the two of them merit making the semifinals of a singing competition," Daniel said.

Alex shrugged as he wrapped the sandwiches.

"They're not terrible. And we don't know how good or bad the competition is. Look, Dani, one thing I've learned in tennis is that if something's meant for you, it will be there, no matter how strange it seems. And if it's not, no amount of talent or preparation will make it happen."

The songbirds were back on fluff-and-fold detail on the ground floor, which rang with laughter.

"OK, tell me what they're doing down there."

Alex whispered in Daniel's ear, kissing it.

"Seriously: They're having a ménage à trois with the washing machine."

"Hey, don't knock it till you try it. Makes a hell of a vibrator."

"What about the dryer, or is it still a virgin?" Daniel wondered. He eyed the dishwasher. "Don't even think about it," he said to the innocent appliance as Alex laughed.

It was good to laugh and be on the open water, Alex thought as he helmed his parents' sailboat, the *Semiramide*.

"I'm impressed with the way you handle her," Dylan said, agreeing to crew.

"You sail?"

"And surf and scuba-dive. I love the sea."

"I would think swimmers would," Alex said with a teasing smile.

"Not all. Not Daniel. He hates the ocean. He never swims in it."

"Perhaps because I'm always in the pool."

"He's afraid."

"Am not, and you sound like my sister."

"Why are you always fiddling with your cell?" Dylan asked Daniel.

"Reception's lousy here."

"Who are you trying to text?"

"Shouldn't that be whom?"

"All right, Mr. Grammarian, whom then?"

"If you must know, Chloë Miller."

"Why?"

"Why not? We've struck up a sort of friendship."

"I don't think Chloë is interested in just friendship."

"Even so, what's the harm?"

"Well, it's cruel to lead her on."

"Who's leading her on?"

"It's just that I know she expects more."

"And you know that because—"

"Because she keeps texting me, telling me she has this great girl for me and wouldn't it be wonderful if we could double-date."

"I told her you were hot-and-heavy with a real babe."

"Glad you think so highly of yourself."

"Thought you'd be. Look, I'm sorry she's bothering you. But wishes don't make dreams come true, right, Alí?"

He shuddered.

"All I know is she's best friends with Victorine, who's the wife of that full-of-himself Étienne, who has no love for me. I'd steer clear of them."

"He's not that bad," Alex said.

"Really?" Alí said. "He seems to have cooled to you."

"Well, he has a wife now. And besides, he knows we're friends."

"Meaning?"

"Well, as you said, he doesn't care for you."

Alí's phone pinged, and Alex couldn't help but notice his agitation.

"Don't tell me Chloë Miller is texting you, too," Alex teased.

"Hmm? Oh, no, it's just Papa, wondering if we're practicing. 'Yes, Papa,'" Alí texted back, "'we're spending every spare moment of our vacation practicing.' Dearest Papa: He really puts the kill in killjoy."

Alex sensed there was more to it than that but let it go. He knew how fathers could push your buttons. Dylan's, he had heard, was a disaster. And even though Ari Kahn had proved a charming host at the post-Olympics party, Alex had no illusions that he was an easygoing parent. Alex was sure Spyros Vyranos was more than their equal.

"Don't forget, Alexandros," he had said. "The *Semiramide* is not a toy. Sailing is like driving. No wildness or drinking. I don't want to see pictures on the Internet of Alexandros Vyranos—the savior of Greece—and his friends partying aboard the *Semiramide*, especially as Eleni is about to make such a fortunate marriage. What a comfort she and Geo are to your mother and me, as much as you will be when you bring a bride home to us."

That, Papa, will be an icy day on the plains of Hades, Alex thought, taking a swig from a bottle of Dom Perignon as he steered.

Still, Papa would've been pleased at the way he showed off Delos to the other members of the quartet.

"It's just stunning," Dylan said.

"It's the birthplace of Apollo, the most beautiful of the gods," Alex said.

"Also not above having a few boy toys," Daniel offered.

"That, too," Alí said as they threaded their way up the amphitheater of the uninhabited isle.

"I have an idea," Alex said to Alí. "Why don't you and Dylan stand down there in the center and let's hear how your voices carry."

"Watch," Alex said to Daniel, "Alí's going to ask if we want to hear 'Incomplete.' I've only heard 59 million choruses of that, 'My

Immortal,' and 'I Am The Warrior.' After the first million, it gets real old real fast."

"How about 'Incomplete'?" Alí asked, his voice carrying beautifully.

"What a surprise," Alex said to Daniel. "Good choice," he said, applauding and nodding.

"'Empty spaces fill me up with holes,'" Alí and Dylan began, as the other tourists applauded.

"Showoffs," Daniel said. "And those lyrics make no sense: How can empty spaces fill someone up with holes?"

"Oh, Daniel, it's going to be a long winter for you."

"I know what will make it shorter: When we get back to your house, let's you and me whip their asses in the pool and on the court."

But Alex and Daniel lost, badly.

"Tomorrow, Alí plays with me; and Dylan, you're with Alex," Daniel said, frustrated.

But Alex and Daniel still lost at their respective sports with the team of Iskandar/Reiner-Kahn dominating on the court and that of Roqué/Vyranos in the pool.

Later Alí and Dylan breezed through the semifinals at Thaïs with an affecting rendition of Joan Baez's "Diamonds and Rust."

"Not many men can pull that off," a woman tourist said, patting Dylan on the shoulder as he and Alí made their way back to their table. "You know Baez wrote that about Bob Dylan."

"I know," Dylan said. "I was named for him. My grandmother knew him and sang his and Baez's music."

"Who's your grandmother?"

"She was Debo Norquist."

"And you're Dylan Roqué."

"Yep, and this is Alí Iskandar and our friends Alex Vyranos and Daniel Reiner-Kahn."

"Oh, my goodness, I have to take a picture. My girlfriends are never going to believe it."

Many photos later, Alí said to Dylan, "Back in Baghdad, my mother had all of your grandmother's records. She gave her a voice in a troubled time."

"And now in another time and place, your mother and my grand-mother meet again through us."

Alex smiled as he leaned in to whisper to Daniel, "I know one arena where we can win."

In the bedroom, Alex moved to undress Dylan, who looked uncertainly at Daniel, who nodded his approval.

"So lovely," Alex said, slipping Dylan's shirt off a molded shoulder and kissing it. "You are so lovely."

Dylan leaned back against him and drew his arm behind Alex's neck, rubbing it. Alex buried his head in the curve of Dylan's neck, stroking his smooth, ribbed chest before cupping his crotch.

As they moved to the bed naked, Alí and Daniel sat opposite them, mesmerized. Alex pinned Dylan by the wrists as he thrust into him. Alí reached out to Dylan, who turned his face to him, his expression caught between fear and desire.

"No, no," Daniel said, pulling his hand back. "You're with me tonight."

"Dani," Alex said, panting and mouthing the words, "Easy with him."

Daniel smiled at Alí, rubbing noses.

"All this gorgeous man fur. May I see if it goes all the way down? Oh, look: It does."

Daniel lay Alí down gently, looking into his eyes as he drew up his legs and began rimming him. Alex watched as the hood of Alí's cock retracted against Daniel's hard belly and Alí arched his back with a sharp breath.

"It's OK, angel," Alex said as he raised himself up on his arms to thrust deeper into Dylan. "I want him to have you. It's only love, and it's beautiful."

Afterward, Alex watched as Dylan and Alí sought each other's arms.

"I know," Dylan said, kissing him and stroking his back. "They don't understand. We don't want to hurt them. We just want to be the best."

Evidently, Daniel had decided that if you can't beat them, join them, for the next morning, he announced to Alex as they prepared strawberry-stuffed French toast, made with thick slices of braided egg bread, "I think we should have a whole day of preparation for the singing competition. I intend to win this thing—as coach, of course."

"Of course," Alex said. "So much for vacation."

Coaching involved running, yoga, more tennis and swimming—all to increase lung function—followed by Alí-led vocal exercises, then wardrobe, choreography and, most important of all, song selection and rehearsal, since the finals allowed participants to pick three numbers of their own choosing.

"We thought we'd open with 'Incomplete,'" Alí said, "followed by 'My Immortal,' and close with a rousing 'I Am the Warrior.'"

Alex looked at Daniel.

"What a surprise."

"And is that how you're going to sing them?" Daniel asked after hearing the set.

"Apparently not," Dylan said, hand on hip, pouting.

"Alex," Daniel commanded, "go make a pot of your strongest coffee. We have work to do."

The finals were on a Friday night. Alex and Daniel took their seats at a table in the center of the balcony overlooking the dance floor. Or at least Alex took his seat. Daniel preferred to pace in the back of the balcony near the waiters' stand. As a tennis player, Alex knew a stage parent when he saw one, and Daniel was a classic stage parent, mouthing the words and doing the gestures.

Alex didn't know why Daniel was so worried. It was clear that one of the reasons Dylan and Alí had made it this far was that the competition was, well, awful. No, actually that was too kind. A guy dressed up like Gaga. A Russian group doing heavy-handed country western. A women trying to warble Mariah Carey melismata. All Alí and Dylan had to do, Alex figured, was remember the lyrics, not trip, and look adorable in their slim jeans and pastel shirts, and the $5,000 prize that they intended to give to a Mykonos children's charity would be theirs.

"Incomplete" was a strong opening, a bit too boy-band perhaps but solid nonetheless. "My Immortal" was surprisingly touching with Dylan shining on the lyrics, "I've tried so hard to tell myself that you're gone. But though you're still with me, I've been alone all along."

"I Am the Warrior" had everyone on his feet, although Alex couldn't help but wonder if Alí was aiming straight for his heart when he sang the line "I Am the Warrior" and pulled an imaginary trigger.

When Dylan and Alí were announced the winners, the crowd went wild.

"Well, Steven Spielberg?" Alex said to Daniel.

"Not bad," he said, smiling and shaking his head. "Although I think you're the real orchestrator of this production."

Alex smiled: "I'm sure I don't know what you mean."

"What a night," Dylan said as he arrived at the table.

"One of the best ever," Alí said, raising a glass. "To Daniel."

"To Dani," Dylan said.

"To the victors," Alex added.

"To friends and lovers," Daniel said.

They all laughed then. How good it was to be young and laughing with your friends, pulling them close, just us, the Four Musketeers, Alex thought.

"This calls for a special treat."

He wasn't thinking hot fudge sundaes.

. . . .

ALEX'S IDEA OF A TREAT INVOLVED SKINNY-DIPPING IN THE moonlit Aegean. "Come on," he said, stripping. "This is my family's private beach. No one can see us. Besides, we'll stay near the shore. Who's game?"

"I am," Dylan said. "Come on."

"Maybe Dani and I will wait for you here," Alí said.

"Chicken," Dylan said, making a clucking sound.

"That does it," Daniel said, stripping quickly to rush in after Dylan. "Come on, Alí."

"Ugh," he said, tugging at his shirt and jeans.

They splashed each other, the bracing water up to their necks.

"Let's swim out," Dylan said.

"Are you crazy?" Daniel said. "There's no light."

"There's a few lights in the distance and from the restaurants on the other beaches," Alex said. "Let's race out to that buoy."

"What buoy?" Alí said. "I can't see anything."

"We'll race alongside one another, listening to each other's voices," Dylan said.

"It's nuts," Daniel said. "I'm headed to shore."

"Fine. You could only beat me in a pool anyway," Dylan said. "Hey, wait."

Daniel took off then, with Dylan in pursuit and Alí and Alex struggling to keep up. After a while, Alex couldn't hear the others, only the lapping of the waves. It was dark, cold, terrifying, and he decided to turn back. He prayed the others decided to do the same, and he was relieved to find them waiting for him on shore.

"Who won the race?"

"Alí was the first back."

"But only because I didn't swim out that far," Alí owned. "That was insane."

"But in a good way," Dylan said.

"We could've drowned," Daniel said.

"Then why'd you do it?"

"I wasn't going to let you get the better of me."

"Hey," Alex said. "The race isn't finished."

And he took off up the stone steps, with the others trailing him all the way to the shower in the master suite.

"Let's warm things up," Alex said, turning on the massaging jets, soaping up the others. He grabbed the belts from two terrycloth robes and began tying Dylan's hands to the faucet overhead with one. He threw the other to Daniel, who did the same to Alí.

"Don't worry," Dylan said to Alí. "Dani would never hurt you. It's just a bit of fun, one of the games men play."

He kissed Alí then, the two of them cooing, kissing and talking. Did they ever stop talking? Alex wondered.

He and Daniel took Dylan and Alí from behind then, pressing Dylan and Alí's erect cocks together as they enveloped the group in a hug.

"Is this what they call a clusterfuck?" Dylan asked, and they all laughed.

The next morning, Alex joined Daniel on court along the sidelines as Dylan and Alí, shirtless, squirted each other with tubes of sunscreen that they held between their legs.

"So juvenile and yet so adorable," Alex said. "What's the matter, Dani? You look too serious for what they're doing."

"I was just thinking, Today's our last full day on Mykonos. Tomorrow it's back to real practice and meets and schedules and appearances and answering the same stupid reporters' questions you've answered a thousand times and decisions that have to be made."

"And has being on Mykonos helped you any with those decisions?"

Alex watched him look at Dylan with a mix of longing and loathing.

"I don't know. I wish I could stay longer."

"So stay longer. Stay forever."

"But then this wouldn't be a special moment, would it, Alex?"

"What makes a moment special? Living it as we will later remember it. And that's tricky, my friend."

Alex got up then and called to Alí and Dylan, who were fooling around on the court.

"Good news: We're all staying on a few extra days."

"Yay," Alí and Dylan said, clapping their rackets.

"*Allons*, Alí, let's show these American swimmers how tennis is really played."

Alex picked up a handful of the court's terra-cotta dust, then washed his hands of it. It fell on portions of his sleek black outfit like iron pilings. He thought it looked like flecks of dried blood.

He motioned for Alí to take up a position at the net while he stood at the base line. Dylan went to stand near the net on the opposite side, and Daniel joined him on the base line there.

Alex hit a ball between his legs to Daniel.

"The ball is, as they say, in your court. Your serve, my friend."

Alex squatted slightly to read that serve, swaying from side to side, twirling his racket, a devilish grin on his face.

"Come on," he said, "let's play."

Dylan

WHEN DYLAN LOOKS BACK ON MYKONOS NINE MONTHS LATER, he thinks of it as an emotional fault line dividing his life with Daniel—if you can call it a life.

Before Mykonos, he was happy with Daniel. After, well, he really doesn't need to go there, does he? Perhaps, he thinks at first, it's just his imagination.

Mykonos itself was a kind of demilitarized zone of bliss laced with a tension that made the heavenly moments more poignant for their brevity and elusiveness.

Now Mykonos is a memory as the texts and calls become more infrequent; the space between visits, greater; the hugs and handshakes in the pool, less heartfelt; and the moments together more distracting, filled with furtive texts to her.

Chloë isn't entirely to blame, of course. Something has clicked—on or off, Dylan's too heartbroken to be sure which. Something has changed, though, between him and Daniel, and Chloë is only part of the reason.

Still, she is a most definite, annoying factor, with her insinuations and manipulations, which are as strong and slimy as a spider's web and just as difficult to extricate yourself from.

"Dylie," goes a typical text, "pls, pls, pls come to dinner w/ me, Dani, and Tina. She's so anxious to meet you and will be so, so, so disappointed if you can't make it. XO, XO, C."

"Tell her you have to file your taxes early/late/on time," Caro advises. "Tell her you're busy counting all the grains of sand on all the beaches of the world. Tell her anything. But don't let that vampire bitch into your life."

Caro is sitting across from him in the cafeteria of the team's training center in Boulder a week before the World Championships in Shanghai. In some ways, Dylan thinks, she is a female Daniel: brilliant, beautiful and not one to suffer fools gladly. With her still-damp brunet tresses gathered by a clip in a casual upsweep and her statuesque figure swathed in a chocolate velour tracksuit with pink piping, Caroline Quinnick, the No. 1 female swimmer in the world, is a real Athena. Dylan wonders why he couldn't fall for her. He knows she wonders the same.

"Look, tell her we've hooked up," Caro says. "I don't mind."

Dylan reaches out to touch her cheek, and she clasps his hand, resting that cheek in his palm before kissing it.

"Oh, Caro," he says.

She reaches out to return the favor, exposing a bruise on his neck.

"All I can say is I hope whoever's really fucking you appreciates you, but I doubt it."

"It's how you like it, isn't it, baby?" Daniel says later, pinning his wrists as he mounts him from behind, biting his neck, and raking his fingers down his back. "Nice and rough."

"Is that the way she likes it?" Dylan says.

Daniel pushes Dylan into the mattress.

"Why would she have to?" Daniel says. "That's what I have you for. When you think about it, a man makes the perfect mistress. I don't ever have to worry about my seed being here." Daniel rubs Dylan's tight belly for emphasis. "Actually, my seed could be here. But you know what I mean. It's not as if you, my vampire lover, can bear a life or anything else—except pain. But then, you're so strong, baby. You can take it."

He can take it. He's had a lifetime of taking it.

. . . .

"YOU'RE SO STRONG, MY DYLIE," HIS MOTHER WOULD SAY TO him, "and beautiful and brilliant and talented and kind. You have so much. That's why you must give, even if it hurts. That's what Jesus says in the Bible: 'To him to whom much has been given—'"

"Yes, I know, Mama, 'much will be required.'"

That was on a good day. On a bad day, she could've burned the house down.

"You're such a stupid bitch," he remembers his father saying to his mother then. "Is this what you call making dinner? Who puts a box of frozen peas on a stove burner?"

"It's OK, Dad," he hears his fifteen-year-old self saying. "She doesn't understand. Rosa why don't you take Mama upstairs, OK? I'll clean up."

"Look at this mess. The whole house could've gone up in flames and all of us with it."

"But it didn't, did it, Dad? I said I'd take care of it."

"You're so dumb. Dumb and crazy," his father repeats, lunging for her. As Rosa cries out, Dylan steps between his father and the women.

"Rosa, take her upstairs now please, and tell the boys to stay in their rooms."

His father tries to push him out of the way. But Dylan blocks his path and, placing his arms protectively about his head, braces himself as his father hits and kicks him.

. . . .

HE FEELS THE RHYTHM OF THE PUNCHES STILL AS DANIEL HUMPS him, then collapses on top of him, biting his neck.

"So good, so good," he says, licking Dylan's tattoo of interlocking Ds before drifting off to sleep.

He doesn't mind. In such moments—with Daniel snoring into his neck, oblivious—he can pretend nothing's changed, snuggle against him, and cry himself to sleep before it begins again.

"Dyl, Dylan, come on, wake up."

"Dani, please, it's too early. I need to sleep. You need to rest, too. We have practice in a few hours."

"All the more reason not to waste our precious private time together. I'll do everything. You don't even have to move. Come on, baby."

And before Dylan can say anything—not that he would, he never denies him anything—Daniel flips him on his back and pins his arms above his head, imprinting his thumbs on his wrists. Dylan can feel their throbbing cocks pressing into each other's bellies. No condoms, no lube, just raw and naked, and it's almost more than he can bear. But he does, because that's who and what he is and because he believes it gives him power over Daniel.

Then Daniel is gone and back just as quickly, slipping on sheer black-ribbed condoms, drawing up Dylan's legs and pushing himself between the molded globes of his cheeks.

"Now arch your back," Daniel says, his voice dusky with lust. "Meet me. Find me."

As Dylan cries out, Daniel groans and shortly falls back to sleep. Though Daniel's all-consuming passion hurts, it pleases Dylan no end. This is how much he wants me, he thinks. This is how much he needs me. This is how much he loves me and not her.

Still, he worries about the telltale bruises and scratches, though he knows it's possible to fool some of the people some of the time, particularly when some of the people see only what they want to see.

. . . .

"SHE MUST BE SOME TIGRESS."

Carter Cabrera is standing at the locker next to Dylan's. The big blond speedster wears his hair close-cropped and duck-billed. That his brain works as fast as his mouth and body is yet to be determined. Dylan has always thought of him as one of those Victorians he passes on his way to visit Daniel in Scarsdale—a big, beautiful, blond Victorian with a wraparound porch and absolutely no lights on.

Earlier, Carter swims the last leg of one of those relays that they own, helping them smash the world record in Shanghai, and they're whooping and hollering and hugging each other tight, wet and wild and hot and shivering, and it's all good as Daniel pulls them close into a group hug.

"Excuse me?" Dylan is saying to Carter, back in the present.

"I said she must be quite a handful," Carter repeats, leering at the marks on Dylan's body. "Just make sure you give as good as you get."

He remembers the sting of his father's hand across his face as he takes the blow meant for his mother. He will feel it forever.

"I would never hit a woman," Dylan says softly.

"And yet, you would let her do to you what you would never do to her. Man, that is SFU, seriously fucked up."

He thinks then maybe Carter is not so stupid after all. Or maybe Dylan is just that strong. There's that word again: You're so strong, Dylan, his coaches say, you can do another set, another rep, an extra mile in the pool. You've such a strong mind, Dylan: You can take the advanced placement chem class, early decision to Stanford, work that after-school job so at least you'll have some money for groceries when that jerk-off of a father gets a bug up his ass and decides not to leave any cash around, which your crazy-ass mother will only hide anyway.

You're so strong, Dylan. Until the day you're not.

"Dylan, I don't think I've ever said this to another athlete, but you have the potential to be the best there is, even better, believe it or not, than Daniel."

Coach Walsh is talking to him privately after he edges out Daniel in the 200 IM in Shanghai. He's the kind of man whose most distinctive feature is just how undistinguished he is. With his close-cropped salt-and-pepper hair, round features, average height, and paunch, he has the look of a man who's always been middle-aged. He could be a car dealer in one of those strip malls you pass on the highway and take note of only for a moment, knowing the moment will never come again.

Yet he is one of the most powerful men in their sport. He must've been young once, must've been a swimmer. Maybe he was good or even good-looking. Where is the youth in the man now?

Dylan is wondering this, because it staves off what he's really feeling: panic, sheer panic. No one begins a conversation with such praise without following it up with a big climbing-out-of-a-hole-only-to-be-shoved-down-again "but." Maybe it's about his times in the pool. He's been pressing a bit at the championships.

"As I was saying," Coach is going on, "your potential is unlimited. Your work ethic, outstanding. Your times, your form here, excellent."

"Thank you."

"That's why I want you to swim the anchor of the 4 × 200 freestyle relay Sunday."

"But Dani always swims the anchor."

"I know, but I think we'll be stronger with Daniel leading off and you on anchor. It's not open for discussion."

"Oh, OK, yeah, then fine."

"And there's something else I've been meaning to discuss with you. I'm not one to pry, but—"

But here it is, Dylan thinks, right on time.

"I don't know how to broach this," Coach says, "so I'm just going to jump in, because if I don't I may be derelict in my duties. OK, here goes: Are you in an abusive relationship?"

Pounding. Heart pounding. Like when he's ready to hit the wall, lungs burning, a thousand knives in his body, and he thinks he can't stand another moment, but he does, 'cause he's strong, right?

"No, no," he protests. "No, Coach, everything's fine."

"Because I see the marks when you're on the blocks, and I hear the whispers, and I gotta tell ya: I'm a live-and-let-live, don't-ask–don't-tell kinda guy. But because of a few bad apples in other sports who didn't report stuff when they should've, I'm left to wonder if you're OK. I wonder if maybe you're involved with someone older who's intimidating you. I know you take some acting roles when you can, which is perfectly fine, but I hear that's a nutty business. I wonder if maybe they're making you do stuff you don't want to. Or maybe you're just young and having a wild time. None of my business. As I said, Don't ask, don't tell."

And right away, Dylan thinks: Coach knows. He knows without even knowing how or why he knows.

"Look, Coach, you don't have to worry about me. I can take care of myself. And I would never, ever do anything to hurt the team—ever. It's just that sometimes things get a little passionate, and I forget the souvenirs."

Coach seems relieved.

"Well, it happens. We've all been there."

We have? Dylan wonders. Et tu, Coach?

"Frankly, I'm glad," Coach says, as giddy as a man who's just learned the test was false positive. "Good for you. I'm glad you found someone. I know how tough it's been since your mom and all."

. . . .

DON'T, DYLAN THINKS, DON'T GO THERE. BUT DYLAN DOES. HE is eighteen years old, trying to cover her nakedness, and the tub is overflowing with bloody water, and he's splashing around trying to staunch the blood and feel a pulse though he can't 'cause the veins in her arms are ripped open, and, anyway, he knows she's gone.

And right then, Dylan thinks, What dumb animals we humans are, we who look for life where there is none.

He keeps lifting her arm and watching it flop down, hitting the overflowing bath with a splash that drowns his tears in soapy water. He draws her to him then.

"Oh, Mama," he says, holding her. He lays her back in the tub and covers her with several big bath towels as if they were a blanket for this Ophelia's watery bed, her watery grave. He hears sirens. Quickly, he closes her eyes, kisses them, and removes the mermaid pendant around her neck, placing the necklace in his pocket.

"I love you, Mama. I always will. Thanks."

Be with me now, Mom. Give me your love, your courage and your strength.

. . . .

THEY ARE SEATED IN THE READY ROOM IN THE ORDER IN WHICH they will swim in the 4 x 200 freestyle relay. Dylan thinks they look more like condemned men than swimmers: Daniel, always so focused anyway, seething and glaring straight ahead; Carter, oblivious as usual, drumming on his thighs to his own beat; Vada Wilson, known as "Dark Vada," for his ebony charisma, chatting away with Dylan, who nonetheless feels so lonesome he could puke.

They head out amid bursts of lights, holding hands, raising arms, and bowing. Showtime. It's a race they've won many times, often with the same cast, only they're a little off tonight. Daniel never quite finds his rhythm, setting them back, especially against the French, who turn out to be very good indeed. Carter's, well, Carter; Vada does his thing, which is solid but not spectacular, which means it's up to Dylan.

Nervous, he takes it out too fast but manages to close strong, hanging on for the win, huffing and puffing, red-faced. He spies Coach Walsh on the sidelines, shaking is head in disgust, relief, and disbelief.

There's the usual huddle, the poolside banter with Kendra Kimball, the gold, the flowers, the anthem. But it's not the same. There's a space, a skipped beat. No one wants to acknowledge it, but everyone senses it. Even at dinner with Dee Dee, Daniella, Jordan, and Austin, there's a tension, underscored by the clicking of a cell phone and secret glances.

Back in their room, Dylan thinks about their first time together in Shanghai and how much they love this Asian New York, how they wished they had time to explore it and promised to come back there together. He glances at a mirror over a dresser and remembers how they stood before another one in another room in the same hotel and watched themselves make slow, sweet love.

Dylan caresses Daniel's neck as he strokes his cock and enters him from behind. But this time Dylan sees no reflection when he looks in the mirror. Finally, he says, "What the hell was that all about?"

"What was what all about?"

"You know."

"No, for the life of me. I don't."

"You, out there, tonight. Jesus, Dani. We nearly lost to the French. The fucking French. I mean, what were you doing? Taking a slow boat to China? 'Cause I gotta tell ya, we're already here."

"Wow, how long did it take you to come up with that one? You Stanford boys sure are clever."

"Meaning?"

"Nothing. What's your meaning? Are you accusing me of deliberately swimming slow? Because I don't think you want to be accusing me of that."

"I'm thinking if you swam any slower, you'd have been treading water."

"We won, didn't we? But I don't think that's what this is really about. No, what this is really about is jealousy. You're jealous that I have a girlfriend and you don't."

Dylan laughs. "Jealous? Of you? All right, I am jealous. But not of you. Of her. I thought I was the girlfriend, you know, bucking you up every time your father made you crumble, urging you on in practice, celebrating your victories, taking a backseat all those years. God, when I think of the times I bolstered you, defended you, explained you to others, even when I didn't understand you myself. When I think of how I love you, how you loved me. But that was only when you were top dog, right?"

"You think I don't love you anymore? I'll show you what love is."

Daniel grabs Dylan then and kisses him, thrusting his tongue into his mouth and ripping open his shirt.

"Come on, stop it," Dylan says, breaking free. "I'm not in the mood, and we're not teenagers anymore. Leave me alone."

"Well, you want to be loved. I'm going to show you what love is."

He wrestles him to the ground, but Dylan wriggles free again and staggers into the bathroom where he bolts the door, which Daniel kicks open with his foot. He tackles Dylan, who hits his head on the sink on the way down.

"Get off me," Dylan shrieks, punching upward with his fists. One of his blows connects with Daniel's nose, and he's stunned for a moment.

Daniel smacks him across the mouth—once, twice—then yanks his shirt off his shoulders and sucks his tits hard. He pulls down his pants and takes him.

After a while, Dylan doesn't resist, doesn't move, doesn't seem to be breathing. The only thing that conveys life are his large eyes, pooling.

"Oh, Dylan, I'm so sorry. Please forgive. I shouldn't have. I never meant. Forgive me. Forgive me," Daniel sobs into his shoulder. "I never meant to hurt you."

Dylan looks around. It's another bathroom filled with blood and tears.

"But you have, Dani. And you do."

Alí

WHEN ALÍ LOOKED BACK ON MYKONOS, HE THOUGHT OF THE Garden of Eden that scholars believed had been nestled on the banks of his beloved Euphrates. Mykonos, too, was paradise: fair weather, good friends, and love. But there was a snake in that Garden, and it slithered in the form of a ten-word text that filled him with a sense of dread and panic: "I know who you are. I know what you are."

It was the message he received on the *Semiramide*.

"Don't tell me Chloë Miller is texting you, too," Alex had teased.

He played along but he didn't have a very good poker face, and he was sure Alex knew something was up. Still, he tried to remain calm, tried to ignore the message's increasing frequency and portent.

It could've been a scam. It could've been a stalker. It could've been anyone or anything. He thought of going to the police, but as when he was young, fear held him back. What did the sender mean: "I know who you are?"

A gay man? Had someone seen him with Alex? An Iraqi-American? Was it some kind of slur? Or was the message more personal: I know you. Could it be a member of his guardian's family? But then, they didn't want to be reminded of him any more than he wanted to be reminded of them.

Still, there were times when he looked up into the stands and swore he saw his guardian come back from the grave to finish what he started.

"This is crazy," he told himself and shook it off. He couldn't let it affect his play. He prided himself on the notion that nothing ever had— and nothing ever would. He had suffered too much, sacrificed his body, his very soul, which he was sure had been rent from his tender flesh, along with his innocence, as he lay cowering, wishing the mattress, the floor, the very earth would swallow him whole, like one of those poor, tortured creatures in the Greek myths whom in the end the gods take pity on.

"I know who you are."

Who was he? Like everyone else, Alí was something of a mystery, even to himself. But the question was one he would be forced to consider, if not answer, very soon, and oddly, the seeds of that urgency had been planted in his greatest triumph, atop the Olympic podium where he clutched tiny Iraqi and American flags, embedding them in the nosegay that had been presented to him.

Now fourteen months later, he was watching a cable news program one morning when he came upon the headline "Senator Questions Athlete's Loyalty." While Alí watched some sports reports to keep up with friends and favorites, he never clued into anything about himself, not even the flattering links Kathy texted him. So he was astonished to discover that the allegedly disloyal athlete was none other than himself.

It seems that a Senator Morris Severance, running in a tightly contested race in Kansas on the platform of "Keeping America Safe, First," was intimating that Alí was not only un-American but perhaps worse:

> What do we really know about this young man, who represented us at the Olympics and will now represent us in the David (sic) Cup finals? What we do know doesn't much add up or bode well. We do know that while our boys and girls were dying in Iraq, he was brought to this country to train to bounce a tennis ball over a net. We do know that he speaks, reads, and writes many languages fluently, including Arabic and Farsi, which is modern Persian—skills that might be better employed at State or Defense or the New York City Police Department than in checking into a Hilton in Dubai or Monte Carlo or Hong Kong.
>
> Or are those skills already being employed, by a sleeper cell? We don't know. And that is my point. There is too much we don't know about this young man, who lives in our nation's capital, with no family of his own. Let's hope when we do find out more, it's not too late.

Alí was stunned, flabbergasted, gobsmacked. If he weren't so terrified, he would've been deeply hurt. His voice mail and email, along with his Twitter and Facebook accounts, were instantly flooded, overwhelmed with death threats and attacks of the most scurrilous kinds, along with words of encouragement, support, and love.

Kathy had already launched a counteroffensive. "We can't allow him to drive this narrative," she told Alí. "Whoever controls the story controls public opinion."

Dylan, Daniel, and Alex immediately came forward.

"Here's a guy who came to this country alone at the age of thirteen," Daniel told CNN, "and after his guardian died, finished high school, worked his way up to become the No. 1-ranked player in the world, and put himself through college and now graduate school. He not only helped the widow and child of the soldier who befriended him in Iraq, but he has also helped support his family and represented this country with an almost unbearable grace. I'm proud to call him my friend."

Dylan's message was more succinct, but perhaps even more heartfelt: "All I can say is that I love him, and anyone who thinks he's a terrorist is nuts."

Alex took out a full-page ad in the *Washington Post* that was signed by more than a hundred top players: "It is our great good fortune to know Alí Iskandar as a colleague and a friend. On court and off, he has exemplified the highest standards of sportsmanship, national pride, and compassion for the less fortunate. We are grateful to number him among our 'band of brothers.'"

To which Alex added to a reporter, "This is a fine young man, a good Christian and a family-minded person. I have played him many times and even dined with him on occasion. He's just a great guy."

Even Étienne lent his support, if you could call it that: "Do I socialize with him? No. His parents are," here Étienne paused to sniff, "merchants. We move in very different circles. But I doubt anyone who has a drop of French blood and whose parents live in Paris, as he does and they do, would be anything less than a gentleman."

It didn't help, however, that Ken Ransom had just come out with another of his psychological portraits in *Sportin' Life*, this one called

"The Brittle Brilliance of Alí Iskandar," which suggested that he suffered from post-traumatic stress disorder and featured pictures of him dancing at Thaïs on Mykonos with Dylan and some women. Nor did it help that the ad campaign for Dusk, the new men's fragrance he represented, made its debut in that issue. It featured an image of a dreamy, pensive Alí, head resting on one arm amid a silk, midnight-blue coverlet that had been drawn back to expose his back and right hip, making it quite clear that he was nude beneath.

"Think post-coital glow," Elliott Gardener had instructed him before taking the shot. "You're thinking of the lover who's just left or perhaps is about to return. I want people to think of Dusk as the scent of sex."

That was easy enough. All Alí had to do was think of Alex and Mykonos.

The photo, an Internet/Times Square sensation, only fueled Severance's fire: "You see, this is what I mean. He calls himself a good Christian boy. But what God-fearing young man poses naked, exposing all that dark skin for the world to see?"

What God-fearing young man indeed? Alí was as conflicted about sex and his body as he suspected Severance was. He loved God. He loved Alex. He enjoyed sex. He didn't understand why they had to be mutually exclusive. It didn't make him feel any less guilty though. Severance was getting under "all that dark skin."

The phrase was a tip-off to Severance's true meaning. Thanks to a no-longer-obscure banking scandal, he was deadlocked in a race with a candidate who was a Bhutanese immigrant. So he chose to paint a bull's-eye on the newly crowned No. 1-ranked tennis player to divert attention from his own troubles. Typical.

And successful. For the first time, Alí heard scattered boos in the stands. Even Glenna Day Costa was nervous when she conducted interviews with him courtside.

"You're nothing but an Iraqi whore," one man screamed during an otherwise innocuous final in Seattle that Alí went on to win.

Signs reading "How many died so you could play?" and "Take off your clothes in your own country" began popping up at tournaments. The controversy even revived accounts of Nutgate.

"Crikey, that old thing," Evan said when he was tracked down on his honeymoon with Bridget. "Listen: Alí Iskandar is a mate. There's none finer. And anyone who says otherwise will have to answer to me."

That prompted headlines of "Bad-boy Tennis Star Defends Nutgate Mate," complete with video of Evan and Alí being escorted from the plane and incongruous images of Alí, Alex, Dylan, and Daniel partying in New York's Meatpacking District post-Olympics.

Apparently, like old soldiers, old scandals never died. They just waited for another YouTube moment.

All the while, the "I know who you are" messages continued, along with words of admonition, encouragement, worry, and confusion from Papa.

"You must be more careful how you present yourself," he messaged Alí. "The least little thing can fuel these hate-filled people."

Privately, Papa might criticize. Publicly, he was a tiger-daddy.

"I am the father of Tariq Alí Iskandar," he began his email to the editor of the *New York Times*. "From the moment he entered the world twenty-three years ago, he has been nothing but a joy to his mother and me, a comfort and support to his brothers and sisters, and the pride of our people. In short, he's a gift from the God who made us all.

"Once the Americans came to Iraq, it was Alí's dream to do two things: play tennis and become an American. I know my son, and I know he would never do anything to dishonor the sport and the country he loves so dearly. Sincerely, Makmud Iskandar, Paris."

It wasn't enough, Kathy was certain.

"Listen, babe," she told him. "There's only one thing that's going to stop the bleeding. You're going to have to take your case directly to the American people."

She booked him on the must-see prime-time newsmagazine *This About That*, where he would be interviewed alone for an hour by Everett Dewey-Smith, a bow-tied blowhard whose questions were at times so long-winded that the subjects often sat in stunned silence, forgot what the question even was, or stalked off in anger, like movie star Trey Fleck, who punctuated his departure by tossing a glass of water in Dewey-Smith's face.

Not good, Alí thought as he sat alone in the green room waiting to go on. Kathy had insisted on being there with him. But she would only fuss, brushing his lintless jacket and straightening his tie for the umpteenth time and making him even more nervous than he was. Besides, Michaela, who was a teenager now, still needed some of that attention.

"Don't worry, A," she texted him. "Me and my girls got your back. We're blasting Facebook and Twitter to let everyone know we love you, and we'll be watching."

Yet as he sat there—trembling in his trendy, new, skinny black designer suit—he had never felt so alone. Usually, he liked that. People tended to make him edgy when he had something important to do. And he hated to be a burden to anyone.

Besides, self-possession was part of every tennis player's makeup, the sense of one individual against another, the individual against the world. But never—not even at Wimbledon—had he been more acutely aware that this was entirely up to him. How he "played" was going to determine his future.

He straightened his periwinkle tie, yet again; checked his fly, yet again; had a sip of water; and smoothed his hair.

"He is drop-dead gorgeous," he had heard the makeup artist whisper to an assistant.

Alí smiled to himself, then glanced at the monitors in the green room, which showed two groups of protesters outside: supporters of Senator Severance and his "Keep America Safe, First" campaign and members of the Iraqi-American Anti-Defamation League, who were furious at the senator's insinuations.

As he did in any tournament, Alí went deep inside himself to gather and channel his emotions and focus on the task at hand.

"You're on," an assistant with a Bluetooth headset said, escorting Alí to a set where, under hot white lights, he was greeted by Dewey-Smith, a pillar of pomposity in the way many political reporters were. God, Alí thought, these people really do believe the world begins and ends with the Beltway. Dewey-Smith informed him in the loftiest terms how he would be introduced and why there was nothing to worry about.

"Good evening," he intoned, "and welcome to *This About That*. I'm your host, Everett Dewey-Smith. Tonight we continue our series on cultural lightning rods. Tariq Alí Iskandar is the No. 1-ranked tennis player in the world, the first American to hold that ranking in twenty years, and the first Iraqi-American ever to hold that position. Born in Baghdad to a family of Franco-Persian descent, he came to this country as a child during the height of the Iraq War after a soldier, the late Private Michael Smeaton, befriended him and spotted his talent.

"Since then, he has won numerous titles, including the Grand Slam this year—only the second American to do so—and the Olympic singles gold medal last year. But his background has also led some to question his motives. Now as he prepares to lead the US Davis Cup team possibly to its first championship in twenty-two years, he sits down with us to talk about the charges. Welcome, Tariq Alí Iskandar."

"Please call me Alí. It is my privilege and pleasure to be here."

"Well, Alí, I can't recall a time recently when a tennis tournament has taken such hold of the American imagination."

"I think you have Senator Severance to thank for that. But if this inspires interest in the game, then I'm glad."

"Do you know the senator?"

"I do not."

"And I take it you have never been to Kansas."

"I have not, though I here it is a beautiful state. Perhaps I can play there someday."

"Do you understand all the controversy swirling around you?"

"Not really. But then, we live in a world where someone can say something outrageous about you and others pick it up as if it were gospel. It would be laughable if it weren't so serious."

"Do you see yourself as an Iraqi or an American?"

"I see myself as an Iraqi-American. Mine is an immigrant's story, like many others. I came here to better myself and help my family. It's what people have been doing for centuries."

"Do you think then that yours is a case of racial profiling?"

"Well, you tell me. If I had come to America from Stockholm and won the Grand Slam, would we be having this conversation?"

"Yet you do come from a region that has a long association with terrorism."

"Yes, and it is my hope to show that there is another face to the Middle East, that the people there are good people who want peace."

"Still, your family was targeted for their Christian beliefs. You yourself were the victim of a hate crime."

"I'm glad you brought that up. Yes, some children carved a small cross at the base of my neck with a knife. But we must understand that this was nothing more than a response to the brutality of war."

"You count yourself a devout Roman Catholic, don't you?"

"I'm a practicing Catholic, but I'm no saint."

"Still, you posed for an ad that some consider highly sexual."

"I consider the photographer Elliott Gardener to be an artist. And art always tells the truth."

"Advertising, though, is about selling."

"And the sales of the men's fragrance displayed in that ad help me support myself, my family, and a wide variety of causes, including UNICEF and the Women's Health Project founded by Dr. Daniella Reiner, of which my two sisters, both doctors, are now a part. They are fighting the good fight, bringing badly needed health services to some of the poorest women and children in the world. I cannot tell you how proud I am of my big sisters. Tennis, modeling, these are nothing compared to the work they and Dr. Reiner are doing. These are the real heroes of our world."

"You speak of causes: Do any of them hold the United States responsible for the brutality of war you experienced?"

"I think America has done what she felt she had to do to protect herself in the wake of 9/11. I think all action is reaction. Someone serves, you return. It's instinct. We are all products of the past. But though we live with the past, we can't live in it."

"That kind of thinking might lead some to vengeance."

"I don't have a vindictive nature."

"There are those who say your unique vantage point, talents, and background would be better employed elsewhere, say, in the Foreign Service."

"But that's like saying because you know how to ride a bicycle, you would make a great cyclist on the Tour de France. We do what we do not only because we have the talent for it, but also because we don't have the talent for something else. I speak any number of languages well, but none with the proficiency of a U.N. translator."

"You could acquire that proficiency."

"I probably could. But then, I might not have time for tennis. What we do in life, if we're lucky, is about temperament as well as talent, timing, training, and technique. I call them 'the five Ts.'

"Besides, in this country, we are free to pursue our dreams, not just what some government official says those dreams should be. But I must really thank Senator Severance again. He has reminded me why I became an American and a tennis player. It's a great game, and if there's anything to come from this, I hope it is a greater appreciation for our democratic country and our beautiful sport."

Afterward, Alí couldn't resist sampling the reaction on the *This About That* blog, even though it was against his better judgment, and Kathy had said he aced the interview:

Oldervet writes: "All I saw was a young man, a quivering boy really, left on his own to defend himself and do so magnificently. Bravo."

Ryderinthesky says: "Are you kidding? Those people are all good at lying through their teeth. Look, it was a pitch-perfect performance. But a performance nonetheless."

Tennisace12 says: "I don't care who he is or what he's done. He is to-die-for hot."

Tennisgirl30-15 says: "Yeah, I'd be happy to terrorize that body any day. LOL."

Quietamericannomore says: "Who gives a fugh? He's a tennis player—a tennis player! They wear shorts. Come on. He's a bore. And probably gay. LOL."

Alí closed his iPad and glanced at the roses that had arrived earlier at his new apartment at the Watergate. His heart leapt when he saw them. He was sure they were from Alex. How he wished he could've had him with him in the green room and off-camera. But he knew the rules of that game: Such appearances tended to set off people's gaydar. Indeed, Alí thought one of the few good things to come out of stupid, venal Morris Severance's comments was that he didn't play the gay card—and instead had sent everyone barking up the wrong bamboo. *Celebrity* magazine had even done a cover on Alí called "Inside His World: His Pals, His Women."

Apparently, some buxom blonde had come forward as Alí's self-appointed girlfriend. She was a model, of course, and confessed that she rarely accompanied him to tournaments, because watching him play made her nervous.

"You just can't make this stuff up," Alí said to himself as he leafed through the magazine, "or perhaps you can."

He again read the card that came with the pale pink flowers: "I love you, and I'm proud of you. DAR." Dylan Anthony Roqué.

That was so like Dylan, so passionate and compassionate. Still, he was disappointed. Why weren't they from Alex? OK, so he couldn't be on set. But he should've been there, now, holding him as he shook, comforting him in the night as he cried out, stroking that throbbing vein that brought him so much pleasure and anguish.

But since Mykonos, since Alí had become world No. 1, Alex had been, well, more than his usual ironic, detached self. The same issue of *Celebrity* had a spread on Eleni and Geo's opulent wedding on Mykonos, including a photo of Alex hugging the maid of honor.

There was no invitation for Alí, nor could there have been. It was all right. He understood the rules of a game in which love was zero.

Alí went into the bathroom that was almost as big as the efficiency apartment he had had when he first left his guardian's house in what seemed a lifetime ago. He was rich and famous, only now he had crossed a threshold, stepping beyond fame into cultural iconography and notorious legend. His life would never be the same.

He splashed his face, the water mingling with his tears. His phone pinged.

"I know who you are," the text read.

He looked hard into the mirror.

"I doubt it," he said as he shut off the light.

Daniel

WHEN DANIEL THOUGHT OF MYKONOS, HE THOUGHT OF HIS family's vacations on the Jersey shore and all those other summer idylls that gleamed in his memory. He would've been happy to stay there and stop time. But he was no magician, and now Mykonos flickered like a Camelot or Shangri-La that once savored could never be bridged again.

The year since passed in a blur of practices, meets, promos, and fundraising events. There always seemed to be some urgent email or text from his sponsors, charities, publicist, agent, coach, family, and, of course, Chloë.

She was the easiest to ignore, at first. He knew her game and was determined to beat her at it, using her as a convenient beard as he pursued his relationship with Dylan. However tough he was on him—something that panged him when they weren't together—he had no illusion about whom he really loved. God or no, Dylan was a piece of his soul. Whereas Chloë was a manipulator, which made manipulating her in turn easier on the conscience. Why then, Daniel wondered, did he use her like a knife to carve up Dylan's heart?

He had to give her credit though: Since that post-Olympic party almost a year and a half ago, she had wheedled her way into the affections of both of his parents, which was no small feat since they were complete opposites whose only common interests were the child they had lost and, possibly, the one that remained.

Worming her way into Daniel's cloistered, brambled heart would not be so easy. It wasn't that he was averse to sex with a woman, say, a Rubenesque beauty who struck him as the female equivalent of Dylan, with a high chest to go along with high coloring. It's just that he planned to withhold sex as a way to one-up the woman who was so determined to control him. That at least was his thinking. But Chloë was like water over a rock. Over time, water wears a rock down. Eventually, Daniel had to cave and do the deed, if for no other reason that to keep his hetero mask in place. He found himself completely repulsed not by the female form per se, but by her own glorified coat hanger of a body, which may have looked great in couture but offered nothing undraped except the sense of being undernourished. He was also convulsed with shame at his betrayal of Dylan.

So when he met his mother for lunch at one of those places frequented more by ladies than the members of his sex, he was not surprised that Chloë immediately popped up in the conversation. Indeed, he was bracing for it.

"So how's it going?" Daniella said, leaning across the table after they had ordered in the way she did when she was about to say how it really was going with you.

"Have you heard from Chloë, because I have to tell you, she thinks you've cooled toward her, or, at the very least, are sending mixed signals. I said I don't know, it's not like you to be less than straightforward."

She patted Daniel's hand.

"I told her maybe you needed some space, and you know what? She completely agreed. God, she is just so wise and intuitive. But I could sense she was a little hurt. I mean, a girl expects to spend some time with her beau."

Daniel was seething. If she wanted time with him, she should've approached him directly instead of running to his mother, which would only ensure in his mind that she wasn't going to get it.

"Well, Mom, Chloë's a big girl. I'm sure she can talk to me about her disappointments."

"And though I know she didn't want to say so, I could see she was upset, too, that Dylan never got together with her friend Tina. Not that I blame Dylan. God knows he has enough on his plate. Now might not be the time. And then I had heard he was seeing that lovely Caroline Quinnick."

A double pang: The websites were full of pictures of Dylan and Caro being honored as male and female swimmers of the year. Daniel made it a point of not attending the event, even though he won a couple of lesser awards. His mother just had to rub it in.

"They looked so adorable together on the red carpet. I texted Dee Dee my congratulations. I know she's thrilled. Now if I could just see you settled."

"Why? Why, Mom? Why is it so important?"

"I just thought it would be nice if you had someone to share your life with. Dylan and Caro make such a nice couple. And I saw a photo of your friend Alex with one of the bridesmaids at his sister's wedding. That must've been quite an affair. Did you see her dress? The lace was exquisite. And Alí—I never could imagine that sweet boy as a terrorist—is dating that pretty swimsuit model."

Daniel had all he could do to keep a straight face. Another insinuating model. Turned out Kahrin Klaus knew Chloë. Or so Alí texted him after she approached him at a tournament to apologize for lying about dating him, then proceeded to have herself photographed with him, further perpetuating the lie. Small world and what a surprise.

"Don't believe everything you read, Mother. And anyway, you never cared about my having a steady girlfriend before."

"But you're older now, and your father and I won't be around forever."

"You and he aren't even fifty."

His mother had him and Ani when she was an intern, and his father was working as a trader on Wall Street. Daniel didn't know how they, especially his mother, did it.

"It's just that, I thought if you had someone special, you'd feel more rooted and you'd take more of an interest in your father's business."

The entrées had arrived, and Daniel smiled at the waitress before resuming in a low voice: "So that's what this little get-together is really about. I thought it suspicious, your nagging. It's not like you. Now I know it's not really concern for me. Did Chloë put you up to this or did your ex?"

"Please, Dani, it's—" Her eyes welled and lips trembled as she waved a hand and took a bite of grilled salmon.

That also wasn't like her, and Dylan was suddenly in uncharted territory. He was scared.

"Look, I'm sorry," he said. "What's wrong, Mom? Tell me, and I'll make it right. You want me to see Chloë, I'll call her up."

"It's not that. It's . . . your father's sick."

"What do you mean *sick*?"

"He has prostate cancer."

Silence. The world skipped a beat.

"But that's like breast cancer, isn't it? I mean, common but curable, right?"

"You know, it's ironic that a doctor should have a child who knows so little of the sciences. Your sister inherited the science gene. She would've made a fine vet. What might've been, right? They're all gone. Your grandfather died of prostate cancer."

"Jeez, I had no idea."

"No, you don't know much where your father and his family are concerned, do you? Listen to me, Daniel Reiner-Kahn, your father needs us now. His business needs you. He built that company up from nothing into a multibillion-dollar enterprise, and if you think for one moment, that I'm going to let it go to anyone but my child, my child," here she struck her breast, "you and everyone else have another guess coming.

"When they pulled your sister and then you out of me—a breach birth no less—on that hot April night, I swore by everything I suffered at that moment, and the ashes of my family and your father's that mingled with the dust of Dachau and Auschwitz, that whatever we had in this world no one would take from us and our children. You're all that's left.

"I don't give a damn about Chloë Miller. I mean, she's a nice enough girl, and if you loved her, I'd embrace her like a daughter, though don't think for a minute I'm blind to her flaws. If you don't want her, fine: There are plenty of other fish in the sea. We're not meant to be alone, Dani."

His mother's tone softened.

"Break bread with your father. Make peace with him. Help him. You're all he's got."

· · · ·

ARI KAHN CERTAINLY DIDN'T LOOK LIKE A MAN WHO NEEDED anyone or anything, Daniel thought when he met him for lunch at one of his clubs a few days later. He was the very picture of the guy the tabloids liked to photograph occasionally jogging around Battery Park.

Daniel didn't know how to broach the subject of his health, but since their lunches were usually stilted affairs, the small talk punctuated by long stretches of silence, Daniel didn't feel any more awkward than usual. Finally, having exhausted the weather (unseasonably warm for late autumn in New York); the local sports teams (fair to middling now that the glow of the Yanks' latest World Series triumph was wearing off); Daniella (good, busy); their careers (fine, busy), there was nothing to talk about.

So Daniel took the plunge.

"How have you been feeling?"

"Fine, good, never better."

"That's not what Mom told me."

"Well, she had no right to tell you."

"No, you're right. It should've come from you."

"Perhaps if we had a closer relationship."

"Yeah, well, I guess, maybe. But still, you know. Perhaps I can help."

"How? Your mother's hooked me up with a great oncologist, I'm on hormone therapy, my PSA levels are good. I'm lucky I was diagnosed early, lucky my ex is a brilliant physician, lucky in the team that works for me."

"Maybe I could help at the office."

"Doing what? Swimming into the fish tank to clean it out? I don't want my son to come in expecting to be vice president of paper clips. You'd have to learn the business from the ground up, and I don't think you have the stomach for that."

"Maybe I do."

"No maybes. You either commit to Ari Kahn, LLP or you don't. Because I have no intention of one day handing this over to a dilettante who's only in it for the paycheck, no matter what your mother says, and don't think I don't know she put you up to this."

"No one put me up to anything."

Just then, Chloë arrived at the table. She was wearing one of her trademark nondescript black outfits: sheath dress, jeans jacket, boots.

"I hope I'm not interrupting anything," she said, interrupting everything.

She went to kiss Dylan on the lips but the buss wound up on his cheek as he turned his head.

"What a pleasant surprise," Ari said, rising to kiss her on her cheek, his eyes glowing. "Waiter."

"Oh, nothing for me, thanks. I'll just have some sparkling water. I'm on my way to a fitting for an assignment. But when your office said you two were having lunch here, I just had to stop by with the name of that acupuncturist."

"You could've just texted it and saved yourself the trouble," Daniel said, smiling broadly.

"Oh, I just needed an excuse to see my two favorite guys—apart from my dad, of course."

She stretched her hands, patting one of Daniel's as she squeezed one of Ari's.

"Ari, I've taken the liberty of including the name of a good masseur and a psychotherapist, should you need to talk."

"Is this girl a treasure or what?" Ari said to Daniel as he kissed her hand.

"I'm just doing what I can," she said with a tuck of her head.

And what she could do, Daniel realized, was considerable. He had thought he understood. But it was only now that he realized the extent of her reach. She didn't want merely to be Daniel's wife. She wanted to replace the daughter Ari lost. It appeared Ari wanted that, too. And what was even more frightening: they didn't care what Daniel wanted. Suddenly, he saw his life unspool before him, each day programmed like the next, calibrated to the millisecond in a seamless demonstration of just how noble Chloë was in pursuing her own agenda.

It was a good thing she had to go on to her fitting, because Daniel might've fitted her right then.

"You'd better snatch her up before someone else does," Ari said between bites of his sole almondine.

"Why don't your marry her, Dad? You can't seem to get enough of her."

"Don't be malicious and ridiculous. She has eyes only for you."

"I'll bet."

"All I'm saying is don't let this one get away."

"Like you did with Dee Dee?"

"Come again?"

"I mean you let true love slip through your fingers, because you were too proud and had to have a Jewish wife."

"Jesus Christ," his father said, slamming the cutlery against his dish. It made a clattering sound that drew the attention of some other patrons.

"Is that what you think? Is that what she told you, no doubt to make herself look good? Let me tell you something, since you've been on this from the moment you met that Roqué kid. I didn't break up with Dee Dee Norquist because I'm a Jew and she's Catholic, or because I live on the East Coast and she lives on the West, or for any other such cocka-mamie reason. None of that mattered a damn to me. I would've done whatever she wanted. But what she wanted was to be a great artist, and she didn't want a husband and kids tying her down.

"Those Norquists and Roqués are crazy all right, but they're crazy like foxes. They never lose sight of what they want. I'll prove it to you. Before you met Dylan, you were the premier swimmer in the world. After, he became the best. But I'll say this for them: At least they believe in themselves and something larger than themselves. What about you, Daniel? What do you believe in?"

After that, he simply had to get out, away from Chloë, Ari Kahn, Ari Kahn, LLP, even his mother. He fled up the Henry Hudson Park-way to his mother's home in Scarsdale, knowing she would still be at her office, threw some things in his duffel, and tore down to Kennedy Airport.

"Get me on the next flight to LA," he said to the young woman at the Delta Airlines counter.

"Oh, sir, that's not departing until 9:30 p.m., and we only have standby. I can get you on the red-eye, but I only have first class."

"Fine, whatever, just get me out of here."

He was about to pay for his ticket when he got a text from Dylan:

"Heard about your dad from Aunt Dee Dee. I'm so sorry. Am here for you in NY at our usual place, Room 722."

His mother must've told Dee Dee, who told her nephew, who—well isn't that whom he was going to LA to see, anyway? Daniel arrived at the Elixir Hotel several hours later, seriously pissed in more ways than one.

"Dylan, open up," he said, banging on the room door.

When a sleepy, stunned Dylan finally opened the door, Daniel barged in.

"Christ," he said, "you'd think with all the endorsements you have now, you could spring for a suite."

"I don't need much. Besides, when we were kids, a dorm room was more than enough for our love nest."

"Yeah, well, that was a lifetime ago."

"Have you been drinking? 'Cause—"

Before Dylan could finish that thought, Daniel yanked his T-shirt over his head and, pinning his arms behind his back with it, kissed him roughly.

"Don't move," he told Dylan. He traced the dunes of his chest with his tongue, sucking the nipples of his high, broad chest—"the best tits in swimming—"he called them.

He pulled down Dylan's sweats and took his cock hungrily in his mouth. Daniel heard him gasp, felt him shudder. He knew when his lover was about to come. Right before he could, Daniel drew himself up and thrust his tongue into Dylan's mouth.

"I want you to taste yourself," he said in a husky voice.

Then he swept Dylan off his feet, lugging him to the bed, threw him across its width and unzipped his own trousers.

"No, please, not like this," Dylan pleaded.

Afterward, Daniel lay on Dylan's back, his ragged breaths keeping time with Dylan's sobs.

"Is there never to be any tenderness between us again?" he said, the words staggered by sorrow.

Daniel rose slightly and flipped Dylan over to face him.

"My father may be dying," he said.

"I know. I understand. But all the more reason for us to be gentle with each other. Couldn't I hold you and comfort you and you could hold and comfort me? If we married—came out and married—we could hold and comfort each other all the time."

Daniel laughed almost maniacally.

"Are you kidding me? You must really be crazy like that family of yours. You're all nuts and skanks, like your Aunt Dee Dee. My father loved her, loved her, and she took that love and betrayed it."

"How? How? My aunt is a lovely woman. She would never betray—"

"He was ready to give up everything for her, everything, and she wouldn't have him, no, because she wanted to be free to make her crappy artwork."

"First off, it's not crappy. And anyway, if she didn't want to marry him, that was her choice. She wasn't under any obligation, just because he tried to force his affections on her."

"Force his affections? My father was a timid, bookish kid who wanted to be a math teacher before he met the clay goddess. But you know what? I'm glad it didn't work out, that the Kahn blood was never tainted by insanity. And just as she would never have him, I would never marry you."

He looked into Dylan's eyes and saw that a light had gone out of them. Right then, Daniel realized he had crossed a bridge, and everything had changed forever.

They slept together fitfully, Daniel listening to Dylan's stifled weeping as he clutched his pillow at the edge of the bed.

In the early hours of the morning, Dylan stirred.

"Where do you think you're going?" Daniel asked.

"I have to go to the bathroom. I feel sick."

"I didn't give you permission to get up. But since you are."

Daniel took him then as Dylan lay motionless, silent. After a while, Daniel fell into a heavy sleep. Later in the morning, he woke and reached out for Dylan, only to find the bed empty.

"Dylan, Dyl, I'm sorry. I don't know what got into me. Are you in the bathroom?"

But he wasn't in the bathroom, nor were his clothes and duffel in the closet, and that's when Daniel realized that Dylan was truly, really gone.

Alex

WHEN ALEX THOUGHT OF HIS OWN PRIVATE MYKONOS, HE thought of how impossible it was to recapture a moment. Hadn't he told Daniel as much?

It didn't stop him, though, from trying to rekindle the playfulness and passion he had found with Alí, Dylan, Daniel, and, to an extent, Étienne. But time is another country and can turn a once-familiar landscape foreign. Alí was no longer the boy who had watched in awe as Alex practiced with Étienne five Wimbledons ago. He was now the undisputed world No. 1, albeit a controversial one, thanks to his equal status as "polarizing cultural icon"—or so the press called him. As a connoisseur of irony and human frailty, Alex relished the laziness with which the media latched onto a phrase and then dragged it around, like a dog with a bone, whether or not it still fit or ever had.

But Alex, too, had changed. He was world No. 2, and he didn't like it one bit. It was hard climbing to the top, harder still to stay there. But nothing beat the pain of having been to the pinnacle only to slip.

Do what he might, he rarely beat Alí now, and the fear it instilled in him created a self-fulfilling prophecy. So he had to savor the occasions when he did. One came nearly two years after the Olympics at a tournament in Cincinnati, one of those colorless corporate events that played out in a string of indistinguishable American cities. It just so happened that the Elyria Championships, sponsored by Elyria Oil, had a prime Sunday afternoon slot on an American network. This was a big moment, and the sponsor let the tournament officials know it.

"Here's our inning, guys," tournament director Frank Abernathy said, choosing a metaphor that was lost on Alex. "So we're going to shine even if the weather doesn't."

Of course, it rained and not just a light summer drizzle but a deluge of biblical, Brontë-esque proportions that let up enough to allow play, but not so much as to make it pleasant.

The hard court was slick, and Alex was worried for himself and for Alí, too, who had to battle hecklers everywhere now, thanks to stupid Senator Morris Severance. What a jackass, Alex thought. Severance had won reelection the previous autumn but at what cost to others? All he had done was paint a bull's-eye on Alí and every player who shared the court with him. It was a good thing Senator Severance wasn't playing him, Alex thought, because he would've happily shoved his tennis racket down his throat. Instead, he was left to battle Alí, the tournament officials, the fans, and the elements. Great.

After Alí slipped during an intense point and grazed his elbow, Alex approached the chair umpire.

"Bravo," he said, applauding sarcastically by hitting his racket with his hand. "Someone may break his neck out here, but hey, as long as you guys get your precious final in and the network fills its slot and the fans get their entertainment, that's all that matters, isn't it?"

The chair ump started to respond weakly, but Alex cut him off, shaking his head. "You people make me sick."

The crowd, just as wet and disgruntled as the players, began rooting against him, booing him and Alí equally.

"Thanks," Alí said at the changeover, "but don't get in a jam for my sake."

"I did it for me, too," Alex said.

He had adopted the kind of cool, distant, passive-aggressive attitude to Alí that Étienne used to visit on him.

"Come on, angel," he would whisper in his ear as he held him close from behind in yet another equally anonymous hotel room, "you don't mind. Just a bit of fun, that's all."

And he would tie him to the bed and gauge the discomfort in those nutmeg eyes as he took him slowly, exquisitely.

Or Alex would wait for Alí to return to his room from some late semifinal, exhausted.

"Hello, angel," Alex would say, lounging in a chair, his robe falling open just enough to hint at his naked hunger. "I'm glad to see you."

"Please, Alex, maybe later. I'm tired now. I just want to crash."

"Come on. You know what I want, what we both want. Don't be shy."

And reluctantly, Alí would perform a slow striptease, the superb abs seeming even more ripped than usual.

"That's not all I want. You know."

And Alí would begin to stroke himself.

"Slowly now. Let me see you pull back the head. And don't close your eyes. You can't hide anymore."

How well Alex knew that. Wherever Alí played, he was plagued either by teenage girls with posters of his ads, longing to cut off a lock of his thick, coarse hair, or xenophobic Americans looking to exile him—or worse. Alex couldn't tell which group was more dangerous. It was beginning to play on Alí's psyche. As a lover, Alex found it troubling. As an opponent, he was willing to watch it play out to what he hoped was his advantage. The Alí who played him in Cincinnati was even more miserable than he himself felt, sneezing, shaking, his tears mingling with the rain. Even his habit of going deep inside himself—lowering that lush awning of lashes and plucking the strings of his racket—seemed to fail him here, and he fell to Alex 4–6, 6–4, 7–6, 4–6, 6–4.

"You know what this means," Alex whispered in his ear as Alí offered him a congratulatory hug at the net. "I get to win later, too."

That night, Alex stripped him briskly, tossing his clothes aside.

"You don't need these," he said as Alí shivered.

He spun him around and held him tight, hissing in his ear, "You're such a little whore."

"Where did you learn these things?" Alí asked as he choked back his emotions and leaned into Alex's caresses.

"No, don't tell me. I can just imagine. It was from Étienne, wasn't it? It all makes sense now. Well, I don't care what went before. Only I don't want to play his games."

Alex turned him around and held him by the wrists. He saw tears beading on the thick lashes.

"Please, angel, for me. Just a little. I won't tie you too tight. Or should I find someone else to share playtime with?"

Alí lowered his gaze. Alex had never seen him give up, on or off the court. Now he merely nodded.

Alex tied him to bedposts, the shower, table legs, everywhere he could think of. There was a part of him that enjoyed how sex had become an endurance test for Alí, how he rubbed his wrists, wincing, and disguised the bruises with sweatbands, how the inner game had begun to make inroads onto the court.

But it didn't make Alex happy. Whenever he released Alí, his lover would throw his arms around him.

"Please, please, hold me," Alí would say softly.

And the flashbacks to Iraq—the screams and the dreams—had become much worse.

Alex was starting to feel guilty and distracted. Daniel had begun texting him more often, inquiring about whether he'd heard from Dylan, whom he had broken up with. Dylan rarely texted Alex, no doubt intuiting rightly that Alex was more a Daniel than a Dylan friend. He was probably in touch with Alí, but as Alex was discovering, there were rooms in Alí's psychic mansion that lay behind locked doors. He wasn't about to betray a confidence.

. . . .

AND THEN THERE WAS ÉTIENNE.

"I miss us," he said, apropos of nothing after he had beaten Alex in the final of an exhibition in which Alex had beaten Alí.

"What us?" Alex said, smiling as he patted him on the back at the net, suggesting to the crowd that they were discussing the match. "There was only you, me, our kinky off-court game, and now your wife and baby. There are some lines even I won't cross, like adultery."

"Oh, Alex, why not drop your little brown boyfriend and give it a try?"

Alex was many things, but he wasn't a snob, and he wasn't prejudiced. So he had mixed feelings when Étienne suggested they meet for a drink at his suite at the Elixir Hotel a week before the US Open.

Alex arrived more than a little on edge. What could Étienne have up his pale pink polo shirt sleeve? It had to be something. He was not surprised to find him in the cavernous living room with a young man he didn't know. Alex relaxed a little. The man in question was the kind of fanny-packing tourist Alex had often seen in New York, even at the Open: stocky, almost pudgy in build, ruddy of complexion, and sweaty of demeanor, with a short barber's haircut that revealed a pinky tinge to the fleshy neck. This must be what Americans meant, Alex thought, by a redneck.

His nondescript attire—checked shirt, jeans, sneakers—underscored that he was not a New Yorker. And he certainly was not in any way attractive enough to catch Étienne's eye. Still, who was he, and why was Alex there to meet him?

"Alex, *je voudrais presenter* Greg. Greg, Alex," Étienne said.

Alex offered his hand.

"Pleasure."

"Likewise."

Silence. Awkward.

"Alex, help yourself to a drink."

"No thanks, a bit early for me. And anyway, I have practice. You do, too, I assume."

"In a bit. But first a little warm-up."

Alex didn't like the sound of that.

The doorbell rang.

"*Entrée, si vous voulez.*"

"Hello?"

Alex recognized Alí's voice.

"We're in here," Alex said.

The two were practically living in Alex's suite on another floor. Why hadn't Alí told him he would be here? For that matter, why hadn't he himself mentioned this to Alí, or Étienne said anything about Alí to Alex?

"You," Alí said, looking at Greg as if he had just witnessed someone come back from the dead. "What are you doing here?"

"You know Greg?' Alex asked.

"You do?"

"We just met. How do you two know each other?"

"That," Étienne said, sitting down with a Scotch on the rocks and clearly relishing the moment, "is actually a fascinating story. Shall I tell it or will you, Alí? No, I see by the expression on your face, *cher*, that you would prefer I start.

"There once was a poor little boy who wanted more than anything in the world to become a glamorous tennis player and escape the dirt and poverty of his childhood. The little boy already knew he was attractive to a certain type of person, so he ingratiated himself with a good-hearted American soldier. But the soldier, who taught him to play, and possibly a few other things, lacked the money and the power to advance the boy. Yet he could bring the boy's dream to the attention of people who could, including a contractor who worked for the American Defense Department in the early days of the Iraq War.

"Now this contractor was a fine, upstanding man with a wife and children of his own. Out of the goodness of his heart, he brought the boy to America, educated him, trained him, and helped the boy's family. And how did the boy repay this extraordinary generosity? By seducing the man with all the tricks he had learned on the streets of Baghdad, driving a wedge between the man and his family. And when the man died tragically in a car accident, the boy blackmailed his widow to the tune of 500,000 US, which he used, along with other people, to rise to the top."

Here Étienne clapped, delighted with himself, then stretched out his arms along the buttery ultra-suede taupe sectional sofa.

"It's a great American success story," he added.

Alex turned to Alí. "Is this true?"

"Do you think it is?"

"I'm asking you."

"Of course it isn't, not entirely, not as presented. But if you have to ask, it doesn't matter, does it?"

"Of course it matters. That's why we're here," Alex said. He now turned his attention to Greg, who was grinning like an idiot.

"And just who are you in all this?"

"I was his son," Greg said bitterly, the grin crumbling suddenly into trembling tears, "and this thing corrupted my father, drove him from his life as a good Christian husband and father. He supplanted my mother, my sister, and me in my father's affections. He did this, and I have waited, waited all these years until I found someone who would be interested in my story. You, you," he spat at Alí, "are a seducer and a blackmailer and a murderer. My father had a heart attack and died on that highway, 'cause of you."

"My God," Alí said, "you're the one who's been sending me all those texts."

"And why shouldn't I? You killed my father, broke my mother's heart, and took away my childhood. Why shouldn't I take away your peace of mind?"

"I was a child, a child," Alí said, hitting his own chest for emphasis. "I came to your country with no other thought than to work hard, learn, and help my family. And I learned all right. Your father raped me night after night, and I suffered it, because I felt one day, one day I would be free, and somehow it would all have been worth it."

"If you weren't such a schemer, why did you take the money, huh?" Greg shouted, triumphantly. "Oh, your little boyfriend here didn't know about that or any of this, did he? No, look at his face. I bet everyone's interested in the money."

And with that, Greg produced a copy of the canceled check for $500,000 made out to Alí and deposited in a Chase account nine years earlier. "This was the money he forced my mother to pay him to keep quiet."

Alex felt as if he had been floating underwater and having at last managed to surface, had finally sighted land. The full import of his relationship with Alí had come into focus at last: the nightmares, the shrieking, the shaking, Alí's inability ever to feel warm. How could he? Here was a child who had suffered horrific abuse and he, Alex, who told himself he should've known and must've suspected somewhere, was nothing but an unwitting reminder of it.

When he thought of the nights he had stripped him, tied him up, commanded him to play with himself—the very things his guardian might've forced him to do—Alex was filled with revulsion. He hated himself, he hated Alí, he hated Étienne, he hated Greg, and most of all, he hated Greg's father, who had ruined the world for them.

"Why did you take the money?" Alex asked Alí, icy with anger.

"What was I supposed to do? I was sixteen with nothing and nowhere to go after my *guardian* died. His widow offered it to me as she kicked me out."

"You could've called your parents. You could've called the police. In fact, you could've done this while your guardian was still alive and demanded he send you home."

"How could I? He watched my every move, kept me locked in a basement bedroom, had Greg and his sister shadow me at school. Had I said a word, he told me, he would've seen that worse happened to my mother and my brothers and sisters. And I believed him. He was that much of a monster.

"And what home? My parents had already moved to Paris. That wasn't my home. And neither was Baghdad anymore. So I took the money, and I went to school, and I got a job, and I played every tournament I could, and I scratched and clawed my way up the rankings, and I repaid every cent with 10 percent interest. Where's that canceled check, Greg? Oh, that's right. I have it and a copy of the brief note I wrote: 'Paid in full.' I'm not stupid."

He turned to Alex, with what Alex would later remember as a terrible hope in his eyes.

"You believe me, don't you?"

"Yes."

"And yet, I've lost you, haven't I?"

"You took the money," Alex said, exploding. "Regardless of why, don't you see how it looks? I can't believe this. I cherished you as if you were a virgin bride. I protected you like you were my baby brother. All those nights, I felt guilty and worried and wondered if it was all too much for you. I should've known. Perhaps I did somewhere. I thought you were so sweet and innocent."

"I was. I am sweet and innocent."

"Then why did you take the money?" Alex screamed.

"Because I wanted to escape, to forget!" Alí shouted. "Him. What he did. Everything. The war, I wanted to escape the war. But I see now how wrong I was. I left the war behind only to find it had moved with me. Everywhere is war."

Alex watched Alí glance around the room. He could tell that for him, it had fallen away, and he was back there.

"Alex, you're not buying his phony trance, are you?"

"Shut up, Étienne."

After a while, Alí collected himself and, turning to Alex, said, "Don't let them do this to me, to us. Fight for us, Alex, the way you fight on the court. I love you."

"I know," Alex said sadly.

"I should've trusted you," Alí said at last, resigned.

"You should've," Alex said, "because where there is no trust, there can be no real love."

Alí nodded, turned, and left without saying anything more.

Alex smiled. When all else failed, he could at least retain his dignity, his sense of irony, which stung his moist eyes and burned his soul.

He turned to Étienne and applauded. Suddenly, everything was clear.

"Game, set, and match. Well played. This was never about him, was it? It was always about me. I took something from you, and now you've taken something—someone—from me more important to me than any Slam or No. 1 ranking, although I never realized that until now. Too late. Bravo. Only I think you missed your true calling, Étienne. Chess should've been your game."

Still smiling, he walked over to Greg, who, cretin that he was, mistook Alex's irony for bonhomie. Alex punched his stupid, grinning mouth, drawing blood.

"If I ever hear that you contact anyone else with this, if you ever go near him again or any of your family approaches any of his, I will kill you."

Alex punctuated the message by hitting Greg again and smiling at Étienne.

"Check," he said, "and mate."

Dylan

DYLAN IS DISTRACTED. NO, THAT'S NOT IT. HE'S NOT SURE. Something. He can't quite put his finger on it. Maybe if he could, he wouldn't be whatever it is he is.

Preoccupied. That's it. That must be. How else to explain the little things—the constant misplacing of his keys—and the bigger ones—forgetting his lines at an audition and even swimming the strokes out of order at practice? How many times had he recited them as if they were a mantra: butterfly, back, breast, free? He's even thought of getting them tattooed on his forearm, which shows you how paranoid he is. Silly. He's Dylan Roqué, the No. 1-ranked swimmer in the world. This stuff is a second skin.

Experts say when you're stressed out, you start making stupid mistakes. Dylan isn't buying it, though. He's always thrived under pressure, congratulated himself on his ability to keep all the balls in play. He's strong, you know?

Except when he isn't. Now something's different. He's tired, bone-tired. And disheartened. All his Olympic dreams have come to naught, because for Dylan, it's never been about the medals, the fame, even the money. It's about what the medals could yield: opportunity, security for his family. And that's not gone as expected.

He thought the sponsorships and the success would mean a big new apartment for him and his brothers. Yet more than two years after the Olympics, he's still living in the same modest "dump," as Daniel called it, because he likes it, and anyway, what's the point of a larger space when there's no family to share it with?

Jordie, having graduated from Stanford, has moved back to Malibu to live with their father and their father's pretty young bride, Lauren, whom Dylan understands is very nice. He doesn't know. He wasn't invited to the wedding. He didn't expect to be. But still, it hurts, as does what he sees as his brother's betrayal.

"You have to allow for different personalities," Aunt Dee Dee says in one of their weekly phone chats. "Jordie wants to be a Hollywood big shot. Who knows? Maybe he'll produce the next *Gone With the Wind*."

"If he doesn't cut down on the partying, he'll be the one who's gone with the wind."

Dylan can hear the pain in Dee Dee's sigh.

"I know. But there's nothing we can do. He's a big boy now. He has to make his own decisions. At least Austin's on the straight and narrow."

Austin had won a film scholarship to UCLA but decided to attend Berkeley and stay close to Aunt Dee Dee.

"Your brothers are on their own paths. Now that Austie's eighteen, your father has dropped the custody suit—finally. Soon I hope to have your grandmother's estate settled—finally. It's time for you to live your own life, Ducky, perhaps even turn it up a notch with a certain teammate of yours."

It takes Dylan a minute to realize she means Caro, not Daniel. She and Dylan have been spending time together, which is good and not so. He doesn't want to mislead and mistreat her the way he's been mistreated. At the same time, why shouldn't they try to make each other happy?

Because there's the matter of the 800-pound gorilla—make that the 195-pound swimmer—who's not in the room but whose presence lingers in Dylan's mind.

"Look, I know you've been seeing someone," Caro says, so like Daniel in her directness, among other things. "And I won't build my happiness on the back of someone else's misery."

"Shh," Dylan says, kissing her. "It's over. It's over."

And it is. And it isn't, which is the hell of it, this inertia that keeps him transfixed and pinned like a butterfly.

Dylan loves Daniel. He always will. He whispered as much in the wee hours of the morning as he closed the door on that room in the

Elixir Hotel and on their relationship forever. But relationships are stubborn. They hover like ghosts.

Dani, my Dani, I love you. I just can't be with you anymore.

Caro is good for him, with him. For once, it's about him, them, rather than a certain you-know-who. She helps him learn Hamlet for an audition, playing all the supporting parts. He's so nervous about forgetting his lines that he over-prepares, and by the end, he's sure she could play every part as well.

It's only a workshop production, but what the hell. It's the way he sees his career going if he wants to be a serious actor, the movie thing not working out. Apparently, Hollywood thinks "Olympic swimmer" means "stupid sex symbol." Something that happened to his mother.

His mother: He tries not to think about her at the audition, but he can't help remember her, Grandma Debo, and Great-grandpa Declan, who all had memory lapses. Ironic, isn't it? That's what Alex would say.

"I am a product of all that I have met": That's what Tennyson's Ulysses says. Touché.

Dylan's too emotional, he thinks, in his reading of Hamlet's first soliloquy, because he gets it, you know? He understands that suicidal people don't want to die. Who wants to die and journey to the "undiscovered country, from whose bourn no traveler returns"? What they want is not to live, which is something else entirely. But how can you not live without dying? It's an untenable situation.

By the time he comes to the words, "Oh God, God, how weary, stale, flat and unprofitable seem to me all the uses of this world," he can hardly get them out, which is good in a way since he's sure he messed up some lines. He thinks he blew the audition anyway. But the producer and director love him, and at the performance, he gets a standing ovation and even some critical praise for a "youthful, lucent reading that recognizes the play's real subject: dying."

Aunt Dee Dee and Austin come down from San Francisco and even Jordie is there, with Caro leading the cheers. Funny, no one mentions Daniel. Maybe they sense something. Or maybe they assume what the press and everyone else does, that they are friends who lead fairly separate lives, especially now that they have girlfriends. Maybe he's a better actor than he thinks.

Back at the apartment, there are flowers. For a moment, Dylan thinks they're from Daniel. But the note is from Alí, who's playing an exhibition in Philadelphia.

Here Caro giggles. But to Dylan, it's no laughing matter. He and Alí have grown closer, texting all the time. Alí's fragility appeals to the protector in Dylan. But also, who better understands the death of their particular relationships than the other? That is the hell of it, too—a grief that is as secret and silent as the relationships and the loss that it mourns.

"I'm here for you," Alí texts.

"Right back at you," Dylan types.

But how are they there for each other? As friends? Lovers? Friends with benefits? Something more permanent? He doesn't want to think. It's too, too, too much.

He turns his attention back to Caro. They're still celebrating his little triumph a night later, alone with some pasta and wine, snuggling on the sofa. Dylan is surprised by how inviting her comparative softness is, how arousing her firm, high breasts.

She pulls her sweater off her shoulders in a gesture of commitment, and he cups those breasts, fingering the petal-pink nipples until they pucker in lust. She's even bolder, undoing his shirt and mirroring his gestures on his chest with one hand while the other slides down to palm his swelling crotch. He blushes, typically.

"You don't ever have to be ashamed of being a man with me," she says.

It's so easy and comfortable, no drama, no ego, Dylan thinks as they recline on the couch and he reaches for the lights and the remote. He hits mute instead of the off button, the images flickering in the darkness. His eye catches Alí on a news report as Caro glimpses the expression on Dylan's face.

"This isn't going to work, is it?" she says. "It's all right. I understand. I think I always have. It was Dani, wasn't it? God, how could I have been so stupid? But then, what a fool he was to throw you away, for I know that's what he did. Anyway, it doesn't matter now. Alí's needs you. Go to him."

Dylan buries his face in her neck, inhaling her scent and hugging her tight.

"Oh, Caro, I'm so sorry, so sorry for so many things."

And he begins to sob with these great, uncontrollable gasps and shudders that seem to rise from an unknown deep, like the groan of the sea.

Alí

IN HIS DREAM, ALÍ WAS ON THE COURT WITH ALEX AGAIN, playing in the finals of Wimbledon. There was a taut silence as Alex, the chair umpire, the crowd—everyone—waited for him to serve.

"But I have no arm," he said, motioning to an empty sleeve.

He woke with a start then and instinctively touched his left arm. It was all there, albeit with a bandage and stitches that already itched. Still, it was seemingly none the worse for wear, though time would tell. He looked around the private room at Memorial Hospital in Philadelphia to find the blinds closed, an array of "Get Well" bouquets and balloons and Dylan sleeping in two chairs pushed together, a light blanket drawn up to his chin. As Alí watched him with a smile, Dylan stirred, stretched, and yawned, returning the grin.

"Hey, how are you?" Dylan said, getting up to kiss him and tousle his hair.

"Happy to see you and a little tired."

"I'll bet. You've been through quite an ordeal."

Perhaps that was inevitable. Alí seemed to have been on course to meet calamity for quite some time, certainly from the moment he broke up with Alex. He had trudged through match after match, winning most, enjoying few.

Now I am alone, he thought, really alone. He kept checking his Twitter account, his Facebook page, and his messages for word from Alex. How he must hate me, he thought. He didn't blame him. Alí failed to trust his lover, which was as good as saying he really didn't love him. He thought, though, Alex should've understood. There were extenuating circumstances. He had been a child. He had been afraid. He had been ashamed. He had just wanted to forget.

He wondered if Alex's reaction to his "betrayal" was nothing more than a mask for his jealousy and an excuse to undercut Alí's success, for who could concentrate fully when a piece of his soul had been ripped from him? At least his guardian had ravaged only his body. Alí knew what to expect then and so sheltered his heart. But Alex, despite his gentleness, had breached that heart, leaving him completely unmoored.

Now when Alí encountered him and Étienne, as he often did in the semifinals and finals of tournaments, there was a heartbreaking coolness that he sensed but doubted any but the most sensitive of fans would've noticed. Otherwise, everything proceeded as before: handshake, pat on the back, "Good match."

Oh, for the days when the politesse of post-match rituals would be stretched enough for Alex to hold him, cupping his head. Alí would inhale Alex's sweet-sweaty musk and muscular heat then in a hug that lingered just long enough for him to feel a ripple of pleasure that crested to a wave in his groin.

He loved Alex and missed him not in the way you miss a friend on a business trip but in the way a deprived addict misses heroin. Maybe that was why his erotic dreams of him were more frequent and more violent. He saw Alex smiling, holding him as Étienne carved the number one between his naked shoulder blades with a knife.

"Shh, angel, you know it's necessary," Alex whispered. "It's something we've all been through."

After, he would nestle between the pair and feel Alex caress his shoulder as he said to Étienne, "This could be our child."

"What? This dark, scrawny, unworthy thing?"

Worse were the dreams in which Étienne would barge into his hotel room.

"What do you want?" Alí would ask defiantly.

"I think you know," Étienne would say, grabbing him and holding him tight. "I want to fuck you till you're dead."

Then he'd strip, bind, and whip him, morphing into his guardian before returning to the Étienne he knew, one who was capable of saying the filthiest, most disdainful things to him, but always with a smile and the most elegant French accent.

Alí would wake from these dreams drenched in sweat, shrieking but also with an erection or sometimes covered in his own come. How sick was that? How disgusting was he? No wonder Alex rejected him.

But why had Daniel rejected Dylan? Dylan was as close to pure goodness as Alí had encountered in this world. Salt of the earth, "sui generous," as Alí liked to tease, playing on the Latin. All it took was for him to mention casually how his mother had grown up in Iraq idolizing Dylan's grandmother Debo, how Debo had given voice to an oppressed, frightened young girl, and within days, Alí's mother had a complete set of Debo's recordings, digitally remastered with a companion book. A small gesture perhaps, but a grand one to Alí.

"My pleasure," Dylan had texted. "Glad Grandma still has her fans."

Now here was Debo's grandson, holding out a lifeline to the Iskandar family once more. Alí watched Dylan as he tried not to doze in the chair near his bed, fetching him ice water and tissues, helping him to the bathroom. Daniel was an idiot to cast aside great love, especially when it was in such short supply in the world.

The more inured Alí became in the No. 1 ranking, the more hatred he encountered, on the court and off. In his native country, whose government let it be known that it would welcome his presence in an exhibition match and reward him with a choice house in Baghdad and, it was implied, an introduction to the daughters of the city's finest families, there were those, including some of Iraq's religious leaders, who intimated there would be consequences the moment he set foot in the nation he had abandoned. Imagine, Alí thought, if they knew he was gay.

Iraq's and America's ambivalence to their native and adopted son did not seem to faze Alí's father.

"You have been graced by God with every imaginable gift: beauty, intelligence, talent, fame, wealth, a caring family, fine friends, and a loving heart. In the words of Jesus, 'to him to whom much has been given, much will be required.' This from our Lord himself, who, though God, suffered death on a cross."

Let's leave aside the odd construction "to him to whom" and the notion that God would sacrifice his own son, which was not exactly confidence-inspiring. How much was much? Something? Everything? Did celebrity require the sacrifice of his very self, or was there a statute of limitations on gratitude?

As it was, he never refused an autograph, a charity, or an interview request. He smiled and waved at the fans, no matter how fickle they were, and after he won, indulged the crowd's calls for him to sing and dance. Perhaps Patrick, Private Michael's buddy, had been right all those years ago in Baghdad: He really was nothing more than a little trained monkey.

All right then, he would play his utmost, smile and sing and dance, no matter how spent he was, because this is who he was, this was what he did, this was all he had to give.

Which brought him to that night before a bullfight crowd in the not always aptly named City of Brotherly Love, where he played a seesaw match with Ryan Kovacs, who, despite an Achilles temperament, had emerged as a fan darling in contrast to Alí.

"At least he's a real American," one fan shouted about Ryan, a blond, blue-eyed, corn-fed beauty from the Midwest.

About the only people in the arena who were rooting for Alí were two movie actresses, who often turned up at his matches and had driven in from New York City for this one.

"I just love to watch him hug other players at the net and change his shirt," he heard one say to the other. "You can see every rib. I wonder what diet he's on."

"Who cares?" the other replied. "I'd just like to tie him up naked and lick every one of them."

It was, Alí concluded, going to be a long match, made longer by the fact that though he had unwittingly embarrassed Ryan 6-0 in the first set and was up by 3 in the second, Ryan, who had a big serve and enormous, unharnessed talent, battled back. Now the crowd was in it, rooting for the underdog.

Once that had been Alí. Once he had been the fresh face, the darling, the pet. Now when he looked across the net, it was like looking into a mirror of the past. Alex told him it would happen someday. How right he was and how ironic and how he longed to tell him how ironically right he had been. Only Alex wasn't there. Not anymore.

At that point in the match, Alí thought, why not chuck it all? It's just an exhibition, his top ranking was secure and there was a new season to prepare for. Just then a young man stepped out onto the court.

"May I have your autograph?" he asked.

"You may after," Alí said, smiling but apprehensive. "Right now, though, we're playing to raise money for UNICEF."

"I even have a pen," he said, as if not hearing. And with that he produced a knife, with which he tried to slash Alí's face. But Alí deflected the stroke with his left arm and wrestled the young man to the ground, holding him there.

As angry as he was, he couldn't help but feel compassion for the young man, who was laughing, his blue eyes blank. He was so lost, and the choice he'd just made was about to plunge him into a Kafkaesque hell.

"It's all right," Alí said to him softly. "Be at peace and free yourself."

"Easy with him," he told the security guards who came onto the court. "He's not well."

But they paid him no heed and roughly hauled him off while solicitous tournament officials, the chair umpire, and even Ryan, who looked like he was about to have a nervous breakdown, swirled around him. It was then that Alí felt a warm, stinging stickiness on his left arm.

"We understand that you'll want to retire from the match," a tournament official said as the others nodded.

"The hell I will," Alí said.

If Alexander the Great could wage a battle and walk among his men with a punctured lung, he thought, I can do this. He motioned for a towel from a trembling ball boy, and smiling to reassure him, ripped it in two and wrapped it around his arm.

"Let's play," he said to Ryan.

Alí rebounded but still lost the second set tiebreaker. At 3-all in the third, Ryan sent a blistering serve slicing through the air that Alí had no business returning. But he did for a crosscourt winner.

That was the turning point. Alí went on to win the point, the game, the set, and the match. At the net, Ryan sobbed on his shoulder. Alí couldn't tell who Ryan felt sorrier for, Alí or himself.

"It's all right, Ryan," Alí said. "You played a great match, and we're both still standing."

Alí turned to acknowledge the crowd that five minutes before was all but calling for the blood that was seeping through the towel. Now the fans were on their feet for him.

He smiled then, waving with his bloody left arm, and walked off to the post-match press conference, in which he refused to blame his attacker, calling him "a lost soul," and then insisted on a shower. The water burned his gash, but he managed to towel off and dress.

The last thing he remembered was sitting in front of his locker. He must've passed out then, for the next thing he recalled was the emergency room, lights, voices, excitement, then another room, and Kahrin arriving and weeping and leaving and returning. Then the police with their questions, and then the doctors with different questions. And then dreams. And Dylan.

. . . .

WHEN ALÍ WOKE TO MOVE HIS BANDAGED ARM AND SAW DYLAN, he felt as if he had been saved.

There was a knock on the door.

"Hello, I'm Dr.—"

"Harrington?" Alí asked, incredulous.

"Well, I guess my reputation precedes me."

"No, it's just that you look exactly like my lawyer."

Dr. Harrington laughed: "It really is a small world. He and I were one and a half minutes apart. But we're very different. I became a healer, while he works for some big multinational law firm in Washington. I guess that makes him the evil twin."

Alí and Dylan looked at each other and giggled, somewhat nervously.

"How is he, doc?" Dylan asked.

"Oh, he's really a lot nicer than he pretends to be. But don't tell him I said so. We get along great."

"No, not your brother," Dylan said. "I mean, how is Alí?"

Alí smiled, looking from Dylan to the doctor expectantly.

"Oh, his arm is going to be fine," Dr. Harrington said, which relieved Alí until he realized it was not an answer to the question Dylan asked.

"Are you two married?" Dr. Harrington asked.

Whereupon Dylan blushed and Alí began to stammer.

"No? Oh, I'm sorry. It's just that you two. Well, never mind."

Dr. Harrington—Matthew was his first name—looked at Dylan: "Would you mind stepping outside for a bit? I want to check his dressing."

"Oh, no, of course not," Dylan said, trying not to show he felt put out, Alí thought. "I'll grab some coffee. Can I bring you something?"

"A Snickers bar, please," Alí said, as excited as a child.

"Snickers it is."

Alí turned his attention to Dr. Harrington.

"Need a sugar fix."

"Tired, are you?"

"A little. Guess that's to be expected."

"Mmm," Dr. Harrington said as he examined his arm. He patted the other.

"I'd like to do another blood test. Your white count is elevated, and I just want to make sure we haven't missed an infection."

"OK," Alí said, trying not to panic. "If not that, what then?"

"Well, let's do the test first."

"Come, doctor," Alí said. "You don't strike me as the type who'd miss an infection. You're just looking to confirm your suspicions. What do you think it is?"

Dr. Harrington looked him in the eye.

"Leukemia."

Alí was sure Dr. Harrington said something after that. Indeed, he could see his lips moving. Yet he heard nothing except the sound of the word "cancer" reverberating to a heartbeat that was like a pounding surf in his head. He fought for control as he began to weep.

"I'm sorry," Alí said, looking frantically for the small box of hospital-issue paper tissues that never seemed to be there when you needed it.

"No, no. You're entitled. Indeed, you're taking the possibility better than most, but then, I've always thought you had a lot of guts. You can tell from the way you play. Let's you and me hold off on the tears, though, shall we? We don't know for certain. And if it is leukemia, we'll deal with it."

"Can I come in?" Dylan said at the door.

"Sure," Alí said, drying his eyes and blowing his nose quickly.

"Everything all right?" Dylan asked, his antenna up.

"Fine, fine," Alí said. "The doctor was just saying that I might have a touch of anemia. So they're going to do another blood test just to be certain."

"Well, that's good. Might as well check everything under the hood while you're in for the oil change, right?"

"Right," Dr. Harrington said with a chuckle. "All right, I'll leave you guys to your sugar fix. We'll talk more about when you'll be released, physical therapy, etc."

"Oh, doctor," Alí said, sitting up as he started to leave. "Might I do that therapy in New York? I've been thinking of moving there, and I'd like to find an apartment, and, you know, set up everything I'll need to do there."

"I'm sure we can work something out."

"What are your plans?" Alí asked Dylan.

"My plan is to spend time with you."

"Then are you up for New York?"

Dylan grinned: "Why not?"

Later, when Alí looked back on his time with Dylan in New York, he did so with a mixture of gratitude and sadness. For there love had dwelled amid thoughts of death, which clung to his mind like the autumn leaves that hugged the sidewalks—wet and fetid, curled and withered.

Mornings, Dylan took the subway from their Upper East Side hotel—he wanted no reminders of the Elixir and Daniel—to the Olympic-size pool at Chelsea Piers for his workout. That gave Alí, who hadn't yet been cleared to resume practicing, time for the team of physical therapists, psychotherapists, and "anemia" specialists that Dr. Harrington and the hospital social worker had put in place. Or so he told Dylan. Alí rationalized that there was no point in telling him about his treks to Memorial Sloan-Kettering and thus worrying him, or anyone else, since he knew Dylan would text Alex, who would text Daniel. But truth was, he couldn't bear to share the news. His guardian had made him self-protective, and any attack automatically made him shut down the vulnerable part of himself.

"I am so very sorry," Dr. Malcolm Avery had said. Avery, the oncologist, had been a classmate of Dr. Harrington's at Johns Hopkins. Far from being the stereotypically cold or merely objective clinician, he seemed to be on the verge of tears when he confirmed the diagnosis, and Alí found himself in the unusual position of having to console the consoler.

"The good news," Dr. Avery said, recovering, "is that with chronic leukemia, you may go for years without having to have any elaborate treatment."

"Is that what you recommend, wait and see?" Alí asked.

"I do. You're young and otherwise healthy. Your white count has stabilized. I say we monitor it and see how it plays out."

"Then let's do that," Alí said. "I have no desire to let my opponents, or for that matter, the world, know about this. If I were taking medication, I'd surely have to inform the officials. It's better this way."

"It will mean checking in here with me regularly."

"Absolutely."

"The very first sign that things are headed south, we become proactive."

"Certainly."

"And I want you to make some lifestyle changes: more rest, better nutrition, less stress."

Alí laughed.

"Easier said than done, huh? Most of all, I want you to believe you will conquer this opponent."

Here Alí fought for control. He'd be damned if he'd pity himself.

"I will," he said, smiling, barely able to get the words out. "I will."

When he got back to the hotel suite, he hurled himself into Dylan's arms.

"Wow, that must've been some B-12 injection the doc gave you."

Alí laughed.

"Come on," he said, "let's go shopping and explore the city."

"Shall we be tourists then, and shall I be your new love?"

Alí grinned at him. "Why not?"

They wandered through the Greco-Roman wing of the Metropolitan Museum of Art, strolled through Central Park, and had pumpkin ravioli at a little trattoria they discovered on a side street near the hotel, arguing and laughing over latte as Andrea Bocelli's recording of "Cantico" played in the background. Alí thought it a fitting soundtrack for love amid the embers of a dying season.

They bought matching crosses at the religious articles shop across from St. Patrick's Cathedral. In the cathedral itself, they lit candles before a beautiful mosaic of Veronica's veil with its exquisite image of Jesus's face, and prayed their silent, separate prayers.

At Rockefeller Center, they watched the skaters eager to test the rink, just opened for another season. It was all Alí could do to keep from reaching out for Dylan's hand. But they were already attracting enough attention. Everywhere they went, people wanted to know how the "wing" was, when Alí would return to the court, what events Dylan would be swimming in the upcoming short-course championships, what they were doing together in New York.

They were mostly well-wishers now, the incident in Philadelphia and Alí's brave, compassionate handling of it having turned the tide of public opinion, although there were still some naysayers who thought he had staged it. Dylan, wary of Alí's fans and sensing how tired he was, would smile at the questioners and after a while say, "You know what? He's still recovering. Let's give him some space."

Back at their suite, they tumbled into each other's arms, tugging off clothes and luxuriating in a warm shower. Afterward, they faced each other in bed, naked, the covers drawn back as they moistened their fingers with their saliva and traced each other's nipples, plumb lines, and members. Alí focused on the watery nature of their dance – the damp tendrils that shadowed their armpits and tented their manhood, the juiciness of their well-shaped mouths, the come-slick bellies. In a way, it was all so easy and light. No fuss, no competition.

And yet for all that, they strained for a raw release that Alí could barely stand but was reluctant to relinquish, their well-muscled legs entwined, their powerful buttocks quivering. It was as if they were two negative charges grasping for a positive one. There was something missing, and they both knew what it was.

"Why did he leave you?" Alí asked.

Dylan shrugged.

"He wanted something else, someone else. It's OK."

Alí shook his head.

"No, it's not."

"And you?"

Alí hesitated.

"It was my fault. I'm afraid I wasn't as honest with him as I could've been, as innocent as he thought I was."

"So you had a boyfriend before. So what."

"Did you, before Daniel?"

"No, we were each other's first, and I thought maybe one day, each other's last. I thought we'd marry. How crazy was that?"

"I don't think it was crazy at all. I think it's beautiful to love someone so much that you share everything, your lives, your very souls. It's what I hoped for me and Alex, only I betrayed him."

Here Dylan raised himself on one elbow.

"How, how could you have betrayed him, you who are sweetness and innocence themselves?'

Alí started to weep.

Dylan took his face in his hands.

"Alí, look at me. Look at me. You can trust me."

"My guardian, the man who brought me to America, raped me repeatedly."

And with that came a release of sobbing and emotion and pain and relief.

Dylan held him tightly, though careful of his left arm, and kissed him, then drew back, framing his face with his large, webbed hands.

"Alí listen to me. You did nothing wrong, do you hear me? Nothing wrong. You were a child, a child who was brutalized by a monster. You didn't deserve what happened to you any more than I deserved to be beaten by my father, but it happened. We each cope as best we can."

"I should've loved him more. Alex, I mean," Alí said. "I should've trusted him with the truth. I shouldn't have been so afraid."

"Alí, you did what you had to do to protect yourself. Doesn't mean you didn't love him."

"I did. I do. Oh God, I loved him. I love him still."

"As I love Daniel. We loved them, and we lost them. Live on in the memory of that love. Can you do that? Can you find the courage to try?"

He looked into Alí's eyes.

Alí nodded.

"I think," Alí said, regaining his composure, "it's time for me to grow up."

"And for me to go on, too," Dylan said, kissing him.

Dylan stayed another week, long enough for Alí to close on a loft with a panoramic view of lower Manhattan.

"I think," Dylan said, looking around, "you're going to be happy here, Alí. You're going to be all right."

Alí took in the comfortable expanse.

"Even though it's empty, it already feels like home."

They hugged at the door with a gesture of finality that neither would've admitted.

"We'll see each other soon," Alí said.

"Count on it."

But Alí was not about to let him go, not just yet.

"You know, you got me through one of the worst moments in my life. I'll always be grateful to you for that."

Dylan flushed, pleased.

"You'll be getting my bill."

Alí watched from the window as Dylan, shouldering his duffel, made his way to a taxi across the street. Before he got in, he looked up and waved.

It was the last time Alí saw him.

Daniel

IN HIS DREAMS, DANIEL SAW HIMSELF DROWNING. IT WAS NOT as he imagined the end would be. There was no gasping, no struggle for the air, only a gentle surrender beneath the relentless waves.

Still, it was drowning. It was death. Perhaps it was merely some subliminal, remedial fear of water. (He preferred to think of it as a healthy respect.)

So he didn't swim in the ocean. Big deal. Professional swimmers didn't any more than opera stars signed up for glee club. It was for amateurs. No, professional swimmers didn't need the sea. They preferred nature, water, to be tamed, as in a pool. Except for Dylan. California boy, he breathed water. He belonged to the wild.

How he missed Dylan. How he loved him. How he craved his return. But it was not to be, Daniel was sure of it. He had overplayed his hand, and it didn't take a card shark to know that those who do rarely win.

He had behaved scandalously, blaming Dylan consciously or unconsciously for everything: Chloë, his father's cancer, the fact that he was not quite as brilliantly natural a swimmer. And Dylan had borne it all with the grace with which he swam, until he could take it no longer—even saints had their limits—and had walked out of his life. Why was Daniel thunderstruck by that gesture? Dylan had always been the stronger of the two, the better man, Daniel knew that now. But how to tell him, how to win him back? He saw the pictures of Dylan and Caro in LA and him and Alí in New York.

They were mere blocks away. But apart from a feeble get-well card, Daniel couldn't bring himself even to text Alí, couldn't bear the possibility of no response. He saw the images of Dylan and Alí together. They seemed happy. He, however, felt like he had been stabbed in the gut.

Well, maybe they've found their soul mates. Good for them, he thought. Not.

"You should go to him," he texted Alex about Alí.

"Don't know if I have the strength to try" came the response.

Stasis: Dante had been wrong. The Ninth Circle of Hell wasn't ice per se. It was inertia, which could take many forms: ice, mud, even water. No wonder he was treading it, in danger of drowning.

At the office, Daniel was subsumed by digital paperwork; rules that were no less strictly enforced for being unwritten (black attire, in at 7:30 a.m., gone by 6 p.m.); and above all, plenty of passive aggression. Indeed, Daniel's experience at Ari Kahn, LLP was like that of a gifted middle-school student who finds himself nonetheless adrift when he arrives at high school. There were two kinds of people at Ari Kahn LLP: those who were awed by Daniel Reiner-Kahn, one of the world's two greatest swimmers and scion of the company's owner, and those who resented him. The former were constantly sucking up as a way to use him. The latter were always looking for their cobra-like moments to strike.

Among the latter was the second-in-command, Jim Lipnicki, who thought his position threatened by Daniel's mere presence. Jim was the kind of average, mediocre white guy—light gray hair, doughy features, belly spilling over his belt—who might've been an accountant, banker, or athletic coach. He was everyone's friend, on the surface at least. Beneath the bonhomie lurked a killer instinct.

"Dan is a smart guy, and I'm sure if the city is ever submerged again in a superstorm, he'll come in handy," he wrote in an email to Ari. "He can always swim us out of the crisis. But I doubt he'll prove to have the skill set necessary for Ari Kahn, LLP day-to-day."

Of course, the email hadn't been intended for Daniel. But emails had a way of ending up in the wrong inboxes.

"Jealousy, pure, evil jealousy," his mother spat when he showed it to her over dinner. "Don't worry, sweetie. I'll take it up with your father."

"You'll do nothing of the kind, thank you very much," Daniel said. "Don't you see? He doesn't know that I have this, that I know what he's up to. That gives me real power over him."

"So how do you intend to use that power?"

"I intend to use it by doing absolutely nothing."

"Well, for now anyway, Mother," Chloë chimed in, squeezing Daniel's arm.

She had taken to calling Daniella "Mother" about the same time she started thinking about wedding dresses. I suppose it's inevitable, Daniel sighed. And she did have her uses. Her passive aggression blocked Jim's effectively.

Chloë had given a party for Ari Kahn, LLP bigwigs at her parents' Sutton Place penthouse, issuing an invite that contained the vaguely confounding "black tie optional." Of course, to Chloë "black tie optional" meant "optional only for clods." When Jim and his wife, Marge, arrived—he in his best blue suit, she in a too-tight black dress that exposed exceedingly fleshy upper arms—Chloë greeted them triumphantly, looking them up and down, then proceeded to ignore them for the rest of the night. Daniel felt sorry for them. Well, almost. One too many "Oh, didn't you get the memo I sent?" grins from Jim had robbed Daniel of the last drop of sympathy he might've otherwise had for him.

Dylan would've complimented the wife, chatting her up, even though she was the dowdiest woman in the room. Dylan would've made small talk with Jim, regardless of how many backstabbing emails he had sent his father. Dylan would've been attentive to everyone, not just his crowd.

Dylan, Dylan, Dylan: I love you. I need you. Flood my memories. Drown me in your lust.

"I see he's in New York with your friend Alí. Shall we have them for dinner?" Chloë wondered.

"I think we should have steak instead," Daniel teased.

"I'll text Alí our thoughts and prayers and invite them anyway," she said, phone at the ready.

"Why not let me handle it?" Daniel said. "Alí's had quite a shock. He may not be ready for more than our good wishes."

"Still, a tasteful fruit basket is in order," she said.

As it was, Alí sent her a thank-you note and a gift, a black scarf with a gold Sumerian design from the Metropolitan Museum of Art. They were both so lovely that Chloë didn't realize that he had declined her dinner invitation.

"What a sweet guy," Chloë said, marveling at the scarf's pattern. "How brave he is, and what a jewel Dylan is to care for him. You're certainly lucky in your friends. I'm counting on them and Alex to be groomsmen at the wedding, with Dylan, of course, as best man."

"Hey, don't I get a say in any of this?" Daniel asked, trying to mask his pique with humor.

Apparently not. He saw his future laid out before him like the lane markers in the pool: as husband to Chloë, father to their children, and custodian of his father's health and legacy. And he wanted to swim away from it as fast and as far as his muscular limbs could carry him. Yet he felt powerless to do so. Perhaps this was the price he had to pay for his treatment of Dylan.

The next few months drifted by, and Daniel found himself increasingly drawn to Central Synagogue on Lexington Avenue, no doubt in part because Chloë already had her heart set on a wedding at Temple Emanu-El on Fifth. But also because from the time he was a child, he saw Central Synagogue's cerulean onion domes as a kind of beacon for all things familiar, comforting, and beautiful. That they served as signposts to neighboring Shun Lee—his favorite Chinese restaurant and a promised childhood treat for him and his sister, Ani—may have helped. Now, his heart heavy, he bypassed the restaurant and instead climbed the synagogue's stone steps slowly, wearily, in search of, he guessed, the God he still confidently dismissed.

He sat down and found himself overcome by a pressure, an emotion, welling up within and bearing down upon him. He remembered the only other time he had felt like that. His mother had taken him and Ani to the American Museum of Natural History. Tired, hungry, and annoyed at the attack of wildebeests that was the horde of visiting schoolchildren in the fourth-floor dinosaur hall, he had balked at his mother's suggestion that he amuse himself by walking over the Lucite bridge that contained a bit of barosaurus bone while she and Ani found a ladies' room.

"All right, I'll do it, but there better be lunch in the cafeteria under the blue whale afterward," he said, pouting.

Something made him look down at the blanched bone halfway across. Suddenly, he was filled with empathy for this dead animal that had lived millions of years before. He realized that he, the dinosaur, and everything that had come before, since, and after was connected by the life force, and that life force was what he understood to be God. He felt then as if a strong hand were pushing down on his head while another pressed up inside him. And he knew that he would never be alone.

When he stepped off that bridge, it was as if he stepped into another world.

"Boy, what happened to you?" his mother said, staring at him with Ani in wonder.

"I honestly don't know," he said.

What had happened to him in the succeeding years? Why hadn't he remembered that moment and lived his life accordingly? Recalling it now, he began to sob—great, gasping, out-of-the-body, who-can-this-be? sobs.

"Forgive me, forgive me, forgive me," he cried over and over.

"Who is it you seek forgiveness from, my son?"

Daniel looked up to see a man he assumed was the rabbi standing in the pew, concerned.

"Oh, I'm sorry, rabbi. No, I have to go. I'm late for an appointment."

"If you'd like to talk some other time."

"No, yes, no. I have to go."

He was late for one of Jim's many interminable meetings. He shouldn't have left the office even for this brief respite. No one ever left Ari Kahn, LLP unless he was in a box, Daniel imagined bitterly. The discipline of swimming—all those hours in the pool, beginning at 5 a.m.—not even that had prepared him for the stultifying, deadening straitjacket that was the corporate world.

He checked his messages and saw several that caused him to stagger in the street.

"Hey, man, you all right?" two young passersby asked.

Just then, his phone rang.

"Dani? Alex. Don't do anything. I'm on my way to New York."

Alex

THE MOMENT ALEX HEARD ABOUT DYLAN'S "DISAPPEARANCE," he knew two things: Dylan hadn't actually disappeared and he was already dead.

People did not just disappear. Oh yes, perhaps some scoundrels who murdered their spouses or absconded with bank funds or government secrets did. But that wasn't Dylan. Nor did it seem likely that he had been kidnapped. People who "disappeared" were either murdered or committed suicide, and given what had transpired between Daniel and Dylan, Alex just knew it was the latter.

It hit him in waves, that he would never see his friend again, not in this world at least. At times, that thought was like so much wallpaper or background music, part of the environments through which he moved—until the moments when it was thrown into sharp relief. Alex would start to text Dylan, or catch his image on a TV screen in Madrid, where Alex was playing Étienne in the finals of that city's Open, and then the irrevocability of what he knew had happened would wash over him, threatening to unmoor him.

The plane ride to New York after he beat Étienne in that final was as interminable as the match itself, with plenty of time to think about Étienne, Dylan, Daniel, and, above all, Alí.

He had missed the Australian Open in January and the beginning of the clay court season in Europe in the spring, which positioned Alex to regain the No. 1-ranking. Ordinarily, Alex would've been ecstatic. Now with Alí absent from the tour and Dylan surely gone, it was a Pyrrhic victory.

He missed Alí, missed being with him certainly, but also missed playing him, missed the way he pushed him to be larger than himself. Without Alí, Alex was left more often than not to face Étienne across a net that seemed an impenetrable border and contemplate the train wreck that was their relationship.

For comfort, he amused himself at dinner with the parade of attractive, young female companions that Eleni often lined up—"the bridesmaids," he called them—and one guest in particular, Dr. Miriam Iskandar, who texted him during a stopover in Athens on her way to Paris from Mozambique, where she worked at a clinic sponsored by the Women's Health Project.

If Alex were going to get seriously involved with a woman, he thought, it would be with one of purpose like Miriam, not one of the bridesmaids, who gave the illusion of substance—swanning through the board meetings of their daddies' companies—but who were really biding their time until an Alex Vyranos came along.

Miriam wasn't waiting for him, which is part of what made her so intriguing. She was so like her brother, perhaps not as much a beauty but handsome nonetheless with the same large, dark eyes and loving heart.

"We've all been so worried about him, but you know Alí," she said. "He wouldn't hear of us coming to New York to take care of him or coming to Paris for a rest. He is so independent, so afraid of being a burden, always the big little brother."

She smiled at that.

"How fortunate he is to have Dylan and you and Dani," she said, covering Alex's hand with her own.

He returned her smile, listening to her words but hearing only how much he had lost.

Despite his persistent fear of flying, which he realized was odd, given the amount of time he spent in the air, Alex dreaded the moment the plane touched down at Kennedy Airport, bringing him closer to a reunion with Daniel and Alí.

Though immaculately groomed as ever, Daniel was barely holding it together at his father's office. His face was ashen; his eyes, puffy and red-rimmed as if he'd been weeping and had barely slept. It was clear to Alex from the minute they exchanged a manly hug in Ari's presence that Daniel thought Dylan had taken his own life and that he himself was to blame.

Ari, too, looked much altered, his trademark vigor and magnetism subdued.

"You guys take one of the gulf jets, of course," Ari said, "and all the time you need, Daniel. Jeez, Tony Roqué's boy. How he must feel. Please give him my best. Tell him if there's anything he needs, anything, I'm here for him."

Alex saw Daniel flinch then as if he had been slapped across the face. Ari had a way of giving with one hand and taking with the other, Alex thought. Of all the people to be worried about, Dylan's abusive father was hardly at the head of the list. Alex was glad his own father had simply said, "Anything you need, you know you have only to ask. One of our boats will meet you in Los Angeles, along with Quentin."

Alex had already heard from lawyer Quentin Harrington. He seemed at once shocked and yet unsurprised by Dylan's disappearance.

"All I can tell you is that he contacted me several weeks ago, at Alí's recommendation, about having a will drawn up. So I passed him along to the firm's Estates and Wills division."

Alex sensed Quentin knew just what he was thinking but only said, "Look, whatever's happened, we'll sort it out together."

Certainly, that was the way Alí approached it.

"Whatever our differences in the past," he said to Alex and Daniel on the plane, "we need to pull together now to rescue Dylan."

Of all the players in this drama, Alex thought, Alí was the most changed. He was sleeker, the muscles more taut, the hair shorter and spikier, with flecks of premature gray, the planes of his face more sculpted. But the physical transformation was nothing compared to his attitude, which was sober, mature, commanding even.

"What may I offer you from the galley?" the flight attendant asked. "Some wine to start?"

"How about some of your terrific omelets?" Daniel offered.

"That sounds great," Alex said.

"Nothing for me now, thanks," Alí said.

"You have to eat," Alex said.

"Yes, I insist," Daniel said.

Alí smiled at the flight attendant. "If it's all the same to you, I prefer to wait."

"Very good, sir," she said.

Perhaps it was all that he had accomplished. More likely it was everything he had endured, but Alí was all grown up, Alex thought. In some ways, though, he remained the naïve, optimistic man-child Alex had fallen in love with. He alone held out hope that Dylan was still alive. He took comfort and courage from the texts he got from photographer Elliott Gardener; Kathy Smeaton, who offered to handle any press; and her daughter, Michaela. He was also buoyed that Quentin would be there.

"If anyone can figure out this mess, he can," Alí said. "Dylan's probably just taken a few days to think. He seemed distracted of late. So many career decisions. I think he was just exhausted. He'll probably be waiting for us when we get there."

"Christ, Alí," Daniel said, getting up to stretch. "They found his clothes neatly folded on the beach below his father's home in Malibu. His stepmother told the police she had encountered him there scattering his mother's ashes on the sea, his mother's ashes, which he kept in that mermaid cookie jar and wouldn't have parted with for anything. Does that sound like someone who was distracted or going off for a holiday? Or does it sound like someone bound and determined to end his own life? I know that's what he did, and I know why."

"Don't," Alí whispered. "Please, don't, Dani. He loved us. He loved you most of all. He would never leave us."

"He never will," Alex said.

They fell into a silence then that underscored the claustrophobia of air travel for Alex. It felt good to get off the plane, even if it meant making their way past the hyenas with their cameras and notebooks who were outside the gate of Tony Roqué's estate.

Waiting at the door was a young woman who looked remarkably like Dylan—or rather, a younger version of Dylan's mother. His stepmother Lauren was a stunning blonde with flowing hair. Her long Pucci top and white slacks did nothing to conceal her advanced pregnancy. She had been crying.

"Please," she said. "Welcome. Come in."

Alí greeted her first, embracing her.

"It's all right," he said. "We're here, and we'll take care of everything."

Yes, all grown up, Alex thought.

But he mourned for the child.

Dylan

NO ONE EVER KNOWS ANYONE, DYLAN THINKS, NOT REALLY, not truly.

As he makes his way to Chelsea Piers for his daily swim practice, his gut tells him that Alí is not being completely honest with him about his visits to his anemia doctor. He thinks Alí is far sicker than he's letting on. But he doesn't want to call him on it, doesn't want to pry or embarrass him, because people are entitled to their privacy, you know?

There's a fine line between being helpful and being nosy, and he's never been one to cross it. Of course, there are those who would use that as an excuse not to intervene at all. But surely, that's not him. Besides, he's harboring a secret of his own. While Alí was asleep at Memorial Hospital in Philadelphia one afternoon, he caught Dr. Harrington alone in the hallway.

"You know I can't discuss your friend's case," he said sympathetically but firmly.

"Ah, yes, I know," Dylan said, trying not to sound hurt. Why was he hurt? He ran his fingers through his short, coarse hair.

"I know in my heart you're a good doctor. I know I can trust you. So I need you to recommend the best neurologist you can."

"OK," Dr. Harrington said, drawing out the *K* slowly, his medical curiosity piqued. "Why don't you call my office and make an appointment, and we'll take it from there."

So while Alí is at his appointments, Dylan cuts short his practice and goes to see Dr. Isaiah Mercado, not far from the boutique hotel in Manhattan where he and Alí are staying.

Dr. Mercado is portly, white-haired, old school, brilliant. Dylan lays out his fears.

"People forget things all the time," Dr. Mercado says. "From what you've been describing, you've been under tremendous pressure, and you've endured a painful breakup. Frankly, it sounds like you need a psychiatrist more than a neurologist. But I understand your concerns about your grandmother and mother, a similar pattern, although it seems that drugs and alcohol played a huge part there. Still, these can mask other issues. I'd like to run some tests, and I'm wondering if you would have access to any of their DNA, a hairbrush, for instance. I know that's unlikely."

But it isn't. When his mother died, Dylan impulsively packed the mother of pearl hairbrush, mirror, and comb set she kept on her vanity. How many times had he watched her brush her hair or later, brushed it for her?

When he arrives back in LA, he sends strands from the brush to a lab as instructed by Dr. Mercado, along with a swab from his cheek. It confirms his worst fears.

"Your mother passed along to you a rare gene for a form of early-onset dementia," Dr. Michael Slohin, Dr. Mercado's West Coast counterpart, says softly. "And judging from what you've told me, it was probably passed down to her from her mother and her mother's father. I'm so very sorry. But I want you to know there are options. Forewarned is forearmed. You can get your affairs in order and make plans for long-term care. With drugs like Aricept, we can retard the progress of the disease. With any luck, you may have twenty, even thirty good years left. And who knows? By then, we may have finally grappled this monster to the ground. You'll probably want to share this with your family. If you have siblings, they may want to be tested."

Options, care, grappling: Dylan hears these words as if he's underwater. He moves as if in a dream to the medical building's parking structure. When he gets in his car, he turns the radio on loud—it's Evanescence's "Going Under"—and he starts sobbing, screaming, and banging on the wheel. He doesn't recognize himself, which is fitting, because one day soon he won't know himself at all.

"Forewarned is forearmed." He won't be aware enough to be fore-warned later on. That's the hell of it.

Well, he can't be unhappy over what he won't be conscious of. Igno-rance is indeed bliss, right? Except he's aware now, isn't he? He remem-bers playing Caligula in a college production of Albert Camus' play. Even the acerbic local theater critic said he was good. As Caligula is being stabbed to death by the Praetorian Guard at the end, he shouts exultantly, "I'm still alive!"

Dylan is still alive, even if his mind is drowning.

He's always prided himself on being protective, in command. He'll be damned if he'll cede that. And anyway, to whom? To Aunt Dee Dee? Clearly, she didn't have the gene, and he wouldn't burden her with car-ing for him. She'd done enough. To Austin? He's just a kid. His life is just beginning. To his father or Jordan? Don't make him laugh.

Who then? Who would he entrust his death-in-life to? Caro, Alex, or Alí?

To Dani? Sometimes things happen, and you don't know why. It's only later that you know. Now he understands why he endured such a painful breakup. Had he and Dani still been lovers, it would've been hard if not impossible for him to do what he knows he must.

The only thing you can control about death is your attitude toward it. And Dylan's attitude is right out of the Romans and *Madama Butter-fly*: Death with honor, when you can no longer live with honor.

He's sad, of course. He doesn't want to leave. But he cannot remain, not this way. And now that he's set his course, he's surprisingly calm. What is the point, after all, of struggling on? He's already done every-thing he set out to do. So why face another race, another audition, another day that's like the previous day, only less so?

"Tomorrow, tomorrow, and tomorrow."

Tomorrow. Tomorrow, he texts Alí and ask him for the name of his lawyer, under the pretext that now that Grandma Debo's estate has been settled, he needs to draw up a will as one of her heirs.

Alí doesn't think twice about it and immediately puts him in con-tact with Quentin Harrington, who puts him in touch with Mark Errico of the firm's Estates and Wills division in the LA office. Dylan's all devil-may-care heir as he instructs Errico about his last wishes. He intends for this to be his greatest performance.

He cleans up his apartment, leaving a copy of the will in the top drawer of the dresser. It includes small bequests: his cross for Alí, his mother's mermaid pendant for Alex, and the mermaid cookie jar for Daniel.

It pains him to know the pain he'll be causing them and his family. All his life, he has taken care of others. Now he has to take care of himself.

Besides, it's his concern for them that has led him to this moment. Even if they're devastated now, far better that than bearing torturous witness to the slow death-in-life that is dementia. And isn't that a kind of self-sacrifice, a kind of nobility? Surely God can forgive that.

He's tired of thinking about it, of caring. There is fortunately only one task that remains. He takes the can of ashes from the mermaid cookie jar and drives to his parents' home—what was his parents' home—in Malibu. He parks at a distance from the property and sneaks onto it and down to the beach through a neighboring estate. Years before, he and his brothers had eluded their parents through this secret passage. Now he remembers the angry neighbor shouting at his wife, "It's those damn Roqué kids. If I catch them again, I'm going to take my shotgun to the lot of them."

"Oh, Aaron," the wife would say. "They're only children."

"I blame those crazy parents. No wonder they're hooligans."

"Hooligans? They're just high-spirited."

Hurtling down the stone steps, Dylan at last arrives at the appointed spot and surveys the ocean. A storm is coming later, and the wind and the waves are picking up.

"There were two sisters came walking by the stream, oh the wind and rain," he sings. "Older one pushed the young one in, cried oh the dreadful wind and rain."

How can you leave me, when I'm so beautiful? the world seems to say to him.

But I'm not leaving, he answers. I'm coming to join you, to return to you and her. I know she's out there, waiting for me, just as Thetis waited for her boy, Achilles.

"May I help you?"

He turns to see his mother, or rather, a younger version of her: white slacks, loose Pucci top that doesn't hide her pregnancy, flowing blond hair, movie-star face. He recognizes her as Lauren, his father's bride.

"Dylan? What a surprise."

Before he can speak, she's hugging him. He can feel her warmth and her stirring baby, his sibling. Lose one child, gain another, but then, everyone's sunrise is someone else's sunset.

It's been a long time since he's felt maternal warmth. This is what we all want, he thinks, to return to our mother's womb, the earth, to go home.

"What are you doing here?"

"I'm sorry. I should've called. I—"

He points to the can of ashes.

"It's time."

"I understand," she says solemnly. "No need to explain. I'll leave you to it then. But you're always welcome here. Come up to the house afterward."

He smiles then.

"That would be great, but I have an appointment, an audition. Rain check, say, Sunday at 3?"

"It's a date. I'm glad you came."

"I'm glad I met you."

When she leaves, he scatters the ashes, feels them mingle with the spray and sting his face, then undresses quickly down to his jammers, prepared for the swim of his life.

Still, it's hard to die.

Submit, Dylie. Yield and overcome. Surrender to the embrace of the sea.

Just then, he sees something, someone bobbing out on the water. He hears cries for help. Just my luck, he thinks. I can't even kill myself in peace.

Of course, he'll have to rescue whoever it is. Well, one day more or less won't matter in the scheme of eternity, one parting gift to the world.

He swims hard, fighting the implacable waves. "There were two sisters," he sings to himself, trying to center his mind.

He's tired, bone-tired. But he must help, he must reach him, her, whomever.

Only it's not a drowning man, just a piece of driftwood and now he's too far and too tired to make it back anyway. What would Alex say? Oh, yes, ironic, he thinks, as he slips beneath the waves.

Alí

IN THE LIVING ROOM OF DYLAN'S CHILDHOOD HOME, ALÍ THOUGHT the scene reminiscent of the moment in an Agatha Christie novel when Hercule Poirot gathers the suspects in a room to reveal the murderer. All the key players in Dylan's life were there: Aunt Dee Dee, her blond, curly-haired beauty marred by grief; a consoling Daniella and Caro, who sat on either side of her on a pale-blue sectional sofa, each holding a hand; the gorgeously sullen Jordan; and Austin, a blond Dylan, who stood talking quietly with his brother as they surveyed the room.

While Neva, the housekeeper, bustled about, offering food in a vain attempt to distract everyone, Lauren paced with a cell phone, her natural graciousness struggling with tension for control. Alí caught part of her hushed conversation on his way to a pretty celadon powder room with jeweled miniatures of the Taj Mahal and other Indian scenes.

"What do you mean, You're not coming home? Listen to me, Tony. This is your first-born son we're talking about. I don't care what went on before. Your children need you now. I need you. I have a house full of family and friends who are trying to cope with what happened. The least you can do is show up."

Presiding over the proceedings like a dowager Chinese empress was a tiny but formidable woman dressed entirely in black with a cinnamon-roll chignon of salt-and-pepper hair. Alí recognized Dylan's description of his grandmother, Adeline Roqué. She was attended by Fan, a pretty, petite young woman from Singapore, who spoke little English and was so deferential that she said, "Sorry, miss" every time she passed you.

"No, no, Fan," Alí said the second time. "No need to be sorry."

He soon realized, however, that this was her default expression and let her be.

Besides, everyone was in various states of sorry, Daniel in particular. Alí had never seen him like this, not even on the plane. He was usually so confident and commanding. Now in the house where Dylan grew up, where his memory only accentuated his absence, Daniel seemed utterly lost, staring out to sea.

"We should be out there," he said to Alex. "We should be out there, searching for him."

"We will, my friend," Alex said, putting a hand on his shoulder. "Our boat should dock any moment. In the meantime, let the police handle this."

The police had already been up to the house and were soon back at the door. Lieutenant Ed Fowler of the LAPD had the taut build of an athlete and the tired expression of a cop who had done this too often. But he wasn't about to let any world-weariness or his natural sympathy get in the way of his cop's instincts, which told him what Alí surmised: That those present had made an unspoken pact of resistance and obfuscation. It wasn't as if anyone was deliberately trying to be uncooperative. It was just that everyone wanted to put a noble spin on Dylan's evident death and wasn't going to allow any thought to the contrary.

"You were the last person to see your stepson, Mrs. Roqué. How did he seem to you?"

"Fine," Lauren said. "He was kind, friendly—lovely, just a lovely young man."

"Did you know him well?"

"Not really. In fact, it was the first time I had met him."

"Why was that?"

"He and his father had a falling out years ago, as you no doubt know. But I like to think that was all behind us."

"Oh?"

"Yes, I invited him to the house for dinner, and we had set a date."

"I see. Why was he here?"

"He had come to scatter his mother's ashes."

"So he arranged this with you in advance."

Lauren paused before answering. "Not exactly."

"So, what, he just showed up at the door with the urn?"

"No, I encountered him on the beach where I often walk in the afternoon."

"But the weather report called for heavy wind and rain. Didn't that strike you as odd? He picks a stormy day to scatter the ashes of a woman who died years ago?"

"All I know was he said it was time, and I left him in peace to do it."

"Uh-huh. Where was your husband?"

"Same place he is now: Bungalow J on the Paramount lot, which is the home of Tony Roqué Productions. I'm sure the guards can vouch for him."

"Detective, we all know where you're going with this line of questioning," Adeline interjected. "My son Antonio is many things—a terrible son, an abusive father, a miserable husband. No, Lauren, Jordan, save your sighs and protests. The family has had its heart ripped from it. It's time to place the cards face up on the table.

"As I said, my son is many things, but a murderer he is not. Nor do I think we need waste much time with the theory of suicide that has already formed in your mind. People who are about to commit suicide do not make luncheon dates with their stepmothers. Nor do they carefully remove and fold their clothes in the throes of their despair.

"Are you familiar with Occam's razor, detective?"

"The most straightforward hypothesis is probably the correct one?"

"Precisely. My grandson no doubt removed his outer clothes to scatter the ashes. As to what happened next, we can only hazard a guess. But I will venture that with all the recent accidents along the shoreline and storm warnings, someone was in trouble, he set out to help him, and was swept away.

"He simply has—had—too much courage and compassion to devastate his family by taking his own life.

"My grandson was a happy, well-adjusted, deeply spiritual young man of accomplishment, as are his brothers and friends you see here."

Alí thought that Daniel and Caro winced then, while Jordan's set mouth twitched in anger. But no one moved to contradict anything she said, and Alí saw what Lieutenant Fowler saw: a seamless wall of denial and opposition. He would get nothing else from this crowd.

Secure in her triumph, Adeline retreated to her frail-old-lady persona.

"Now if you don't mind, detective, Fan, I need my tea and my nap."

"Of course, Mother Roqué," Lauren said. "Your suite is all ready."

"Thank you, my dear, and if I were you, I would get some rest myself," she added, glancing at her belly. "This cannot be good for you and the baby, nor any of us."

Attended by Fan and Daniella, who offered to take her blood pressure, she moved deliberately toward the stairs. At the banister she motioned to Alí and asked him to contact Kathy, whose blog for war widows she read religiously as a Gold Star mother.

By the time Quentin arrived at the house, Kathy had already tweeted and e-blasted a portrait of Dylan as nothing short of an aquatic angel, who had helped a fellow swimmer in distress and probably paid with his own life. As the family's newly appointed lawyer, Quentin pledged to cooperate fully with the police, which Alí took as code for doing precisely what the family wanted.

Quentin stayed behind on the beach with the investigators as Alí, Daniel, Alex, Jordan, and Austin boarded the boat Alex's father had provided for them. Alí was glad to be out on the water, even though it was now dark, doing something, anything at last.

He envied the women, indeed, all women. They at least had their to-do lists, their projects, their sisterhood. Already, they had organized sleeping arrangements at the house and guesthouse, along with dinner and coffee, sandwiches, and cookies for the police. They handled calls from well-wishers and had the bouquets and Teddy bears accumulating at the gate collected and distributed to local hospitals.

The men, meanwhile, went down to the sea in a ship. But to what purpose? How could they hope to find Dylan in the vast, inky sea that melded with the night?

"Take this to him. He's always cold," Alí heard Alex say to Jordan.

And Jordan appeared with a hoodie, a reminder of Alí and Alex's first time together. Alex had drawn down the hood as if unveiling a bride, and their love affair had begun. Now, Alí reasoned, he was no longer loved but oddly, he was no longer cold either.

"How 'bout some coffee?" he said to Jordan. "I'll help you in the galley."

It felt good to contribute something, however small the gesture, he thought. Daniel in particular felt the uselessness of their predicament. At one point, he made to strip and jump in the water, he who never loved the sea.

"Don't," Alex said, grabbing his arm. "Don't let people see you like this."

"Where is he?" Daniel cried. "Where is he in this world?"

Nowhere, Alí thought as he gestured to the watery expanse.

And everywhere.

Daniel

THEY NEVER FOUND YOU, BUT THEN, I COULD'VE TOLD THEM that.

I could've told them that you made sure you had fled us, fled me, Daniel thought. Why else would you choose the vast ocean for your exit but to put the greatest distance—at least in this world—between us?

That distance was the bourn of our divide; the manner of your death, the depth of your hatred. And yet, I cannot raise my voice in protest, cannot bring myself to shed a tear—not even after you left me the mermaid cookie jar in your will—for that's how much I deserve your abandonment and your contempt.

At your memorial, they—the City Council members, folk legends, movie stars, and athletes who turned out—called you a hero. Your grandmother made sure of that. The priest, echoing her, spoke of your courage and compassion. I used to wonder where the courage was in killing yourself. Now that I'm older, I suppose it takes courage to die, no matter how you do it.

The most moving moment was not any talk of heroism, but Alí singing "My Immortal." The sobs resonated throughout the cathedral. I sat in the middle of the mourners, surrounded by your family and several generations of their friends. Despite their warm embrace, I never felt more alone. The church was a foreign country that offered no comfort. For what God, what loving father, would accept the sacrifice of his own beautiful son on a cross? And if God could do that to his own child, what hope was there for us orphans?

There is no hope, I thought as I sat there, buttressed by Alex to my right and a clinging Chloë to my left. My eyes bore into the back of

Caro's head, which inclined every once in a while as she whispered something to Dee Dee in the front pew.

I should've loved you, should've married you. Then that would've been me, chief among the mourners. Me in the first pew. Me listening to others saying how lucky we were to have had each other, if only for a short time. Me smiling bravely, putting others first. But when had I ever done that? And so I lost what I couldn't properly understand.

Still, I searched for you. I looked for you at the pools and the meets, in those you loved and my memories. I went to San Francisco to see Aunt Dee Dee and slept in the bed where we shared our lust if not our love. I wandered the city, like Hitchcock's Scottie, chasing obsessively after lost love or an idea of that love, an idea of myself, chasing after death.

"What's wrong, Ducky?" Aunt Dee Dee asked. She, too, had changed. Some of the old fire had gone out, though none of the insight.

"I know you miss him. We all do. But he wouldn't want you to mourn like this. He would want you to go on. I can tell you that all the clichés about time are true. In time, your grief will be tempered by the life you lead."

"But that's just it. I don't want my grief to be tempered. I want to feel this pain forever. I want him to haunt me, hound me. It's the only way I can be sure he'll never leave me. It's what I want, what I deserve."

"Why, my darling? Why do you want to punish yourself?"

"Because I killed him by not loving him as I should've, by not being kinder to him, by not being to him what he was to me."

"Oh, I'm sure you're exaggerating. All friends have their differences."

I fought for control then.

"Daniel, what is it? You can tell me. He wasn't just a friend. Oh, honey, did you think I was that naïve or that cruel? I'm so sorry for you. Sorry that you lost him and even sorrier you two thought you had to hide your love, especially from me. I would've understood. I understand now."

And with that, I broke down in her arms. After a while, she searched my face and smoothed my hair like a mother reassuring a child who's skinned his knee.

"Ducky, you won't find him here. You have to seek him where he was happiest, at home and in your heart.

"I know he loved you, and whatever you think you did or didn't do, he forgives."

"What about you, Aunt Dee Dee?"

"What do you mean?"

"Can you, too, forgive? My father's back in the hospital."

"I'm sorry. I didn't know."

"His prostate cancer is no longer responding to treatment. They want to try something else. I have no right to ask this, but I was wondering if you would find it in your heart to go and see him."

"Oh, Ducky, I don't know. After all these years? And he's so sick. How do you know he'd even want to see me?"

"Please. I can't bring Dylan back. But at least I can close the circle between his aunt and my father."

I left Aunt Dee Dee's house then and sought you where you lived and died, where you, too, came full circle.

On the beach, I stripped and waded into the water. I must do the thing I'm most afraid to do, I said. Be with me now, I prayed as you had prayed, as you had taught me to pray. Give me your love, your courage and your strength.

After my swim—my "baptism," as it were, into a new life—I went up to the house and saw your stepmother. Your brother, Julian, reminds me of you. Already, he's fat and sassy, and Lauren is pregnant with his sibling.

I wasn't there long when your father came in. I rose to leave, but Lauren said, "You'll do nothing of the kind.

"Tony, look who's here. You remember Daniel."

"Oh, yeah, how are you?"

"Fine, sir, thanks."

"In town long?"

"Not very. I've got some business for my dad's company and some swimming promos to film, and then I'll be heading east."

"How is your dad?"

"Not particularly well but hanging in."

"Well, there's a lot of that going around these days. Poor Ari. Great guy. Where're you staying?"

"The Beverly Hills."

"Oh, that's ridiculous. Stay here. I insist."

"Yes," Lauren said. "We'd love to have you."

Shall I tell you that he treated me like the son he never recognized in you, that people can be monstrous to their own and kind to others, that I felt compassion for the man who should've been my father-in-law but for my want of a spine and a heart?

But you know this, don't you, probably even instigated it, now that you're pure spirit.

I dream of you and you are as real as when you were alive. I see you and reach out to touch you, but you pass through my fingers like water, for you are water and earth and air.

Shall I tell you, too, that your death has freed me at last, giving me the backbone to question what I want, to take risks and choose what and whom I truly love? I have cut my moorings now, preferring to sail in open waters.

Are you surprised—pleased, vindicated even—to know I broke it off with Chloë? Probably not. You were always too nice for revenge. Or gloating, but I can tell you the rest—Alí, Alex, and my mother— were delighted to see her go. Something she said about you that made me see her for the first time.

"Poor Dylan," she said one day at lunch with my father. "But I'm so glad my friend Tina never got involved with him. Imagine if she had married him only to discover he had no guts."

"What?" I snapped.

"I only meant that suicide is the selfish coward's way out. At least, that's what I heard was the real cause of death."

"I can't," I said. "I can't do this anymore."

I got up to leave, but Chloë followed me.

"Daniel," she said, "don't do this to us, to your father, who's so sick."

"So because his life has been damaged, I should ruin mine? No, Chloë, I'm sorry. It's over."

"You say that now. But in a few days, you'll have a fresh perspective."

I stopped, turned, and looked her in the eye.

"No, Chloë, this is my fresh perspective, one that you won't be able to spin to your advantage. Besides, life's too short to spend it with a woman who takes so long to say a few simple declarative sentences. I just couldn't risk inflicting that on any kids."

That surely would've made you smile and this, too: I took Aunt Dee Dee to see my father at Sloan-Kettering. I watched from the door as she approached the bed and took his hand.

"Hello, Ari. It's been a long time."

"Oh, you," he said, and began to weep.

"Don't cry, Ari. It's taken me a long time to grow up. Maybe we both have. But it's all right. I'm here now."

As I closed the door, I felt your spirit soar, drawing mine up as well. And I understood at last what Aunt Dee Dee meant about time and forgiveness, for I felt a measure if not of happiness then at least of contentment, freedom, and peace.

Until the next time you and my grief wash over me.

Alex

AFTER THE MEMORIAL, ALEX SAW ALÍ AND DANIEL FROM TIME to time. But Dylan's death had not drawn them closer. Alex hadn't expected it to.

"Famously ironically detached people don't expect anything," he said to himself as he shaved one morning in his Tokyo hotel room. "That way they're never disappointed or hurt."

Of course, Alex saw Alí more often as he continued to meet him in the semifinals and finals of tournaments. It seemed to Alex that Alí was less the player he had been and more so. He often played badly. When he was on, however, he was untouchable.

In a way, the final of the US Open the year after Dylan died crystallized the state of his play and their relationship.

Alex got out to a quick two-set lead—the first of which ended in a bagel—and it looked as if the match would be over before it started. But Alí fought back as Alex had seen him do time and again against Étienne, Marius, Ryan, Evan, and even himself. It was excruciatingly exquisite to witness and even more so to take part in. Play seemed to slow to a crawl as Alí fought for every point and, it seemed, every breath, the fan support growing with every save.

If I let up on him, it will do me no good and only seem insulting, Alex thought. So he pushed back hard, though he longed to do nothing more than stop the match, take him in his arms, and whisper, "I loved you once. I love you still."

Even when Alí slipped at one point, Alex didn't move toward him, and Alí, at once embarrassed and relieved, rose quickly, smiled sheepishly, and motioned the ball boy away.

The final set, the final points, were as good as Alex had ever played, and he still lost. Alí watched Alex's last shot sail wide for a moment, as if willing time to stand still. But there was no dramatic dropping to the knees in jubilation, no hands to the head in disbelief, no smile even. Instead, with head down, he jogged to the net and embraced Alex for a long time, burying his face in his shoulder.

"I'll always be with you," he said at last, which filled Alex with a terrifying sadness.

He was still pondering what Alí meant during the trophy presentation. Glenna Day Costa asked Alí if he had a song he'd like to sing.

"Actually, I do," he said, then began:

Of all the money ere I had,
I spent it in good company,
And all the harm I've ever done,
Alas, it was to none but me,
And all I've done for want of wit,
To memory now I can't recall
So fill to me the parting glass,
Good night and joy be to you all.
Fill to me the parting glass
And drink a health what ere befall,
And gently rise and softly call,
'Good night and joy be to you all.'

Of all the comrades that ere I had,
They're sorry for my going away,
And all the sweethearts that ere I had,
They'd wish me one more day to say,
But since it fell into my lot
That I should rise and you should not.
I'll gently rise and softly call,
'Good night and joy be to you all.'
Fill to me the parting glass
And drink a health what ere befall,
And gently rise and softly call,
'Good night and joy be to you all.'

Afterward, he said, "There are just two thoughts, two emotions, I'm filled with tonight: love and gratitude. I love you all. And I thank you for sharing this journey with me."

He picked up his gear and the trophy and waved.

"Good night," he said, blowing a kiss. "And goodbye."

Then he walked into the interview room, announced he had cancer, and quit.

The front page of the *New York Times* the next day carried the news as if it were an obituary more than a sports or human interest story:

> Tariq Alí Iskandar, the only American tennis player ever to capture the Golden Slam, announced his retirement immediately after winning the US Open yesterday. Iskandar, who has been a polarizing figure in American sports since emigrating from Iraq during the war at the age of thirteen, electrified Alexandros Vyranos, the No. 1-ranked player in the world, and the crowd of 22,347 at Arthur Ashe Stadium, with his come-from-behind win, 0–6, 2–6, 7–6, 7–6, 7–5, in a match that took 5 hours and 43 minutes.
>
> He then shocked the sports world by announcing his retirement, effective immediately, citing chronic leukemia.
>
> In his post-match interview, Iskandar refused to blame the disease for his recent erratic play and declined to give specifics about his illness or its treatment.
>
> Instead, in remarks reminiscent of Lou Gehrig's farewell address, he was full of praise for his family, his American sponsors, teachers, friends, and especially, his chief rival, Vyranos.
>
> "His friendship has been the great joy of my life," he told reporters.
>
> He said he would grant no more interviews but vowed that this was not the last the world would hear from him.
>
> "I'll be back when I have something more to say," he said.

Five years later, he was. In his memoir, *Net Gains*, he detailed his tennis career and its lessons for youngsters. There was no mention of his guardian or his love affairs with Alex, Daniel, and Dylan, though the book was dedicated "To My Friend Dylan Roqué."

Biography, particularly autobiography, is the place of reinvention, Alex thought. Besides, they were none of them ever going to be the poster boys for revelations.

He decided to surprise Alí at his book signing, waiting on the line that snaked around Barnes & Noble's Fifth Avenue store. He spied Daniel a dozen people behind and motioned for him to come up.

"He's with me," Alex told the fans immediately behind him, who were less annoyed about someone cutting in front of them than they were intrigued by whether or not he and Daniel were who they appeared to be as they hugged.

By the time the pair approached the table, the murmurs and camera flashes had become their own sound and light show. But still Alí hadn't looked up, absorbed as he was in the task at hand, his left arm crooked awkwardly as he signed elaborate greetings and his name.

Alex drank him in. Gone was the sensuous young man and in his place was an urban sophisticate, dressed in black, his spiky hair flecked with gray, the stubbly leanness underscoring the impossibly high cheekbones, the tempting, bow-shaped mouth, the long nose and always, the bashful fringe of Lamb Chop lashes.

"Whom should I make it out to?"

"To one who knew me," Alex said with a sad smile.

Alí looked up then and grinned. The dark eyes were the same as ever: still large and flashing, still filled with a trepidation trumped by curiosity and hope. Those eyes said with Tennyson's "Ulysses," "Though much is taken, much abides. And though we are not now that strength that in old days moved earth and heaven, that which we are, we are."

"Look whom I found," Alex said, gesturing to Daniel.

"But you guys didn't have to wait on the line. I would've sent you copies or e-books."

"Well, you know, we both wanted to surprise you," Daniel said as if they had planned this together.

"You two," Alí said, shaking his head. "Wait for me in the café."

Alex noticed that he walked very deliberately with a cane, he who used to scamper after every one of Alex's serves and returns. There was no attempt to cover up his increasing infirmity now, nor any trace of self-pity in its presence.

"I hear you've been spending time with Étienne on the Legends Tour," Alí said, sitting down with equal care.

Alex shrugged sheepishly. He wondered if Alí saw him as a hypocritical traitor, given all that had passed among the three. But the matter-of-fact way in which Alí broached the subject told him that he didn't hold it against him.

"He asked me and I thought, What the hell. Life's too short to dwell on who did what to whom. You could join us."

Alí laughed. "I couldn't even serve as ball boy. But one of these days, I'm going to come see you play, just to keep you two honest."

Alex thought of all those years ago when Alí had watched him and Étienne play at Wimbledon. Now it was over: the rivalry, the jealousy, the gamesmanship, and all that remained was the love that had brought them together in the first place.

"Did Dani tell you I've joined the board of the Ani Foundation? I think it's a good fit, given my work for UNICEF. All the proceeds from the book will go to the two organizations.

"It's funny. It's almost like this was what I was meant to do all along, and tennis and cancer were the means to getting there, just as in a way swimming prepared Dani to take over his father's company."

"Oh, yes, I was sorry to hear about your father and sorry I couldn't make it to the funeral," Alex said.

"Thanks, your sentiments, your flowers and your generous check to the Ani Foundation in his honor touched me deeply. No, it was sad, of course, but he was surrounded by everything and everyone he had ever loved. He died with a smile and one name on his lips—Ani. It was a good end."

Alex nodded. "Your mother's doing OK?"

"Fine, fine. She had long ago made her peace with Dad. She has her work, her friendship with Dee Dee. She's happy that I'm settled. Plus, Alí's been a big support."

It hit Alex then like a wave that there was something between Alí and Daniel, something that had blossomed in New York while he was out on the Legends Tour with Étienne. Alex felt a stab to the heart but couldn't help laughing. He had come here wondering if it was time to rekindle his relationship with Alí. Now he saw it had been a prelude all along to other relationships in life's second act.

For Alí, of course, there would be no third act. Maybe that was what he had in mind when he asked, apropos of nothing, "Do you think about him? Because I do. Not a day goes by that I don't wonder if we'll ever see him again."

Alex was surprised to hear Daniel add, "I'm sure we will."

Alí smiled, content. In some ways, he was still such a child, Alex thought, with a childlike faith.

"I'll probably be the one to see him first," Alí added. "Promise me something. Promise me after I'm gone, you'll take care of each other."

Alex couldn't bear it. He saw Daniel's eyes brim as he looked away.

"We could be caring for one another now," Daniel said, boldly reaching for his hand.

"Oh, Dani," Alí said, patting it. "I'm too tired and sick to play house or games anymore. But we could see each other more often, the three of us, couldn't we? I mean, not just at book signings and sporting events but, you know, casually. We could start with coffee."

"I'll buy," Alex said. "Still a vanilla latte guy, Alí, and Dani, a double espresso man, right? Some things never change."

At the coffee bar, Alex watched as Alí and Daniel talked.

"Your drinks, sir," the barista said.

"Do me a favor," Alex said, handing her a big tip. "See those two men over there? Tell them I forgot an appointment, but I'll be in touch."

Alex turned to go but not before he saw Alí and Daniel smile at each other.

Acknowledgments

WRITING IS A SOLITARY PROFESSION THAT NONETHELESS HAS A large cast of supporting players. If I were to name all the people who contributed in some way to this book, the list would rival those speeches cut off at the Oscars. I shall therefore spare you by delving into only the recent past.

A writer needs three things: inspiration, the proverbial "room of one's own," and money.

Dr. Erika Schwartz read *Water Music* in its infancy and was the first to offer encouragement. Novelist Barbara Nachman furnished the example with her devotion to storytelling. Sarah Bracey-White, executive director of arts and culture in Greenburgh, New York, and Karen Rippstein, adjunct professor of creative writing in Westchester Community College's Continuing Education Division, nurtured my fiction writing—and me—at a time in my life when I was looking for a new direction.

Gloria Jeng gave me the room. On Sundays I worked on this book in her Hartsdale, New York, restaurant, Hunan Village II, where Gloria serves up common sense and the space to let thoughts play, along with shrimp and snow pea leaves in ginger scallion sauce.

Financial advisor Elana Milianta provided the money—or rather the means to make the money—to produce this book.

It may take a village to raise a child, but when it comes to creating a novel, never underestimate what a handful of terrific dames can do.

Photograph by Bob Rozycki/Courtesy of WAG Magazine

About the Author

GEORGETTE GOUVEIA IS THE EDITOR OF *WAG*, A LUXURY LIFE-style publication, and the author of The Essential Mary Cassatt. For thirty years, she covered culture for Gannett Inc. She lives in suburban New York. To learn more, visit www.thegamesmenplay.com.